FEAR THE TRUTH

SALLY RIGBY

TOP
DRAWER
PRESS

CRIME FICTION BOOKS

GET ANOTHER BOOK FOR FREE!
To instantly receive **Nowhere to Hide,** a free novella from the Detective Sebastian Clifford series, featuring DC Lucinda Bird when she first joined CID, sign up for Sally Rigby's free author newsletter at www.sallyrigby.com.

Chapter 1

Lucinda 'Birdie' Bird marched into the office, dropped her bag on the floor and collapsed in a heap into the chair behind her desk.

'That's it. Job done. Thank goodness. Next time it's your turn.'

Sebastian Clifford smiled to himself. His partner in the private detective business, Clifford Investigation Services, which he'd set up a few months ago, was referring to their latest job. Following a supposedly cheating spouse. Their client had paid for twenty hours of observation, after which he wanted a report, which is what Birdie had just delivered.

'Was the client satisfied with the results of our investigation?' he asked.

'When I informed him that, as far as we could ascertain, his wife wasn't seeing another man, he pushed me for dates and exact times we had her under surveillance. He seemed okay when I gave him a breakdown. For a moment, though, I was worried that he'd ask us to continue watching her, but luckily he didn't.'

Sebastian stretched out his long legs and made a mental note to buy a more comfortable office chair. At six foot six, he wasn't designed for the antique furniture that currently furnished Rendall Hall. The seventeenth-century house belonged to his cousin Sarah, but he was living there while she travelled abroad.

'I'm surprised you didn't encourage him to continue, considering we'd be missing out on the income,' Seb said, an amused tone to his voice.

'Ha, ha. Very funny. Okay, admittedly we do need the cash, but we've said all along that it's the interesting cases we want. And they're not going to appear out of thin air. You know, Seb, we really need to advertise, or at least do something. Before we become known for investigating marital matters only.'

She was right. They did need to be more proactive. They hadn't been inundated with clients recently.

'I had hoped that the publicity from helping Annabelle might have helped,' he said, referring to their previous case, where Seb's ex-fiancée, Annabelle Frankland, had employed them to find her current fiancé who'd gone missing.

'I hate to say this, but maybe it's because we're not in London.' Birdie let out a frustrated sigh. 'Not that I think we should up sticks and move to the big smoke, because I don't. At least, not yet anyway.'

Birdie had taken the plunge and left a promising career in the police force to join Seb, so it was to be expected that she was worried about what would happen if they didn't get enough work. Since Annabelle's case three months ago, all they'd had was an employee surveillance case for a local company, and a couple of potentially cheating spouses to follow.

'I agree with you. Logistically, Market Harborough, or

East Farndon to be precise, is the best place for us, considering it's close to where you live, and we don't have the sort of extortionate rent we'd have to pay.'

There was his London flat to consider, but that was too small and therefore not conducive to being a business as well as a residence.

'I suppose we should be grateful that you still have the contract work with Rob, even though I know you'd rather give it up,' Birdie said.

On a fairly regular basis, Seb would help out his ex-colleague at the Met, Rob Lawson; it paid the bills, but wasn't ideal for growing their own business.

'One day,' he said.

Birdie restlessly tapped her foot on the floor, a reminder of just how much energy she had. It didn't help that they were cooped up in the office while the outside garden was still full of dahlias, daisies and roses, thanks to the late summer.

'Are there any events you can attend where you can hand out business cards and pick up some clients?' Birdie suggested. 'Considering all the practice you've had mixing with lords and ladies, surely you could get something for us to do.'

'Are you suggesting I ask to attend one of my father's charity affairs?' he asked with a grimace. His father was a viscount, and thankfully it was Seb's older brother Hubert, the heir to the title, who was called upon to do his part for the family. It was only when his brother was out of action that Seb had to stand in, albeit reluctantly. 'It's not something I enjoy, as you well know.'

Despite that, he realised that if all else failed he'd have to do whatever it took to find them some business. He was in the fortunate position that he could survive on his savings and an old inheritance if no work materialised. But it was different for Birdie. They had to make the business pay, especially as she had invested all of her savings into it.

'As Sarge used to say, we all have to do things we don't like,' Birdie said, her voice mimicking her old boss to perfection. Then her tone became more sombre. 'But seriously, Seb, we can't sit around here all day, waiting for the phone to magically—'

Seb's phone started to vibrate on the desk. A number he didn't recognise flashed up on the screen and a smile tugged at his mouth as he raised an eyebrow in Birdie's direction.

'Don't even think of saying it,' she said, giving him a warning look, which was ruined by the gleam of excitement in her eyes.

'I wouldn't dream of it.' He resisted the urge to broaden his grin as he swiped the screen. 'Clifford Investigation Services. Sebastian Clifford speaking.'

'Oh—' There was a pause at the other end, as if the caller hadn't expected anyone to answer. It wasn't a surprise. People had many reasons for contacting the police and private investigators, which could often make them not just reluctant, but downright scared. 'Mr Clifford, I would like to discuss a private matter with you. I heard about your company a while ago when you investigated a case for the Duke of Whittington's daughter.'

The caller was a woman, and her voice was soft and breathy, as if she feared being overheard.

'Do you know Annabelle?'

'We're not close friends, more passing acquaintances.'

'Did she recommend us?'

'No. I read about the case with interest at the time, because of Annabelle's involvement.'

'How may we be of assistance?' He lowered his tone to

try to reassure her. At the mention of help, Birdie leaned even further across her desk, red curls falling across her face. If the caller hadn't been so nervous, he would have considered putting her on speaker. But as it was, the line went silent, and for a moment, Seb thought the call had been cut off.

'I, I think it would be easier if we talked face to face,' the caller finally answered.

'I see.' Seb frowned. 'Can I at least ask your name?'

There was another pause before she let out a soft sigh, as if uncertain how the information would be received. 'It's Florrie Hart.'

He jotted down the name on a piece of paper and slid it over to Birdie.

She made a choking noise and her eyes bulged dramatically.

Was Seb missing something? Clearly Birdie recognised the woman, but Seb was none the wiser. Was she a singer or actress? Or a sports personality? Whoever she was, he hadn't come across her. Which was odd because with his highly superior autobiographical memory, HSAM for short, which was both a blessing and a curse depending on the day, it was unlikely that he would have forgotten the name if he had seen it before. Unless the woman had a cult following.

'Are you aware that we're based near Market Harborough?'

'Yes. I'm in London but can catch the train up to see you. And, Mr Clifford, thank you for your discretion. It's one of the reasons I decided to contact you. I was hoping your family background would mean you would understand the sensitive nature of certain things.'

'We take client confidentiality very seriously. When would you like to meet?'

'Are you available tomorrow? I have the day off and could be there by eleven. I know it's short notice, but—'

'Tomorrow at eleven is fine. I'll text you the address.'

Once the call was finished, Birdie jumped up from her chair and fist pumped the air, much like she did when she bowled someone out when playing cricket.

'Was that really Florrie Hart?' she eagerly demanded.

'It was,' he agreed. 'I take it you know who she is.'

'Of course. I can't believe you don't. She hosts *Hands On*. It's a kids' TV show. It's brilliant, and instead of showing presenters jumping out of planes in far-off places, it has things that regular kids can do. I've watched it for years.'

Birdie pulled out her phone and tapped something on the screen, before holding it for him to see.

It was a photo of an attractive woman in her mid to late thirties standing next to a vegetable allotment. Her hair was scraped back into a ponytail, and there was a smudge of dirt on her nose as she held up a bunch of carrots. The next photo was obviously a publicity shot as the blonde hair was shoulder length and fell around her face in loose curls. In both photos, she was smiling.

Seb nodded. While he hadn't heard of Florrie Hart before, he had heard of the show.

'That explains why she didn't want to discuss her issue over the phone. She seemed very concerned about privacy.'

'And rightly so. She's the longest-running *Hands On* presenter they've ever had, and everyone adores her. Not to mention that one of the previous presenters was involved in a drug scandal, which was all over the media. Why does she want to see us? As far as I know she's not married or in a relationship, which means no cheating spouses.'

The last part was said with an air of relief. Birdie was

quite vocal about her biggest fear in joining him in the business; that they'd be stuck doing surveillance on other people's infidelities.

'True, but it's still impossible to speculate,' Seb reminded her as Elsa, Seb's beloved yellow Labrador, stood up from her spot near his feet, nose twitching, and looked expectantly at the wide French doors that opened out onto the garden. He walked over and opened them up, and they all stepped out onto the patio into the mild September breeze. 'We'll find out soon enough.'

Chapter 2

'Sorry I'm late.' Birdie rushed into the kitchen the following morning. Her cheeks were glowing, making it look like she'd run all the way from Market Harborough. 'I called into the station to see Twiggy for a catch-up. He's had a bit of a setback, healthwise.'

Birdie's ex-partner in the police, DC Neil 'Twiggy' Branch, who Seb had never seen eye to eye with, had been diagnosed with frontotemporal dementia earlier in the year and, although he was determined to work, the prognosis wasn't great.

'Can he still work?'

'Yes, for now. But he's been warned to take his diet more seriously—you know how much he likes cakes and pastries. So, I couldn't even take him out and buy anything, which means I'm starving. I ended up staying longer than I'd intended, but it was great to catch up. And he was certainly more cheerful when I'd left than when I first set foot in the office. He sends his best wishes, by the way.' Birdie's mouth twitched, and then she laughed.

Twiggy had thought Seb was taking Birdie away from

him. Which, technically he was, but the decision to leave the force had been entirely hers.

Since then, the two men had reached an alliance where they were civil to one another for the sake of Birdie.

'Next time you see him, you can return the good wishes. I've been going over some episodes of *Hands On* in preparation for Florrie Hart's visit.' Seb held up the remote control to pause the small television that lived on the Welsh dresser in the far corner of the farmhouse kitchen. He could see the appeal of the series, even though it wouldn't be his programme of choice. The content was challenging and inclusive and Florrie Hart came across as warm and caring. Online, there were numerous articles about her, and how her laid-back attitude came from her parents who travelled the world and homeschooled their only daughter, wanting her to learn about life first-hand.

'I remember that episode. Florrie showed you how to build your own battery.' Birdie spared a glance at the screen before carefully putting a reusable container on the table and lifting the lid to reveal three large blueberry muffins. The warm buttery scent that filled the kitchen suggested they'd not long been out of the oven.

'Breakfast?' he asked.

'Don't be daft. That was ages ago. This is for when Florrie gets here. A muffin and a mug of coffee will put her at ease. Do we know when she's going to be here?'

Seb glanced at his watch. 'In about twenty minutes.'

'Good, because I can't wait much longer to eat one of the muffins. It also means you'll have enough time to make the coffee.' Birdie grinned at him, then pulled out the note-book she always used.

Despite her apparent laissez-faire approach to life, Birdie kept meticulous notes and Seb knew she would've spent last night doing her own research.

He was setting up three mugs on a tray when Elsa barked, announcing that someone had arrived. Moments later, the doorbell rang, and Birdie darted out into the hallway. By the sound of voices, introductions were being made.

The coffee was ready when Birdie reappeared, closely followed by a slim figure whose head was hidden beneath a large scarf. Her face was barely visible behind huge black sunglasses and most of her body was buried under an oversized black coat that almost reached the floor.

If this was Florrie Hart's idea of wanting to be inconspicuous, it wasn't working; it made her stand out even more.

At the sight of Seb, Florrie let out a little gasp, appearing visibly taken aback by his large stature.

'Yes, he's very tall, but you'll get used to it,' Birdie said in her no-nonsense manner as she directed Florrie to the large wooden table. 'You're safe to take off your glasses and coat in here.'

'Thank you. You must think this whole attire most peculiar, but I didn't want anyone to recognise me on the way here. I was utterly melting on the train, but needs must.'

Florrie peeled off the outer layers and placed them on the back of the chair. Her hair was tied back, and she wore no make-up or jewellery apart from the diamond studs glistening from each lobe. She was attractive in real life, but the playful energy that came across on camera was missing, and there were dark smudges under her eyes. Then again, he'd met enough notable figures to know that the public persona doesn't always match the private one.

'You're safe here.' Birdie gestured to the fields and woods that flanked the house. 'No one can sneak up without us seeing them. That's one of the good things about living in a large country mansion.'

Seb frowned. 'It's hardly a mansion, but there is an excellent surveillance system.'

'Well, it's a mansion to me,' Birdie quipped. 'Would you like a coffee, Florrie? It's the good stuff and it might help refresh you after the journey.'

'Yes, please.'

Seb poured her a mug, but she shook her head at the offer of milk or a muffin.

'Maybe you'll want one later,' Birdie said as she reached for one off the plate and took a huge bite. 'They're good.'

'So, Florrie, how may we help you?' Seb stirred milk into his own hot drink. 'You said it was something you didn't want to talk about on the phone.'

'I'm sorry for being so secretive—I couldn't risk anyone hearing me or finding out what I'm doing.' She dropped her gaze and studied the mug in front of her, before finally looking back up. 'I, I, I'm being blackmailed. For two hundred thousand pounds.'

'Bloody hell,' Birdie said. 'Sorry, but that's a lot of money.'

'And that's why I'm here.' Florrie wrapped her arms around her body, as if trying to comfort herself. 'I can't afford it. Especially considering how much I've already given them.'

'Wait. You've already paid them money?' Birdie spluttered, her eyes wide.

Seb's expression became grave. That was not good. Blackmail cases were challenging enough, without the woman having already engaged with them.

'I know it was stupid,' Florrie said, sounding ashamed. 'But when I received the first letter, they only wanted one thousand pounds, and it seemed an easy way to make it all go away.'

'Except it didn't, did it?' Birdie said. Her cheeks darkened with frustration.

Birdie was passionate about equality and making sure innocent people weren't taken advantage of, and Seb felt the same. He'd investigated several complex fraud cases in the past when he worked at the Met, and what they all had in common was that the victims were left with an overwhelming sense of shame.

'No.' She choked back tears as she continued to hug herself. 'Next, they demanded five thousand, which I paid, and now it's two hundred thousand.'

'That's a big leap,' Seb said.

'More cash than I can lay my hands on. To get it I'd have to liquidate some assets, which isn't easy and not something I can do at such short notice. People think everyone on TV is rich. And, yes, some are… but there are still a lot of us who don't have as much money as the glossy magazine features would suggest.'

Seb understood that better than most. He'd grown up in an aristocratic family but while his and the other families in their circle appeared to have the trappings of the wealthy, many of them were as poor as church mice, but too afraid to admit it, for fear of losing their reputation. It made for the perfect storm.

'Why haven't you informed the police?' Birdie asked.

Florrie gave a vehement shake of her head.

Seb wasn't surprised. Blackmail only worked when someone had something to hide. Going to the police and putting something on public record was probably the last thing the woman would want to do.

'What do they have on you?' he asked.

'I don't know. They just told me to pay up or I'd regret

it.' She shook her head, but her eyes didn't meet his. She was lying. Next to him, Birdie also stiffened, which confirmed she thought the same thing.

'Florrie—may I call you that?' The terrified woman nodded. 'I'm sorry, but I find it hard to believe that someone wants two hundred thousand from you, and doesn't give you a reason to comply,' Birdie drilled, never one to shy away from asking tough questions. 'If they have nothing on you, why are you even here?'

It had the necessary effect, and colour crept up Florrie's neck as she tapped her nails against the wooden table-top. Elsa, who'd been sleeping by the window, lifted her head to find out what the noise was. But neither Birdie nor Seb spoke. They both knew that sometimes it was only by allowing silence that they could get to the truth.

Florrie seemed to notice her nervous gesture and quickly put her hands into her lap, but she couldn't hide the fear still clouding her expression. She swallowed and looked back up.

'You have to promise this won't leave the room.'

'Of course,' Birdie said before Seb could answer. 'Everything you say is confidential. But we can't help you if we don't have all the facts.'

'I know. It's just…' The woman's voice fell away.

'If it helps, there's been a rise in extortion, especially with social media and the kind of surveillance capitalism that we live in. You're not the only person to find yourself in this position.' Seb didn't add that with so much information now being stored online, it was getting increasingly easier for complete strangers to have access to private and often damning information, photos and videos. 'Tell us why you're being blackmailed.'

Florrie sucked in a breath. 'This is something I've worried about for so long, like waiting for the other shoe to drop, yet now it's happened, I'm not even sure where to start.' She dabbed at her eyes. Seb reached for the box of tissues at the far end of the table, but the woman waved them away and squared her shoulders. Despite her fear, she obviously wanted to meet her issue head on. 'I'm okay. So… everything you've ever read about me in the papers or seen online about my background, well… it's false.'

'I see,' Seb said while Birdie clamped down on her lips, no doubt to stop the hundreds of questions she had from tumbling out all at once. 'And what *is* the truth?'

Florrie took a deep breath. 'I was born in Peterborough and my real name is Jane Smith. My mother worked as a part-time cleaner, and my father spent most of his time at the unemployment office or the pub. We never had any money, and no one seemed to care where I went and what I did. It was like they'd forgotten about me. Then I met Katie, and for the first time, I had a friend.' Her eyes lost the panicked expression and brightened with some long-ago memory. She stared up at the ceiling.

'That sounds like fun,' Birdie said.

Florrie nodded. 'It's hard to explain how wonderful it felt. Katie lived down the road from me and we'd hang out at the park. And it was brilliant. Then she met Trevor, and we'd spend time with him and his friends. At first it was just to smoke a spliff or drink a beer, if one of us had money. But one night, one of Trevor's friends suggested we do something with our lives. Make some money, instead of hanging around, you know. He told us about a house his brother had seen. The owners had gone over to Tenerife for the whole summer, leaving it empty.' Her mouth flattened into a straight line and her eyes darkened into flint. 'A *whole* summer. I mean that's a long time. My family couldn't even afford a weekend at a holiday camp in Great Yarmouth. I was young and stupid, and felt like the world owed me, so I said yes. And long story short, we were caught and charged with burglary and assault.' Florrie abruptly stopped, as if regretting her outburst.

'What happened then?' Seb asked in a gentle voice; he didn't want Florrie to clam up. 'Did you get prosecuted?'

She nodded. 'I was sixteen, so they gave me community service. But the others went to prison.'

'Is that why you changed your name? To get away from them?' Birdie asked.

'It wasn't like that. No one blamed me. I was young and didn't even get out of the car when it was all happening. But the whole thing woke me up. I could see what my life would be like if I stayed in Peterborough. I'd end up poor, with no future, and going through the motions, like my parents. So, I did an administration course while I was finishing my community service. Then, once it was over, I got on a bus and went to London with no intention of going back. But no one wanted to give a seventeen-year-old girl with a dodgy history a chance. That's when I decided to change my name, dye my hair and reinvent myself. I started working as a receptionist at a television production company and as soon as I could afford it, I got a nose job and a new chin. By the time I landed *Hands On,* Jane Smith no longer existed.'

Seb drew his brows together. Something still wasn't adding up. 'So why have they contacted you now? If this all happened twenty years ago, why has it taken so long for anyone to recognise you?'

'I don't know.' Florrie squeezed her eyes tightly shut.

'Would it really matter if the truth came out?' Seb asked.

The woman's eyes opened up in a flash. 'Yes. It would be devastating. It's not just about me. I have a whole team that only gets paid when I do. My agent, my stylist, and my

assistant. And then there are all the charities I support—'
She broke off, a choking sound coming from deep in her
throat. 'Look, I was guilty of going along with them that
night. But I paid for it, and the idea of being punished
again hurts. You don't understand what it's like.'

'It's definitely hard when you're tarred with the same
brush,' Seb said, remembering what happened before
leaving the Met. How all the hard work and success his
team had achieved had meant nothing when one of their
colleagues was found to be corrupt. 'But you're not responsible for everyone else's lives. You might find it's not as bad
as you think.'

'I wish that were true, but the press is ruthless, and so
are the internet forums. One wrong step and it's all over,
however much my bosses love me. That's *if* they do.
They're more concerned with ratings and the show being
squeaky clean. There's always someone, all young, shiny,
and new, waiting to step in and take my place. I'll disappear as if I were nothing.' The last words were swallowed
up as tears fell down her cheeks.

This time, she didn't try to stop them. The worst of it
was she was right. The British press were notorious for
publishing scandals, truth be damned.

'That won't happen,' Birdie said in a warm voice. 'At
least, not if we can help it. But you need to be completely
honest.'

'I will. I swear.' Florrie nodded her head. 'Does that
mean you'll take my case?'

Seb opened his mouth to reply but Birdie cut him off.
'We must discuss it first. We're partners and that means we
both must agree. If you wouldn't mind waiting here, we'll
go into the next room.'

Birdie gestured towards the hallway, and he got to his

feet and followed her through. Once the kitchen door was closed, she spun around.

'You know we're doing it, right?' she said in a firm voice.

He blinked. 'What happened to being partners and needing to discuss it first?'

'I only said that to make us look professional.'

'We *are* professional,' he reminded her, 'and without wanting to dampen your mood, there are still several things to consider. Blackmail cases are notoriously tricky. Even if we find out who's behind it, we can't control what they'll do with the information they have on her. The fact she's already given them money will make them double their efforts because they'll see her as an easy target.'

'I know that, but we've still got to help her.' Birdie's tone was adamant.

'Okay. But remember we must make sure she doesn't decide to pay them the two hundred thousand.'

'Why would she do that? Isn't that the whole point in her coming to see us, to avoid doing so?'

'Fear, Birdie. Because even though she knows it's wrong, she wants it to be over. But at the same time, the fact that she's already given them six thousand pounds means she'll try to protect that—and make sure that it counts. It's called the sunk-cost fallacy, and it's the reason so many gamblers struggle to walk away from a losing hand, even when they know it's logical.'

Birdie let out a long whistle. 'That's messed up.'

'Yes, it is,' Seb agreed. 'And it's what we'll be up against if we can't find the blackmailer quickly. It's why I'm not sure whether we should take this case.'

'All good points. But I have no hesitation in saying yes. Florrie's clearly terrified. The over-the-top disguise and the constant tapping. The woman's scared to death! Surely you can see that.'

'Okay, if you're happy to go ahead, then I'm in agreement,' Seb said, nodding.

'Great. Come on. Let's go back in there and find out everything she knows. It might be a good idea if you leave it to me, initially, considering that I already know plenty about our new client and I can put her at her ease.'

Chapter 3

Yes. Yes. Yes. Birdie wanted to jump up and click her heels together as she hurried back to the kitchen where Florrie Hart was waiting. Behind her, Seb coughed, as if he knew how much she wanted to celebrate.

Grinning, she forced herself to regroup.

Birdie had always known that she wasn't designed to sit still. It's why she'd hated working on the police desk when Sarge was punishing her for whatever the latest thing was that she'd done wrong. She needed to be busy, either throwing herself into a case, playing cricket, or dancing in a club with her friends. And while she wasn't regretting her decision to leave the force and join Seb, she hadn't considered how draining she'd find the feast-and-famine nature of waiting for work. Especially now that the cricket season had finished. This was only their second major case since she'd left the force, and she couldn't wait.

Florrie was sitting at the table, her hands wrapped around her mug of coffee, which was probably cold by now. Her brows knitted together in confusion as Elsa circled one of the chairs, making a low whining noise.

'Yes, you're a good girl,' Birdie said, her calm voice settling down the yellow Lab. 'Seb, do you want to take Elsa outside?' she asked, using it as an excuse to get Seb out of there for a short while.

Florrie blinked in understanding. 'I didn't realise that's what she wanted. I'm more of a cat person than a doggie person.'

'You weren't to know. I won't be long,' Seb said, escorting the dog through to the boot room.

Birdie sat at the table with her notebook in front of her. Unlike Seb, with his ridiculous computer-like memory, who never forgot a bloody thing, she needed to write everything down. 'Right, we've agreed to take your case, but we have a few more questions before we get going. First of all, how did the blackmailer first contact you, and when was this?'

'By letter.' Florrie reached into a large leather bag and pulled out a folder with three envelopes inside. All they had was Florrie's name printed on the outside, which meant they'd been hand delivered. 'I received the first one three and a half weeks ago, and the latest one arrived on Sunday night.'

'Do you live in a house or a flat?' Birdie asked, reluctant to touch any of them without wearing disposable gloves in case of fingerprints. Except… she was no longer in the police, and her access to those kinds of services would only happen if they were handing over a case or working in conjunction with a force. She kept forgetting that. 'And is there any security?'

'I have an apartment at Canary Wharf, and the letters were left at the front desk with Ernie, the night-time concierge. Whoever delivered them should have signed the book, but for some reason, they didn't.'

'None of them?'

'No.'

Once, she could understand. Twice, even. But all three?

Obviously the blackmailer wouldn't want to sign the book, and Ernie should have insisted. So, either he didn't for some reason, the person delivering pretended to sign, or it was an inside job.

'Were you able to get a description of whoever delivered them?'

'I checked with Ernie, but he couldn't remember. I asked if it was the same person each time, but he didn't know that either.'

'Is he usually so vague?'

'Sometimes. And if it was at a time when he was busy, he might not have noticed.'

Why was she making excuses for the man? He clearly hadn't done his job.

'Is it busy at night? I'd have thought it was an easy time to work.'

'Between you and me, he has been known to occasionally fall asleep in the back office, or watch the TV in there, but he's okay. I wouldn't want to get him in trouble. Do you think they've been watching me, and the building, so they know when to drop the letters off?' Florrie's eyes widened with fear.

'Maybe. Do you think Ernie could have been involved?'

'No. Definitely not.' Florrie waved a hand.

'What makes you so sure? It's not like he's done his job properly so far.'

'I just don't think he would be. And if he was, surely he'd make sure to get the letters signed for, even if it's with a fake name? Because he'd know that no signature would send an alarm.'

21

'Hmmm. I suppose that does make sense. Does Ernie ever leave the building during his shift?'

'He might go around the back for a smoke. But I'm not sure whether he's officially allowed to leave.'

'Where's the book kept for couriers to sign?'

'On the front desk, so if Ernie's busy, they can still sign and not wait for him.'

'It sounds like whoever delivered the letters waited for him to go outside. Would that be possible?'

'It could be, and that would explain why Ernie didn't want to tell me.' Florrie nodded.

'Did you ask your neighbours if they've seen anyone lurking around? Or could the concierge give you access to CCTV footage from the time of the deliveries?'

Florrie recoiled, as if Birdie had asked her to walk out onto a busy motorway. 'In the letters, they told me not to tell anyone. Even this is a risk. Plus, what if the media get hold of it? Then they might start digging themselves.'

Birdie's mouth dropped open, suddenly understanding why Seb had been reluctant to take the case on—because if they can't question the people who might help them, it could seriously hinder their progress.

Before she pointed this out, Seb returned to the kitchen. The September breeze had tousled his dark hair and brought colour to his cheeks. Now that Florrie had recovered from his height, she cast an appreciative look at him. Birdie stifled a smile. Even if Florrie had been Seb's type, he wasn't the kind of person to get involved with a client. Still, it might mean Florrie would open up to him.

'What have I missed?' His sharp gaze immediately settled on the envelopes. 'Are these the blackmail letters?'

'Yes. There are three of them,' Birdie explained. 'And the concierge isn't sure if they were delivered by the same person, or of the exact delivery times. Do you have any gloves here? Mine are in the study.'

'I do.' He extracted a pair of disposable gloves from the wooden dresser and passed them over.

It was a weird place to store them… But this was Seb.

Birdie pulled them on and carefully opened the first envelope. A piece of A4 paper had been folded in half, and when she opened it up, a newspaper cutting fell onto the tabletop. It was brown with age, and the cheap print had started to smear. It was only a single column with a tiny headline and no by-line to identify the journalist.

Four in Jail after a Burglary Went Wrong

A group of thugs, aged between sixteen and twenty-two, claimed to have thought the house on Park Crescent, owned by local business-man, Tom Winger, was unoccupied when they broke in on Saturday, 8 March. But Winger and his two sons had returned from holiday early and were woken by the disturbance. Two members of the group—both known to police—attacked Winger with a hammer, leaving him in a serious but stable condition, while others caused damage to the property before fleeing the scene. Thanks to vigilant neighbours, police were able to make several arrests and today, in court, justice was served.

Birdie sucked in a breath. A hammer attack was serious.

She pushed away her distaste. The fact Florrie had only been given community service proved she hadn't been part of the assault itself.

Along with the newspaper cutting was a note typed on plain paper.

I know your secret and now it's time to pay. Transfer £1000 to the account below by tomorrow. If you tell anyone, then you'll be famous for all the wrong reasons.

The second note was similar, but the amount was for five thousand pounds. Birdie bristled. The idea that someone could so casually demand money from another person didn't sit well with her. She swallowed down her annoyance.

'During the time of receiving the notes and paying, did you notice anyone following you, or acting suspicious?'

'No, though not from lack of trying. This whole thing has turned me into a nervous wreck. After I made the second payment, I didn't hear anything for over a week, and I thought—okay, hoped—that was the end of it.' Her head was dipped to avoid looking at them both, as if embarrassed to admit what she'd done.

'Seb, why would they risk giving Florrie a bank account number to pay the money into? Can't it be traced?' she asked, knowing this was part of his background.

'Technically yes. But the amounts are small and without involving Florrie's bank it would be difficult. Also, while I can see that it's from a UK bank, the account could've been opened solely for the purpose of the black-mail by someone using a fake identity. Or it could be part of a bigger scam, where the money is quickly moved out of the country. The first two might have been to test the water.'

This seemed to break Florrie's trance, and she looked up. 'You think this was just a scam?' Her voice was almost hopeful. As if being scammed by a stranger hidden away in an office block halfway across the world was somehow better than being blackmailed.

Seb shook his head. 'Not necessarily. Scams can be elaborate, but they're usually set up to work on multiple people, not just one. Until we find out more, it's difficult to say what kind of person, or persons, we're dealing with. 'The next amount being so large could be easier to trace, if it was paid. Were you given the same account number in the note you received on Sunday?'

'No.' Florrie shook her head and pointed to the third envelope, which Birdie carefully opened.

Thank you for your commitment. But if you want this to end, it will take more than a few quid. I want £200,000 in cash. You have seven days.

Seb rubbed his chin. 'Notice they say "I" in the notes. This implies we're dealing with a person acting on their own. Also, the fact they're asking for cash means they know a larger amount could be traceable. That is useful to know, because it suggests they're worried about being caught. Scammers work on a numbers game, and a lot of them are quite blatant about what they do. It also means they'll need to give you a location, and that, too, will tell us more about who they are.'

Florrie looked alarmed. 'But what if you can't find out who's behind it before the deadline? Shall I begin liquidating some assets?'

'No,' Seb and Birdie said in unison.

'You've already seen what happens when you pay up,' Birdie said. It was blunt, but it was the only way of getting across the severity of the situation.

Florrie dropped her head into her hands and shuddered, as if sobbing, before finally looking up. 'How will you find them?'

'We need to figure out how this person discovered your identity, and knows about your past? Have you stayed in touch with anyone from those years?' Birdie asked.

'No. My mum died six months after I left home, and my dad used the funeral insurance to buy himself a one-way ticket to Spain instead of a coffin. It seemed pointless to go back when there was nothing left for me.'

'Is your father still alive?' Seb asked.

'I... I don't know.' Florrie shrunk further into the chair, making her almost childlike.

'We'll need his name as well as everyone who was arrested the night of the attempted burglary.' Seb's voice was calm, which seemed to help, and Florrie rattled off a list of names. Birdie wrote them all down while Seb merely sat there, no doubt his superbrain taking it all in. It would be irritating if it wasn't so useful.

'Do you have a photo of yourself from when you were younger? Before, you know… you had the work.' Birdie put her pen down. 'We'd like to see how likely it is that someone could recognise you.'

'Is that really necessary?' Florrie's hands automatically patted her nose, as if checking it was still there.

'It would certainly help,' Seb said in a reassuring voice. It had the desired effect and Florrie tilted her head in agreement.

'What about at work? Have you had any incidents with co-workers or fans?' Birdie asked.

'None. Most of the production team started when I did and we're really close. And the fans are the sweetest. They send cards and photos all the time. Of course, there are a few strange items and requests, but nothing threatening. Besides, surely the blackmailer is someone from my past. Why else would they include the newspaper cutting?'

'The article is their leverage,' Birdie said, not bothering to add that solving crimes would be so much easier if the most obvious theory was always the correct one. 'They could've come across it quite by chance. Or someone might have told them. That doesn't mean we won't follow up people from your past, though. We'll cover everything.'

'I still can't believe this is happening,' she whimpered.

'A lot of people out there do things that we'll never understand,' Birdie said before taking a deep breath. 'There's one other question we have to ask. What's the best outcome here? Even if we find out who's behind it, we can't necessarily stop them from revealing what they know. And, if you don't want to go to the police, this all might be for nothing.'

'Definitely no police. All I want is to find out who they are, then we'll figure out a way to stop them. If we threaten to go to the police, they might back down.'

'What if they don't?' Seb asked in his even tone, though there were tiny worry lines around his eyes.

'I can't think about that.' Florrie once again wrapped her arms around her torso. 'If this gets into the press, I'll never book another job, and my entire team will be affected. Please, you must help me.'

Birdie glanced over to Seb, who dipped his head in agreement. 'And we will. But first we need to discuss our fee...'

Chapter 4

'How was your day, love?' Birdie's mum called out from the depths of the kitchen.

Birdie followed the scent of roast chicken, her stomach rumbling. All she'd eaten was the blueberry muffin when Florrie Hart had first arrived and an apple that she'd picked from one of the trees in the garden at Rendall Hall when she'd taken Elsa out for a quick walk after a taxi had whisked Florrie away, disguise firmly back in place. The rest of the afternoon she'd spent building up a solid profile of their new client, while Seb finished off some work for Rob.

'Excellent. We have a new case.'

Birdie dropped her bag by the door and walked over to the bench where a bowl of raw carrots was sitting. She swiped a couple and then danced out of the way before her mum could swat her hand. It was a game they'd played since Birdie was little and it still made them both laugh.

'That's wonderful.' Her mum beamed, before wrinkling her nose in uncertainty. 'Is it okay for me to be happy when the case might mean someone's in trouble?'

'Let's think of it as helping someone improve their situation. Seb and I are heading down to London tomorrow morning. I'm not sure when we'll be back.' They'd arranged to meet up with Florrie in the morning to get photos and a list of all the people from her past and present. They also wanted her to sign their contract and make the initial payment for their services.

'Again?' Her mum looked up, eyes wide. 'You were there not long ago.'

Birdie bit back a smile. Her parents loved Market Harborough and only went to London every few years to see a musical. 'Now I'm not on the force where we're restricted to our jurisdiction, I could go anywhere. We work where our cases take us.'

'Well, if they take you somewhere sunny, make sure there's room for me in your suitcase. I could use a holiday.' Her mum laughed.

'Chance would be a fine thing.' Birdie assumed that working for yourself meant no more statutory holidays. Although maybe she'd see about getting a week in Spain next year?

'It doesn't hurt to dream.' Her mum sighed as the oven timer beeped. 'Dinner will be ready in fifteen minutes. Would you mind setting the table and bringing in the washing? I'm hoping it's all dry.'

'Sure.' Birdie grabbed another carrot stick and darted out through the kitchen and into the back garden where a line of washing was hanging. Part of her longed to head straight up to her room and finish researching, but it wasn't fair on her parents if she didn't pull her weight.

She'd be twenty-seven soon and even though she loved her family, she hated the fact she was still living at home. The original plan had been to stay there while she saved up for a house deposit, but now she'd used her money to become a partner in Seb's business, she was back to square one.

Not true. She reminded herself. After all, if she hadn't joined Seb, she'd still be in the police. And while she'd loved parts of being on the force, there were other parts that had driven her batshit crazy. Like all the rules. And the trouble she'd got into for her bad timekeeping.

She had other talents, many of them, and even though she sometimes got sidetracked on her way to doing something, it hardly made her a bad person. In fact, she liked to think it showed how focused she could be when—

'Birdie… the table,' her mum's voice echoed from the kitchen.

She burst out laughing as she unpegged the rest of the sheets and hurried back inside. Fine… so sometimes she did get a little sidetracked.

An hour later, she'd finally made it to her bedroom, her stomach full from the second helping of apple pie. She sat on her bed, cross-legged, and pulled out her laptop from its bag, placing it in front of her.

Seb was picking her up early tomorrow morning and, knowing him, he'd be even earlier. She'd pack her bag before going to bed to make sure she didn't keep him waiting. Well, not for too long.

They planned to visit Florrie's apartment building to see what they could discover without going against their client's request not to mention the incident. They also hoped to get their hands on the original police report, with the help of Rob.

But first she had to finish researching TBG, the production company that was behind the *Hands On* programme.

She was about to start when an email notification pinged. Most of her friends sent her texts or DMs, and her older friends, like Twiggy, tended to call. Curious, she opened up her inbox to where an email from k.bakirtzis was waiting for her.

Kim Bakirtzis.

Her birth mother.

Her stomach churned and her skin began to prickle. She yanked her hand away from the mouse, terrified that if she touched the email with the cursor, it might somehow disappear.

Birdie had always known she was adopted, but it wasn't until two years ago that she'd begun searching for her birth mother, only to be told by the adoption agency that the woman didn't want any contact. It had been devastating— like being rejected for a second time. But she'd decided to carry on with her investigation, anyway; even if Kim didn't want to know anything about her daughter, Birdie still wanted to know about her.

A few months ago, Birdie had discovered that Kim, who as a teenager had emigrated to Canada with her family, had returned to England and was living in Croydon. But Birdie's search had stopped when she'd managed to find an old school friend of Kim's. The friend had refused to hand over Kim's contact details but had agreed to pass on Birdie's details to Kim—leaving the ball in her court.

Except it wasn't even a ball. Because Birdie hadn't been able to explain to the friend who she was or why she wanted to talk to Kim. Nor had she been able to get Kim's married name, which meant her trail had gone cold. All in all, it had been a rookie mistake that taunted her every time her phone rang or a new email came in.

Except now, here it was.

Finally, three months since handing over her email address, her birth mother was in contact. Birdie closed her eyes. She wasn't the type of person to get scared. Even as a kid when her friends at school didn't want to go into the haunted house at the local fair, Birdie had charged in, ready to face things head on.

Her fingers once again curled around the mouse, and she clicked to open the email.

Birdie,

My friend Tina told me you were looking for me. She said you sounded anxious and a little scared, and was 99% certain you weren't some kind of scammer or crazy person. But I know you could be. There are a lot of terrible people out there. You read about them in the newspaper every single day. I'll tell you right now that this is a separate email address that isn't connected to my real life, so if you are trying to steal my details or bank account, then I'm afraid you're out of luck.

But, if it's about something else. If it's… no… I can't write it, or even think about it too much. But, if it is about something else, then please email me back.

Kim

Birdie stood up and walked over to the window, which looked out onto the street she'd grown up on. The last of the early-autumn light had gone and the road was damp from rain. Despite living in a detached house, it was still possible to hear next door's television blasting out with the same quiz show that they listened to every night. It was as familiar to her as her own family. Except now, it felt different. Not because the street or the families who lived there had changed, but because she had.

She swallowed. Her parents had been worried when she'd first told them what she was doing, and now she understood why. Because once she met her birth mother, some parts of her would change forever. Space would have to be made in her mind, and possibly her life, for the answers her mother would give her. Even if they weren't the answers she wanted.

Was this why Kim had refused to be contacted? Because she'd been scared of how it would change her own life? And yet, her email suggested that she thought Birdie might be the daughter she'd put up for adoption all those years ago. If so, had she changed her mind about wanting contact?

Well… there was only one way to find out.

Crossing back to her bed, Birdie drew her laptop onto her knees and started to type.

Dear Kim

Thanks for emailing. I wasn't sure if Tina would even give you my details, let alone whether you'd contact me. But I'm pleased you finally did. My name's Lucinda Bird, but I only answer to Birdie. I was born in Leicester Royal Infirmary on 7 November, 1995, but was adopted when I was six months old. I believe you're my birth mother.

My adopted parents are wonderful people and they've given me everything I could have wanted. But there's a part of me that has questions and so I'm reaching out to see if you would think about meeting me. I know you wanted a closed adoption and I can respect that. But, if you have changed your mind, please let me know.

I could travel down to Croydon to see you. I'm free two weeks on Saturday. There is a pub I went to once after a cricket match. It's called the Royal Oak. We could meet there at 12:30 p.m. Please let me know as soon as possible, so I can book a table.

Best wishes,

Birdie

P.S. I was a detective in the police force but now work as a private investigator, so I'm probably better at catching hackers than I am at being one. I hope that helps

She hit send and waited for the swoosh to indicate it had gone.

It was done.

All she had to do now was wait for a reply.

Chapter 5

'You're quiet. Don't tell me you're regretting eating two sausage rolls on the way down?'

Seb slowed down to avoid the white van that had pulled out in front of him. He really didn't miss the London traffic. It had been bumper-to-bumper from when he reached the North Circular Road until now when he arrived at his flat in Notting Hill.

'What?' Birdie, who'd been blankly staring out of the window, stiffened, as if suddenly realising he'd spoken.

He frowned. Something was distracting her. Not only had she been waiting outside her house when he'd driven up to collect her, which never happened, but instead of her usual chatter, she'd been lost in her own thoughts.

'I was asking if you were okay. You've hardly said two words the entire journey. Is it the case?' Seb turned into the parking garage under his block of flats in Notting Hill. He waved a fob in front of the electronic pad and the metal door slid open. The space was filled with a collection of vehicles, from top-of-the-range Jaguars to small Suzuki Swifts, which he drove past until reaching his own spot.

'Nothing like that.' She rolled her shoulders, as if trying to shake off her worries. Then let out a pained breath. 'Okay. I'll tell you. I heard from Kim last night.'

Now it made sense. It had been weeks since Birdie had passed on her contact details to her birth mother. But because she hadn't brought it up again, he hadn't wanted to push. He hoped it was enough that she knew he was always there any time she needed to talk about it.

'That's promising,' he said carefully. 'How are you feeling?'

'Honestly, I've got no idea. It was a weird email. She didn't admit to knowing why I contacted her, but then she sort of implied that she *might* know. I emailed back and told her who I was and when I was born. Then I asked if she wanted to meet me for lunch and suggested a time and place. That was last night, and I still haven't heard back.' The words poured out in a jumble, which was something Birdie only did when she was nervous or excited.

'Waiting to hear is always hard. But the fact she contacted you is good, don't you agree?'

'Part of me thinks yes, but the other part keeps thinking of all the terrible things that could happen. Like she refuses to see me or... I don't know, she takes a restraining order out against me.'

'She's not going to do that. She has no grounds.'

'Okay, maybe that's exaggerating, but you know what I mean. And now there's the extra guilt because I didn't tell Mum and Dad about it last night. I was going to this morning, but I ran out of time. I know they'll be okay about it, but it still feels weird.'

'I understand. Will you wait to hear back from her before booking a table?'

The thought seemed to galvanise her, and a familiar gleam came back to her eyes. 'That's a good point.

Imagine if she says yes and then I can't get a table? What a disaster that would be.' She pulled out her phone. 'I'll make an online booking right now, and then if she doesn't want to meet me, I'll cancel. I wish she'd reply, though.'

'Give her time. It's hard for her as well, remember?'

'Yeah, yeah. I know. What you say makes sense in theory, but you might have noticed that patience isn't one of my virtues.' Her lips formed a rueful grin.

'You're doing better than you think.'

'Thanks. I appreciate it. And don't worry, I'm not about to go crazy on you. We're here to work,' she said as they both climbed out of the car.

'I never doubted it,' he said, smoothing down his trousers and brushing away one of the stray crumbs from Birdie's sausage rolls.

He opened the back door of the car to where Elsa was stirring, her huge brown eyes blinking away the sleep. 'Come on, girl—Jill's expecting you, and I'm sure she'll take you to the park for a walk,' he said, referring to the woman who lived in the next-door flat and who regularly looked after Elsa for him.

An hour later, once Elsa was settled with a delighted Jill, they disembarked from the Tube and walked out from the curved glass canopy of Canary Wharf station to meet Florrie at a day spa.

Seb would've preferred to go directly to her apartment, but Florrie had refused, worried the blackmailer might be watching her every move. Privately, Seb thought it was unlikely someone would be watching her twenty-four seven, but he'd been unable to convince her otherwise.

Jubilee Park was a tree-filled space that had been built above the Underground station. It was filled with office workers and tourists, all making the most of the bright day. Birdie seemed more like her regular self as her eyes glowed with excitement from visiting a part of London she'd never been to before.

The spa was in a shopping complex—another glass-fronted building—which spread out like a rabbit warren of marbled chambers. The day spa was on the second level and had a discreet shopfront with elegant, understated brass features.

'So, this is how the other half live?' Birdie let out a low whistle as her hand touched her red curls.

'Some,' he countered as a woman walked out, sunglasses covering her eyes.

When he'd been dating Annabelle, she'd dragged him along to a couple's massage there. It had been torture, more like being at the bottom of a rugby scrum than a relaxing experience. Still, it was probably no worse than sitting in a car for eight hours on surveillance duty.

'Lucky them.'

'Come on, let's get this over with.'

'At least pretend to enjoy it,' she teased before her eyes drifted down to his clothing. 'Hang on. You're wearing a suit?'

'Well observed,' he agreed, knowing where this was going. Birdie's civilian attire consisted of jeans and a comfortable T-shirt, with a leather jacket thrown in for good measure, and she often teased him about his own neat appearance. 'Too much?'

'A bit.' She grinned. 'Still, maybe the sauna will take the starch out of your collars.'

'Possibly.' They stepped inside to the reception area. A defused mist of peppermint oil greeted them, and the low lighting and ambient music was obviously designed to release stress. In the middle of the room was a light-coloured wooden reception desk, which almost glowed against the dull lighting.

'Namaste.' A middle-aged woman with straight hair and a nose ring appeared from behind the counter. Her smile slipped at the sight of Seb. Was it the suit? Indecision played out in her eyes before she finally turned to Birdie. 'Do you have an appointment?'

'*We* do,' Birdie said, correcting the mistake with her usual bluntness. 'We're meeting a friend for a hot-stone massage.' It was the phrase Florrie had instructed them to use.

'Of course.' The woman's eyes lightened in understanding. 'Unfortunately, Wednesday is a female-only day.'

Next to him, Birdie's mouth opened in surprise. 'Our friend didn't mention that.'

'She might not have realised,' the woman at the counter said before turning to Seb. 'Though you're welcome to book in tomorrow. We do specific sessions for men. Waxing. Skin care...'

'That does sound good. What do you think, Seb?' Birdie's mouth twitched with mischief. 'Shall we book you in?'

'I'll have to check my diary,' he lied, working hard to hide his relief at not having to go in. Then he lowered his voice. 'This will give me a chance to look into who delivered the letters. I'll meet you at the Bird in Hand at five. Don't be late.'

'Moi?' She gave him a wide-eyed smile before lowering her own voice. 'And remember, no direct questions.'

'Agreed.'

Seb waited until Birdie had disappeared from the reception area before leaving. He exited through the shopping complex and made his way onto the street.

He increased his pace, enjoying the fresh air, as opposed to the stifling atmosphere of the spa. Florrie Hart's apartment was a five-minute walk away. It was in one of the area's older buildings but stood right on the water's edge with a small park to one side.

He peered through the wide doors that led into the reception area where a middle-aged woman was at the desk. The lifts and stairs weren't in view, so he assumed they were further inside the building where it would be difficult for anyone to slip past unnoticed.

In terms of Florrie's safety, that was a good thing, but for what Seb needed, it wasn't helpful. He couldn't go against their client's wishes and speak directly with the woman, but he was still determined to discover more about the letters' delivery.

He moved away from the door and positioned himself nearby with a view of the entrance, the slim trees giving him some shade. Several people walked out of the building, including a couple of tradesmen, but it wasn't very busy.

Finally, a twenty-something courier clad in bright yellow cycling shorts rode up on an electric bike, his pannier bags bulging with parcels. He stopped to study a message on his phone, before retrieving a box from one of the bags and striding inside.

Seb stepped out from under the protective shade of the tree and walked over to the bike. Inside, the courier was leaning against the marble counter, talking to the woman behind the desk. Then he handed over the box, followed by his phone, which the concierge tapped several times before returning it. The courier then leaned over, picked up a pen and wrote something into a book on the desktop.

When the courier re-emerged, he raised an eyebrow—possibly at the sight of a six-foot-six man in a business suit waiting for him.

'Can I help you, mate?' He had a broad Australian

accent and ruddy complexion, no doubt from his mainly outdoors profession.

'I hope so. My name's Clifford and I'm the legal representation for Miss Louisa Banks.' Seb dusted off a piece of imaginary fluff from his suit.

'Never heard of her.' The courier shrugged but didn't seem in a particular hurry. Seb had always heard that Australians and Kiwis were more laid back than Londoners. Maybe it was true—or he was being paid by the hour. Either way, even though it was a long shot, based on the number of bike couriers in London, Seb hoped the guy knew the night concierge who'd been working when each of the notes had been delivered.

'I imagine not,' he agreed, pleasantly. 'But she has a private matter to discuss with an Ernest Barstow. I urgently need to contact him and believe he works here.'

'Ah! You mean Big Ern. I never caught his last name.'

That was a relief. Seb had no idea what it was either, but had wanted to make sure he sounded convincing. 'Yes, that's correct.'

'Well, if she wants money, she'd better join the queue —he's a great guy but shit at picking horses.'

Seb widened his eyes. So, Ernie was a gambler. Interesting. Was he on the take and that's how the letters were delivered? 'He doesn't owe any money. But I do need to talk to him.'

The courier rubbed his chin. 'He's on a permanent night shift as far as I'm aware. Starts at seven and goes through seven in the morning five days a week. Poor bastard.' The courier's phone pinged with a message. It seemed to remind him that he was talking to a stranger, and his casual air fell away as he climbed back onto his bike. 'I've got to blaze. But, hey, don't tell Ernie I said anything, yeah? A man's business is his own, and he's not the kind of guy I want to be on the wrong side of.'

'How do you mean?' Seb asked, but it was too late; the courier had gone. Still, the fact he was rattled at least gave Seb some insight into the concierge's personality. A gambler with a temper. Plus, he now knew the letters must have been delivered between seven in the evening and seven in the morning, and that even though Ernie had told Florrie he couldn't remember who delivered it, it didn't mean he was telling the truth.

It wasn't much, but it was a start.

Chapter 6

The Bird in Hand was a whitewashed pub with dark wooden floors and plain furniture. It was around the corner from Seb's flat, and he'd visited on many previous occasions.

He was sitting out in the courtyard, nursing a half pint of Guinness. Birdie was late. Though considering how subdued she'd been on the car ride down from Market Harborough after being ready on time, maybe being late was a good sign.

After visiting Canary Wharf, he'd returned to the flat to do some research into the numerous internet message boards that discussed the programme *Hands On*.

For a children's show, a lot of adults weighed in, although most of them were old fans who'd grown up alongside Florrie. And it was clear they loved her. Of course, there were several trolls and barbed comments, and while it was often impossible to trace them back to anyone, he looked for anything to suggest the blackmail was linked to a smear campaign. But the syntax and grammar were all different, making him think the posts were made by random individuals rather than a particular person with a grudge against her.

Hopefully, it was one line of enquiry they could rule out.

He'd also sent out several emails, trying to track down Florrie's father, but hadn't yet received any answers.

Fifteen minutes later, when Birdie walked into the beer garden, her skin was glowing and her eyes were bright. Either she'd had a successful conversation with Florrie, or the spa treatments really had been excellent. Hopefully both.

'Why didn't you tell me you were going to be out here? I've been scouring the inside looking for you.' Birdie dropped down to the seat next to him. 'I'm famished. Would it be rude to order before Rob arrives?'

'Fine. I doubt he'll have time to eat.' Seb handed her a menu.

'Thanks. I take it that's for me?' Birdie said, pointing at the bottle of cider on the table. She picked it up and took a gulp. 'A bit warm now, but the food smells divine. And I just saw they have jam roly-poly—I hope they don't run out.'

'You and me both. And before you ask, this is my treat.'

'I had no intention of asking. Especially as I'm the one who's had to endure hot rocks on my flesh all afternoon.' Birdie opened the menu and licked her lips. 'Lasagne with no salad, and definitely ask if they can save us a jam roly-poly, but we'll ask for it once we've finished our main course, or it will get cold.'

'When I get back, we'll compare notes before Rob arrives.' Seb got to his feet and made his way inside to the bar. The place was heaving, as usual, and it took him ten minutes to make his way to the front of the queue and place their order. He got another round of drinks while he was there to save going back up for a second trip.

'Right,' he said, once he was seated. 'How did it go?'

'My skin feels like dew and look at my nails.' She proudly displayed her fingers, which were painted in pale apricot.

'I meant with Florrie.'

'So easy... Every time, I get you. Every time!' Birdie flashed him a grin before opening her notebook. 'Anyway, to business. I've got a list of all the places she's worked since moving to London, as well as the names of her school friends. Unfortunately, she has no contact details for any of them, though she did give me some photos.'

She pulled out several and handed one of them to him. It was of a slim girl, maybe sixteen or seventeen years old. Her face was narrow and thin, and her black hair was cut short and feathered around her cheeks, clinging to the back of her neck. 'Is this her? She's nothing like the woman we met yesterday.'

'You're telling me.'

'Well, at least it explains why no one has recognised her until now. Even her eyes are a different colour.'

'She's confessed to using contact lenses.' Birdie handed him another photo. 'Here's one of her with Katie, her best friend. They look close.'

'They do indeed,' he agreed. The two girls were dripping with water and laughing as they held up a hose, clearly having a water fight.

'She didn't have any of the three guys who were involved in the break-in. I also asked her again about her father, but she insists she has no idea where he is. Nor does she have any photos.'

'Did you believe her?

'Difficult to say.'

A waitress dressed in a tight black skirt and a starched white dress shirt appeared with two plates of lasagne.

'Oh… are you joining me on the dark side? No quinoa or salad left?' Birdie said after the waitress had gone.

'It would appear not.' It was true he liked to eat healthily, but it was all about balance. Who said he couldn't enjoy the occasional splurge?

He put the photos down on the table as Birdie talked him through the rest of the conversation she'd had with their client. Most of it involved a walk-through of Florrie's average day, which would help them get a better idea of who she interacts with on a regular basis. Once she'd finished, Seb told her about the concierge and the message boards.

'The one thing I don't understand,' Birdie said between mouthfuls, 'is why would someone bother sending letters? It seems so old-fashioned. Wouldn't it be simpler to email or text? And a lot harder to trace.'

'I'd wondered that as well. There could be two reasons. That they're purposely trying to avoid a digital footprint and go old school. Or they really *are* old school and don't feel comfortable using technology.'

Birdie was silent, as if trying to imagine a world where people didn't use the internet for everything. 'You know, sometimes you remind me of Twiggy. That's the exact sort of thing he'd come up with. And I mean it as a compliment,' she assured him as she scraped the last of the pasta from her plate. Seb wasn't quite so sure, but before he could respond, Rob stepped out into the beer garden.

He was tall, imposing with a barrel chest and thick blond hair. Seb held up a hand and waved him over.

'Sorry I'm late.' He slid into the spare seat, his bulk

threatening to spill over the handles. 'Had to make a detour for chocolate and nappies.'

'Sounds like a dangerous combination,' Seb said as Birdie leaned over to hug Rob. 'How's parenthood?'

Rob turned to Seb and raised an eyebrow. 'Remember that money-laundering scheme in Bethnal Green we worked on and didn't sleep for three nights?'

'The guy was running several betting syndicates and was also dealing in stolen cars. He moved location every seven and a half hours because he was so paranoid,' Seb responded instantly, his HSAM never far away. 'Why do you ask?'

'Because that was a bloody doddle compared with this. I love Leo, but he's on the go non-stop. Anyway, I can't stay long. I promised Maddie I'd be home by six-thirty so she can get a shower. Can you believe it? We have to schedule in showers now.' He spotted the half pint of stout that Seb had ordered for him, and some colour returned to his cheeks. 'This for me?'

'Sure is, and thanks for fitting us in. I know you've got a lot going on.' Several of his friends had families. and as hard it was to imagine one tiny creature could cause so much chaos, he accepted it was true.

'No problem.' Rob opened the leather satchel he'd been carrying and started to rummage through it before producing a folder of case notes. 'Since you're already working as a consultant for us, there are a few less strings to pull. Now, let's see.' He held up the file and began to read.

'Three young men were arrested and charged with assault. Dean Knowles, nineteen; Trevor Blackham, twenty; and Kyle Richards, twenty-two. Knowles and Blackham served twelve months and were released on probation, while Richards stayed in a further four years. He'd been the one with the hammer, and his sentence was then extended for fighting with another inmate. He got out three years later but is now back inside. This time, he's serving life for manslaughter. In other words, not a nice guy. There's nothing else on Knowles and Blackham since then. So either the system is working, or they're too clever to get caught.'

'Let's hope it's the former. Did you find anything else?'

'Katie Wilson, aged seventeen, was charged as an accessory and ended up doing six months in a young offenders' institution, while a second girl, Jane Smith, was given community service. She was only sixteen at the time and had been in the car, so while she was technically an accessory, they took her age into account and the fact she wasn't at the scene.'

'Thanks, Rob. Any addresses or phone numbers for them?'

'I'm not that forgetful—yet.' He pulled out a second sheet of paper. 'Jane Smith seems to have fallen off the planet, and the only address I have for Katie Wilson is for her parents' house from years ago. I can't find a current address for her. No luck with the others either.'

'No problem, it's a good starting point. And thanks for not asking any questions.'

'I trust that if you discover anything illegal, you'll alert the police.' His voice was friendly but there was a hint of steel behind it.

'Of course,' Seb assured him, and it was true.

Over the years, they'd both witnessed too many excellent police officers morphing into something else as their values and good intentions were chipped away under the weight of all the tiny micro transgressions that accumulated throughout their career. It wasn't a path he had any interest in going down.

'Good man.' Rob clapped him on the back. 'One more

thing. I noticed the officer in charge was Colin Reeves. I played for the English police rugby team with his kid brother, would you believe? I tried to call, but he's off on some Caribbean cruise. I've left a message and will be in touch if there's anything else to add. Right, I'd better leave before Maddie goes wild.'

'Give her my love,' Birdie said.

'Consider it done.' Rob grinned at them both before disappearing back into the pub.

'What's the plan?' Birdie asked. 'Do you think we should go to Peterborough to see if Katie Wilson's parents are still at the address? Or shall we tail Ernie the concierge?'

'Peterborough.' Seb swallowed the last of his beer and stood up. 'It still seems the most likely place. Not only do Wilson, Knowles, Blackham, and Richards all know about Jane's involvement in the crime, but we need to consider the victim as well. Tom Winger. We'll look into him at the same time and, since we're on a ticking clock before the blackmailer contacts Florrie again, we need to move fast.'

Excitement filled Birdie's eyes as she shrugged on her jacket. 'You're right. Let's go back to your flat and let Jill know where we're going. Elsa will also need a walk tonight if we're leaving first thing in the morning.'

'She's not the only one,' Seb said, shaking his legs at the prospect of travelling through the London rush-hour traffic. Still, at least they'd got what they'd come for. Now they had to follow the dots and see where they led.

Chapter 7

The house where Katie Wilson grew up was in the middle of a long terrace. The once-uniform red-brick buildings had all undergone a multitude of changes, making them look like rebellious teenagers trying to stand out in a crowd. Number twenty was no exception. A wooden porch, painted a dull mustard colour, had been put in front of the door, and the small front garden had been replaced with paving slabs. A couple of broken plastic tricycles were discarded in the corner, along with a deflated football.

The street was lined with a series of older-model cars and it looked like they'd have to go further up the road to find somewhere to park, but suddenly a car pulled out from a space right outside the house.

Seb reversed into the spot, and once he'd turned off the engine, Birdie climbed out of the car and pocketed her phone, but not before checking one more time for an email from her birth mother. Still nothing.

She waited for him to join her on the footpath outside the house.

'Remember the plan?' Birdie asked, purely to hear his

long-suffering sigh. And he didn't let her down. Teasing him about his memory never got old. 'I'll take that as a yes.'

'Please do.' His voice was mild.

They'd spent most of the drive from London going through various theories, while listening to old interviews Florrie Hart had given over the years. They hadn't learnt much, apart from the fact their latest client was incredibly upbeat, even on the early-morning radio shows where she must have woken up at the crack of dawn.

Some of her later interviews, where she'd been grilled about the drug scandal her co-host had been caught up in, had been more strained. And while Florrie had managed to come through it, the network had almost cancelled the show twice in the last three years.

It explained Florrie's desperation regarding the black-mail, since the entire *Hands On* production team would also be impacted.

Seb and Birdie's plan was simple: they were investigators working to locate Jane because of an inheritance.

Seb opened the black wooden gate, and a low growl came from the house next door as a tiny black-and-white terrier appeared on the other side of the short privet hedge that separated the two properties. The dog continued to bark, while prancing back and forth on its thin legs.

'That's enough, Bluebell.' A woman appeared out of the mustard-coloured porch, untying an apron from around her waist as she walked over to the hedge. The dog immediately stopped barking and trotted back into its own house. The woman then turned to them. 'Sorry about that. My neighbour's dog is convinced it's her duty to act like a warning bell for us as well as them. It doesn't help that they keep the front door open all day so it can do its business on the front lawn. Still, there's nowhere else to do it because there's no grass out back.'

'Are you Mrs Wilson?' Seb gave her a charming smile and held out his hand. The woman didn't take it.

'Last time I checked. Who are you?'

'My name's Clifford, and this is my associate, Miss Bird. We're hoping you can help us. We're looking for someone we believe used to be friends with your daughter. Her name's Jane Smith.'

At the mention of Florrie's birth name, the woman stiffened and folded her arms in front of her. 'What's this about? Are you the police?'

'No, definitely not. We work for a firm of solicitors who are handling Jane's late great-uncle's estate,' Birdie quickly said, realising she should have spoken first. While Seb could hold his own in most situations, he seemed to forget his height and posh accent might put some people on the back foot.

Unless there was another reason Mrs Wilson was nervous. Did she know something?

'That's not a name I've heard in a long time.' Some of the tension around the older woman's mouth faded. 'What do you need her for?'

'The case is going through probate, but she's been left an inheritance. We can't find any information about her whereabouts since she went to school round here. Katie's name came up in our search and we found a photograph of them together. We're hoping your daughter might be able to help us find Jane.'

'How much money is she getting?'

'Sorry, we're not at liberty to say.' Birdie shrugged, apologetically. 'Does Katie still live here?'

The woman shook her head. 'No. She's got four kids to bring up on her own, and the youngest two are still in primary school. Can you imagine? We'd be like sardines if they were all here. Not that she has much more room in that shoddy little flat the council shoved her into.' Bluebell appeared by the fence again, barking. 'Look, you'd better come inside before Mavis from next door hurts her neck from all the snooping she's no doubt doing from behind the net curtain.' The last part was said in such a loud voice that it was obviously meant to be heard by the aforementioned Mavis.

'That's very kind of you.' Birdie and Seb followed her into the house.

The front door led straight into a small living room filled with a sofa and two armchairs, all angled towards a large television up on the wall. The surfaces were crammed with framed photographs of babies and groups of people.

'Katie's due round here soon. She's taking me to the doctor. It's the blood pressure. I told her if I wasn't always worrying about her and those kids, I'd be fit as a fiddle. Still, what are you going to do?' Mrs Wilson busied herself, moving a pile of magazines off the leather sofa and wiping it down with the apron that was still bundled in her hand. There was an air of bustle about her, as if she didn't often sit still. 'Can I get either of you a hot drink?'

'No, thank you. We don't want to be a bother,' Birdie said, hoping their host would be more at ease if she sat down with them. It seemed to do the trick, and she finally settled on the far end of the long sofa. 'Do you remember Jane?'

'Oh, yes. She was such a sweet girl. Wouldn't say boo to a goose. Can't say I was surprised with a father like hers. Smithy had a mean streak that went through to the bone. They lived down the road at number ten, though Jane was hardly ever there. She and Katie were as thick as thieves, but never anything bad. Well, not until the... trouble—'

A rattle of keys and the click of a door handle cut off the rest of the conversation, and Mrs Wilson immediately stood up as a woman walked in.

'Katie, love, we've got some visitors.'

'That explains the flash car outside. I was hoping it belonged to some rich sugar daddy.' Katie Wilson was about five foot five, but her shoulders were slumped forward, and her blonde hair had several inches of black regrowth running down the centre. Her skin was fair, and she had heavy lines collecting around her eyes and mouth. If Birdie hadn't known better, she would've guessed Katie was at least ten years older than Florrie.

Curiosity prickled along Birdie's arm, sending the hairs on edge. If Katie had recognised Florrie, would she have tried to blackmail her?

'I'm Birdie and this is my colleague, Seb,' Birdie said, standing up and holding out her hand.

She gave Seb a warning glance to let her speak. He nodded in agreement, probably terrified of being mistaken for a sugar daddy.

Katie ignored the hand and raised a quizzical eyebrow. 'What's going on? Don't tell me Mum owes you money, because—'

'No, it's nothing like that,' Birdie quickly cut in. 'Sorry to give you a scare. We work for a law firm in London and we're trying to locate Jane Smith. You used to be friends with her, so we have a few questions.'

The woman's mouth softened, and she let out a small sigh. 'Thank God. Things are so tight these days, I keep thinking the worst. Though not sure how I can help. I haven't seen Jane in years. What's this all about?'

'An inheritance. Seems there's a dead great-uncle.' Mrs Wilson gestured for her daughter to shut the door and sit down. Katie dropped the two carrier bags she'd been holding and joined them on the sofa.

'An inheritance? Lucky cow. I could do with one of them right now. I paid three quid for a four-pack of yoghurt just now. Three quid.' She pulled a vape pipe out of her jacket pocket but didn't put it up to her mouth. Instead, she fiddled with it, as if trying to fight off an urge.

'Can you remember when you last saw Jane?' Birdie asked.

'It must be nineteen years ago, at least. Before Crystal —she's my oldest—was born. I suppose if you're lawyers, you know what happened?'

'We do. And if you don't mind, we'd like to hear your point of view. How did you get involved?' This time it was Seb who spoke, though he didn't correct her about being a lawyer. He'd shifted his body to give a more casual appearance, obviously not wanting her to think she was being interviewed.

Katie let out a disgruntled snort. 'Story of my life. I met a guy. We weren't really dating. More like hooking up at the end of the night. Anyway, he had a friend, so I got Jane to come along one night to the park, and after that, we all started hanging around together. It wasn't just the four of us. Often there were other guys there, too. Usually, it was just drinking and a bit of hash. But then one of the boys suggested we rob this house and get some proper cash.'

Next to her, Mrs Wilson was bobbing her head in agreement; obviously she'd heard the story so many times she'd become immune to the fact her daughter had been involved in a serious crime.

'And did it bother you that Jane only got community service and you were sent to a young offenders' institution?'

'Bother me?' Katie blinked before shaking her head. 'Hardly. I was relieved. She wouldn't have lasted a day in there.'

'What do you mean? Was it because she was small?' Birdie leaned forward, unable to hide her curiosity.

'Nah. Nothing like that. She was just too... I don't know... Mum, what's the word?'

'Innocent,' her mother supplied, and Katie nodded in agreement.

'Yeah, that's it. She was sweet and kind. That's why I liked hanging out with her. If anything, I felt bad that I got her mixed up in the whole mess.'

'Did you see her afterwards?' Seb asked, his tone still light and casual.

'Yeah. Only once, not long after I got out. She was doing some course or other. Like to work in an office. Sounded dead boring, if you ask me. Anyway, we arranged to go out for a drink, but something came up and it never happened. Then I met the kid's dad, and by the time Crystal was born, I heard Jane had moved away. I don't know where she went.'

Birdie swallowed down her frustration. So far it wasn't anything they didn't know, and going by Katie's body language, she wasn't trying to hide anything.

'You mentioned that you were both seeing guys. Were they involved in the assault?'

This time, Katie's cheeks reddened, obviously reliving some of the memories again. 'Yeah. I'd been hanging with Trevor for a few months, and Jane started getting friendly with his mate, Dean.'

'Were they definitely dating?' Birdie asked, trying to hide her surprise. Florrie had forgotten to mention that.

'Not dating... Just, sort of, you know, hanging out together.'

'And what about Kyle Richards?' Seb asked.

Katie shuddered. 'He was bad news. I know we all went along with the idea, but it was Kyle who suggested it and he was the one with the hammer. Trevor and Dean weren't bad guys. They just got caught up in the moment. We all did.'

'Where are they now?' Birdie asked, hoping to get Katie out of the past. 'Would any of them have stayed in touch with Jane?'

'I can't think why. Dean's still here. He ended up marrying Ginny Fowler not long after he got out of prison. Poor sod. I think she visited him while he was inside. She's a bit on the possessive side. They have a couple of kids, and he has the pawnbroker's shop. Trevor died a couple of years ago. Cancer.' She broke off and dabbed her eyes.

'Terrible, it was,' Mrs Wilson cut in. 'He was skin and bones by the end of it. Nasty way to go.'

Katie nodded in agreement. 'We didn't stay in touch much after it all happened, but his funeral was ever so lovely.'

'I'm pleased,' Birdie said, before exchanging a quick glance with Seb. They already knew that Richards was back in prison, so if Blackham was dead, then apart from Katie, it only left Dean Knowles.

'Do you have the pawnbroker's address?' Seb asked, getting to his feet.

'Sure. It's *Les's Pawnbroker's*, over the other side of the motorway. And if you do find Jane, tell her I said hello. I'd love to catch up with her,' Katie said, desperation clinging to her voice. Was she hoping that Jane and her imaginary inheritance might somehow help improve her own life?

'Will do.' Birdie swallowed back her own guilt at giving her false hope. 'And thanks both of you for helping us.'

'You're welcome, duck.' Mrs Wilson walked them to

the front door and waited under the porch until Birdie and Seb were back in the car. The net curtains next door twitched, and Bluebell appeared again, dancing her way up and down the hedge.

'What do you think? Was Katie telling the truth?' Seb asked, starting the engine and pulling out onto the road.

'It sounds like things haven't been easy for her, but when we mentioned Jane's name, she didn't tense up or look away. And she didn't try and hide her jealousy of the non-existent inheritance. I think we can rule her out.'

'Which leaves us with Knowles, Florrie's ex-boyfriend. Why do you think she didn't mention they'd been involved?' Seb's brows knitted together as he drove.

'Your guess is as good as mine. People have done worse,' Birdie said as they drove down the street and the numbers on the doors flashed past her. Twenty, eighteen, sixteen. 'Hey, slow down. Let's have a look at number ten.'

Seb brought the car to a halt outside a grimy-looking terrace. The windows were boarded up and a metal door had been installed to stop squatters or vandals from getting in.

Weeds had cracked through the paving slabs and discarded crisp wrappers and beer bottles littered the overgrown garden. The houses on each side were in a similar state of neglect, and while it had been twenty years since Florrie had lived there, it was easy to see why she'd been so keen to leave her past behind.

An oppressive cloud hung over the houses, making Birdie's skin prickle. Suddenly, she wished they hadn't stopped.

'Do you want to knock on one of the doors, to see if we can find out where the father is?' he asked her.

She shook her head, not sure how to explain the heaviness pressing down on her.

'No point. It looks like some of these have been empty for a while. I guess I wanted to see what it was Florrie had been running away from.'

'I can't say I blame her,' he said as a couple of youths appeared from one of the houses. Both had pale complexions, stark against their black hoodies. One of them was walking unsteadily, like they were drunk. Calmly, Seb put his foot on the accelerator and drove off. In the wing mirror she watched the youths walk after them, but they didn't attempt to chase the car. Which was a relief since getting into a fight—or worse, getting carjacked—wasn't something she wished to face.

Chapter 8

Les's Pawnbroker's was in a rundown parade of shops that had seen better days, much like the street Florrie had grown up on. It was flanked by a vape shop on the left and a betting shop on the right. However, despite the litter and small blue pens covering the pavement, the shop front was neat and the glass clean.

'We'll use the same story again.' Seb pressed the key fob to lock the car.

'Definitely, because it will seem more suspicious if Katie and Knowles discuss our visits and their stories don't tally,' Birdie agreed, before frowning. 'Though I wonder if I should go in on my own. You saw how initially Katie and her mum clammed up around you. What if Knowles thinks we're police?'

'Probably not the first time he would've been visited by a detective. Is this about my clothes again?' He glanced down at the more casual waterproof jacket he'd chosen today.

Birdie shook her head. 'No, you're about as dressed

down as you're going to get. But you hardly look like you're going in to buy something. Or sell anything.'

'Would it surprise you to know how many rich families have secretly pawned off their possessions? There's been a long-held tradition within the aristocracy of selling off the family jewels after having fakes made to keep up the illusion of wealth.'

'You mean, your mother's diamonds might not be real?' Birdie's eyes gleamed.

'Entirely possible.' He bit back an amused grin while trying to imagine what his mother would think if Birdie ever asked her the question directly. 'Apparently my great-great-uncle was a nasty bugger who liked to gamble.'

'I stand corrected. You probably know your way around a pawnbroker's better than I do,' she teased as they stepped inside.

Seb wouldn't go that far, but he'd been into his fair share while on the force. And while some resembled upmarket jewellery shops, mainly displaying gold and diamond jewellery and luxury watches, Les's wasn't that standard and had shelves of consoles, power tools and musical instruments as well as display cabinets for the more expensive items.

There were a couple of older women leaning over one of the cabinets, pointing at something, while a tall woman with black hair served them, keeping a hawk-like eye on her customers.

A door chime had announced their arrival, and a man appeared from behind a curtained-off area. He was about five foot ten, with a receding hairline and expanding stomach that was covered in a too-tight Ben Sherman polo shirt. Down one arm was a sleeve of tattoos and a collection of thick gold bracelets. There was enough of a resemblance to the photo in the police file for Seb to identify him as Dean Knowles.

'All right.' Knowles nodded at them both. 'Can I help you?'

'I hope so.' Seb crossed the floor with determined steps. He knew his size sometimes intimidated people, and today he hoped for the same, since he imagined Knowles made a living from being tight-lipped. 'We're investigating the whereabouts of Jane Smith.'

'Never heard of her.' The man didn't so much as blink. But the tall woman behind the counter glanced over, her mouth set in a firm line.

Was she Ginny, Dean's wife?

'Maybe we can jog your memory? She was small with black hair and a cute face,' Birdie added, obviously noticing Ginny's annoyance and deciding to fish for a further reaction. 'On the second of May—'

'Okay. That's enough,' he growled, before glancing over at the woman. 'Sorry, love. Do you mind watching the shop? Blake's out the back if you need him. This will only take five minutes.'

Ginny's lips puckered, clearly not happy. But she gave a sharp nod and returned to her customers. Knowles used his hands to herd them out of the shop and onto the pavement outside. Once they were there, he folded his arms across his large stomach.

'You're not police, so who the fuck are you?'

'We're trying to trace Jane Smith in relation to an inheritance. We're speaking to anyone who might know her. Sorry if we caused problems in there—it wasn't our intention.'

At that, Knowles let out a sigh and unfolded his arms, the tough persona melting away. 'It's okay. And Ginny doesn't mean anything by it. We went to school together, but we didn't get together properly until after I got out of prison. She likes to say she's the reason I've stayed on the straight and narrow, and she's probably right. She gets a bit touchy when anything—or *anyone*—from the past crops up. She didn't even want me to go to Trev's funeral.'

'Did you go?' Birdie asked.

Knowles nodded. 'Well, yeah. I had to, didn't I? We'd been mates for years.'

'Did Jane go to the funeral? She might have been with her friend Katie,' Seb asked, hoping that it might lead to them finding out more.

'Katie was there, getting drunk and wearing all black, like she was the grieving bloody widow. Not that I blame her. Her taste in men has got worse as she's got older. But if Jane was there, I didn't see her. Not that I gave it a thought. As far as I know, she left town before I got out and hasn't been back since.'

'Did Jane contact you while you were in prison, or after you were released?'

'Why would she? Oh.' His eyes widened in understanding. 'Because we used to knock around together? Nah. It was nothing serious, and as soon as the court case started, we both knew it was over between us.'

'How did she take it? Was she upset?'

'Upset?' He frowned. 'I don't think so. She was a good kid. I assumed she'd been pleased to see the back of me.'

'Why's that?'

'Because I was the one who brought Kyle Richards along to hang out with us. Biggest mistake I ever made.'

'How did you know Kyle?'

Knowles nodded at the shop window. 'Through this place. Les, he was my uncle, and Kyle worked for him for a while. Kyle's old man had been robbing houses for years and Les used to fence some of the gear. It was easy back then. Not like these days, when everything's gotta be above board. It all goes through the books, now. Anyway, Kyle had been helping sell his dad's gear for a couple of years and had a real eye for it. My uncle called him a truffle hound. I guess that's why he took him on. When I first met him, he was a right laugh. I never had him down for attacking a geezer with a hammer, though. Shows what I know.'

'Does your uncle still work here?' Birdie asked.

Knowles shook his head. 'No. He died nineteen years ago while I was still locked up. It was a hit-and-run car crash. They never caught the arsehole who did it.'

'I'm sorry to hear that,' Seb said. 'When did you start working here?'

'It was impossible to get a job when I got out, so my aunt took me on. She'd been struggling to run the place on her own but couldn't afford to sell it. And while I might not have had the same nose for gold and diamonds as Kyle, I was damn good. I turned the place around, without doing anything illegal, which meant my aunt could retire to Blackpool. She died six years ago and left the place to me and Ginny. We've been running it ever since.'

'I'm pleased things have worked out for you, Dean,' Seb said. 'Do you know what happened to Tom Winger?'

At the mention of the man who'd been injured doing the attack, Knowles' cheeks went red, as if embarrassed to remember the past. 'After I got sent down, there was a big hoo-ha in the papers about how his family were too scared to live here anymore, so he sold his businesses and moved to Australia. People were angry because he owned three supermarkets and when they were taken over, loads of people lost their jobs. My cousin Vera included. She wouldn't talk to me for years because of it.'

'And has he ever come back here?'

'You're joking, right? Why would he come back to this shithole? Last I heard, he'd bought a resort on some fancy bloody island and was raking in the money, so things didn't turn out too bad for him.' Then he frowned as if it suddenly hit him that they'd gone off on a tangent. 'Hang on a minute. What's Tom Winger got to do with Jane? I doubt he'd know where she is.'

'A long shot.' Seb shrugged, pleased Knowles hadn't considered that *before* answering the question. 'Is there anyone else Jane might have stayed in touch with that we can speak to?'

He shook his head. 'Not that I can think of. I'd better get back in there. Last time someone mentioned one of my ex-girlfriends, Ginny got so stroppy that I had to fork out for a holiday to Ibiza. God knows what this'll cost me.'

'What about Ginny? Did she know Jane?' Birdie asked.

'I don't think so. Well, maybe from school, but they're not the same age. Ginny's my age. There was no reason for them to have had anything to do with each other.'

'Okay. Thanks. It was just a thought.'

Seb pulled out of his pocket one of the generic business cards they'd printed. It didn't mention their PI business, just had their names and a phone number that went through to a burner phone. He held it out to Knowles. 'Thanks for your time. If you do think of anything else to help us locate Jane, could you please give us a call?'

'Sure.' Knowles didn't bother looking at the card before putting it into his pocket and stepping back into the shop.

Looking back at the shopfront, it was clear that Ginny had been watching the entire conversation through the glass, and Knowles held up his hands in appeasement as he joined her behind the counter.

'It looks like this will be costing him more than a trip to

Ibiza this time,' Birdie said as they headed to the car. 'So, either he's a bloody good actor, or he really hasn't thought about Florrie in years.'

'Agreed,' Seb said as he climbed into the driver's side and started the engine. 'It also means it's time for another conversation with Florrie. If she wants us to find out who is behind the blackmail, then we need access to the people who are currently in her life.'

'Yeah. And she needs calling out about hiding things from her past. Like the fact she and Dean Knowles dated. If she isn't upfront with us, then we don't have a hope of sorting it out for her.'

Chapter 9

'We've made it,' Birdie called out as she and Elsa rushed into Seb's flat the following morning, having been out for a long walk.

They hadn't arrived back until late from Peterborough because of traffic. With hindsight they should have gone back to Market Harborough and travelled to London first thing. But then, Elsa would have had to stay overnight with Jill, and Seb didn't want to impose on her too much.

'Sorry we're late.' She pushed open the door to the kitchen, and Elsa beelined straight for her water bowl, which was by the back door.

Seb was sitting at the small table by the window. He gave Birdie a quizzical look. 'You were only walking Elsa. I thought even you couldn't be late back from that.'

'Never underestimate me,' she said, laughing. She hung the lead on the back-door hook and joined him at the table. 'Though if you want details, there was a rogue lawnmower that Elsa refused to go anywhere near, which meant we had to walk the long way around the park. And then there was the bakery on the corner. You know, the one that makes those to-die-for chocolate chip cookies.'

'Food? Why am I not surprised?'

'I need to make the most of it while I'm here.' She put her hands on the teapot that was by his elbow. It was still warm, and she poured herself a cup before holding up the cardboard box she'd brought in with her. 'I understand if you don't want one…'

'Thank you,' he said, taking the box. 'Though I'll probably wait until later in the day. Or at least until after ten.'

'You and your weird ways.' Birdie added a splash of milk to her cup and stirred it in. 'Have you heard from Florrie?'

'Yes, she called while you were out. She's on her way over but has to be at the studio by eleven, so can't stay long.'

'Well, that's not much help. We have a lot to discuss. We should have met her at the studio instead of here. You'd think the woman was avoiding us instead of wanting us to rid her of her blackmailer.'

It had been after five in the afternoon when they arrived back in London yesterday, and Florrie had been on her way to a charity event and couldn't cancel, which meant they'd bought takeaway Vietnamese and continued their in-depth research into the names Florrie had given them the day before.

They'd also researched Tom Winger, and Dean Knowles had been correct; he'd moved to Australia and had gone from a rich businessman to a tycoon. His two sons worked with him. This meant the chances of them wanting to exact revenge over something that had happened so long ago was minimal. Seb had also spent time digging into Knowles' business, but it all appeared above board. And while there had been a couple of newspaper articles alleging his uncle had fenced stolen items, Knowles, just as he'd said, had turned it into a legitimate business.

All this meant they needed to dig deeper into Florrie's current life because it was most likely the place where the blackmailer came from. But first they had to convince her to let them investigate.

Birdie suspected it wouldn't be easy.

The doorbell rang, and Seb got to his feet to answer it, leaving Birdie at the table. She glanced down at herself and sighed. She'd hoped to have a shower before Florrie arrived, but instead, she was in her tracksuit bottoms and her favourite hoodie that now had a smear of chocolate on it. Quickly, she took it off and tied it around her waist before finger-combing her wild red curls.

She'd just about finished making herself semi-presentable when Florrie appeared in the doorway. The black coat and glasses disguise had been replaced by a simple grey jacket that reached her knees, and a baseball cap.

'I'm sorry about last night. It was raising money for leukaemia, and several of the patients have been on the show, so I couldn't let them down,' Florrie explained as she sat down at the table.

'We understand.' Birdie leaned forward and reached for the teapot. There was just about enough in there for another cup. 'Would you like some?'

'I wish. Unfortunately, I can't drink too much before filming in case I need the loo,' she explained before a hint of red crept up her neck. 'Sorry, that's probably more information than you need. What happened in Peterborough? Did you have any luck?'

'Yes. We spoke to Katie Wilson and Dean Knowles.' Birdie explained what they'd found out, including the information that Kyle Richards was back in jail and that Trevor Blackham was dead. Once she finished, she folded her arms. 'Why didn't you tell us that you and Dean were dating at the time of the attack?'

Florrie's brow wrinkled. 'Dating? I'd hardly call it that. Katie had been seeing Trevor, and when Dean started hanging around with us, we ended up talking by default. We got on well and started to see each other a bit, but it was never serious. More like we hung around together if we were both at the same place. I didn't see him again after the trial. I'd honestly forgotten about it. I'm surprised he even mentioned it.'

'He didn't,' Birdie admitted. 'It was Katie who told us. Though Dean's wife Ginny didn't seem at all happy when we asked about you, which did sort of confirm it.'

'Ginny? Oh, wait, you mean Ginny Fowler. I vaguely remember her from school. She was in a higher class than me. I had no idea she and Dean were married. Why would she see me as a threat? It's not like Dean and I were a proper couple. It's so weird that you spoke to Katie. How is she?'

Birdie sighed. 'Okay. A single mum with four kids, so it's not easy for her.'

'Four children. Wow! Did you meet any of them?'

'No, the younger ones would have been at school. But we did meet her mum,' Seb said. 'She remembers you fondly. They both do.'

Florrie hesitated, as if considering her next words. 'You might have noticed that I didn't grow up in the greatest part of town, but Katie and her mother were very kind to me, at a time when no one else was. I don't suppose you have a recent photo of Katie? I'd love to see what she looks like now.'

'Sorry, we don't do that kind of surveillance,' Seb interjected. 'But I'm sure you could find her on social media if you look.'

'No, I can't. I promised myself to never look back. That's what I don't understand about the blackmail. I've always been so careful.' Worry lines creased her brow, and she shut her eyes, as if trying to collect herself. When she opened them again, the lines had gone, and her calmness had returned. 'Do you think Katie or Dean are involved in this?'

'No. Body language isn't everything, but when combined with their circumstances and the answers they gave, neither of them appeared to be harbouring a grudge against you. In fact, it was the opposite. They were both pleased that you hadn't been given any detention time following the trial,' Birdie said.

'What happens now?' Florrie pressed her lips together, clearly concerned.

'We understand why you wish to keep a low profile,' Seb said in a gentle but firm voice, 'but we need to talk to people who know you now, or who have information that can help us. Like Ernie the concierge, and the people you work with, including your agent and assistant. The more people we interview, the quicker we can rule them out.'

'I can't believe anyone at work would do this to me—we're like family.'

'Sometimes it's our families who hurt us most,' Birdie said, her throat tightening as she suddenly thought of her birth mother; even if she had done it with the best of intentions, it was still hard to explain the dull ache that the abandonment had left behind. Or the fact she still hadn't replied to the email.

'What if the blackmailer finds out?'

'They won't, because we're not going to mention anything about the blackmail.' Birdie quickly assured her.

'We've come up with a plan that we believe will work. We'll go undercover as journalists writing an in-depth article on you. Considering how many magazines you've already been featured in, it won't seem strange to anyone.'

'It's important we move quickly,' Seb added. 'Time isn't on our side and we've already lost a day from our trip to Peterborough. We can't afford to wait any longer.'

Florrie tilted her head, as if having a mental conversation with herself. Then she nodded. 'You're right. It's stupid that I keep worrying about drawing attention to myself. If we don't do anything, it will only get worse. When do you want to start?'

'Today,' Birdie said immediately. 'It's already Friday, and the blackmailer said they were going to give you just under a week. That means you should be hearing from them on Sunday with further instructions.'

The room was silent apart from Elsa's gentle snoring.

Then Florrie abruptly stood up and gave a nod of consent. 'Okay. I was being naïve to think it would just go away. But it's a good plan. We have journalists coming and going all the time. I'll make some calls and get it approved and then you should be good to go. But please, you have to find out who's behind this.'

'That's what we're here for.' Birdie exchanged a glance with Seb.

His jaw was set tight and his eyes grim. They'd both worked enough cases to know that sometimes what you really needed was time. And right now, that was the one thing they didn't have.

Chapter 10

'Where did you say you were from?' Tanya, the make-up artist, said as she leaned over Florrie's face, carefully blending concealer under the presenter's eyes.

The star's dressing room was smaller than Seb would have expected, reinforcing Florrie's point that her job wasn't always as glamorous or well paid as people thought. Because of time constraints, the make-up artist could only talk to them for a few minutes after making up Florrie, which meant Seb wouldn't be able to probe as much as he'd like to, also she was unlikely to give them her full attention. But it was better than not talking to her at all.

'A new magazine called *Lift*. We're all about supporting and empowering strong women and letting the public see them in a new light.' Birdie's voice was breezy as she tapped her pen against the notepad in her hand.

It was a habit she had when things weren't going fast enough for her liking, and it could be infuriating. However, right now, it was proving a good distraction, and he took the opportunity to use the digital camera he'd brought with him, pretending to take some background shots while instead having a good look around.

At the far end was a low emerald-green sofa and a gold-and-glass coffee table that was artfully covered in scented candles and a large book on interior design. A Kandinsky print on the wall finished off the space, making it seem modern, yet completely impersonal.

He did a second sweep but there were no family photos or anything to indicate Florrie's real identity. It was obvious she was very careful when around others.

'Oh, right. Sounds cool.' Tanya didn't bother to look up at them, which suggested she wouldn't be reading the article or the magazine—even if it had, in fact, existed. She picked up one of her brushes and swiped across Florrie's cheeks a couple of times before finally standing back and nodding. 'There you go. All done.'

'Thank you. Tanya, you're an angel.' Florrie stood up and smiled at her reflection in the mirror.

A girl appearing extremely harassed stood in the doorway. She was in her early twenties and was panting, as if she'd run a half marathon.

'There you are, Florrie,' she said. 'You're needed on set in five minutes. And I've got a bunch of messages for you. Your stylist will also be arriving later to discuss a gown for Sunday night, and Brian wants to talk to you about next week's press conference.' The girl spoke in rapid fire, barely even stopping to take a breath. Stress radiated off her and the ends of her fingernails were chewed down to the quick.

Florrie gave Birdie and Seb an apologetic smile. 'Sorry, that's my cue. By the way, this is Lily, who has the dreadful job of trying to keep my life in order. I think you're down to talk to her later today about the article. Is that right, Lily?'

'Oh, yes. At three-thirty. Can't wait,' Lily replied in an unenthusiastic voice.

Just one more item on a very long to-do list, no doubt.

Seb pitied her. He suspected that working as an assistant in the entertainment industry could be an unforgiving job.

Florrie patted Lily's arm. 'They'll be gentle on you, I'm sure.' Then she turned to Tanya, blowing her a kiss. 'And I really appreciate you talking to Seb and Birdie for a few minutes. They want to make sure they get a well-rounded perspective for the article.'

'How long have you worked with Florrie?' Birdie asked with an encouraging nod once Florrie and Lily had left the room.

'About five years.' Tanya meticulously inspected her brushes before packing each one away. 'Though it's not full-time, which is why I can't talk for long. I need to be on set soon and once the recording has finished, I have an editorial shoot across town.'

'We're grateful for whatever time you can spare us and will make this as quick as possible. How would you describe Florrie as a person?'

'Sweet, kind, thoughtful. Unusual traits for someone of her standing.' Tanya moved onto the bottles of foundation that were spread out across the dressing table. 'Last year, for my birthday, she remembered me saying that I love Turkish Delight, so she brought me the most delicious authentic box of it, all the way from Turkey.'

'Yum. I bet it was to die for.' Birdie's eyes lit up. 'It's one of my favourite sweets, too.'

Seb hadn't known that, but it didn't surprise him; there wasn't much in the way of sweets and cakes that his partner didn't like. But the comment also had the result of capturing the make-up artist's interest and she put down the lipstick she'd been inspecting.

'It costs a bomb, but totally worth it,' Tanya confided. 'That's Florrie all over.'

Birdie gave an enthusiast nod of agreement. 'It sounds like you're all one big happy family here.'

'Well, it can be tricky with television. There are so many egos all competing for space, thinking that their job is the most important. But Florrie's not like that. I don't know whether I should be telling you this, but... well, I guess it won't hurt. About three years ago the network wanted to cancel us. They said we were out of touch with the digital age. Most of us are freelancers and if the show had been taken off air, it would've been devastating for so many of us. But Florrie worked her arse off to convince the network to reconsider, even offering to take a pay cut.'

'Wow, that's amazing. What happened?'

'Eventually, they decided to keep the show going. Thank goodness.'

'Did Florrie have to take a pay cut?'

'I don't think so.'

'Who are the big egos working with Florrie now?' Birdie asked in a casual voice.

Tanya paused for a moment. 'There aren't any. Not really. The really big ones jumped ship as soon as things looked bad. A couple of screenwriters and one of the producers. But the team is better for it.' An alarm went on her phone. 'Crap. That's me. I'm needed on set. Florrie asked me to take you through to the green room. Brian, her agent, is meeting you there.'

'Great, and thanks.' Birdie put her notebook away while Tanya finished collecting her numerous tubes and brushes.

Once finished, the make-up artist gestured for them to

follow her down a long corridor filled with lengths of scaffolding, stacks of metal boxes and random pieces of equipment including an eight-foot-tall cardboard dog.

The green room had a dark red carpet and magnolia-covered walls. A couple of nondescript sofas were set at right angles, facing a huge television monitor that had been mounted on the wall.

'Brian won't be long.' She gave them a quick wave and hurried away, leaving the pair of them alone. The room was empty and they both walked over to the sofas.

'Thoughts?' Birdie asked.

'Tanya appeared genuine enough. If she's to be believed, there's no one working with her now who has any reason to get revenge. But—'

Seb was cut short as the door opened and a middle-aged man with fine, pale brown hair walked in. He was about five ten and had the start of a pot belly. It was Brian Springer, Florrie's agent. Seb recognised him from his research the previous evening. After reading history at Oxford, Springer had taken a job as personal assistant to a well-known academic who'd done several shows for the BBC. From there, he'd segued into being a talent agent and, while most of his clients worked on documentaries, he did have several presenters, actors, and singers on his books. Florrie was the most well-known.

'Thank you for taking the time to meet with us.' Seb held out his hand and Brian took it. 'I know it's short notice.'

Brian raised an eyebrow. 'This is television. There are only ever two speeds and no one knows what the second one is.'

'All the same, we do appreciate it,' Seb quickly continued.

Brian bristled with the impatience of a man who had

better places to be. 'I don't usually like my clients agreeing to media interviews without keeping Missy in the loop— she organises all the PR and marketing—but Florrie said you're an old family friend, and she owed you a favour. So, fire away.'

'Much appreciated. We're interested in showing Florrie as a whole person—the real ups and downs of being in the limelight. I imagine it must come with its challenges. Has there been a time when you've been worried for her safety or mental health?'

Brian blinked, as if waking up from a nap. 'What did you say the name of this magazine was?'

'*Lift*.' Birdie jumped in. Her smile was friendly but her eyes were narrowed. She clearly didn't like Brian.

'The question may sound odd, but we've done extensive market research and our readers want to move away from fake, edited narratives. That's why we want to normalise the complexities of being a working woman in today's world. We believe it can be of real benefit to people,' Seb said.

Brian's facial expression remained static, but he finally shrugged. 'In answer to your question, I've never been worried about her. We go way back and she's always had the most extraordinary ability to shrug off negative comments. I've often wished she could teach my other clients how to remain calm. I think it's been the secret to her success. That, and the way she lights up the screen,' he said, as the overhead television burst into life and Florrie appeared.

'She does have a great presence,' Seb agreed, staring at the screen and admiring Tanya's work. The dark shadows from her pressing anxieties were gone, leaving Florrie looking bright and engaged. 'And resilience is definitely something we'll be focusing on. Especially with what's going on in the world. On that note, what kind of public interaction does Florrie have with her fans? Does she mix with them in person or online? And does she receive much physical fan mail, or is it mainly emails and social media comments?'

'The amount of physical mail the show receives is ridiculous. Most of it's from kids, but there are older fans as well. Ones who watched her when they were young.'

'Does Florrie read them all?' Seb asked.

'That would be impossible,' Brian said, before narrowing his eyes. 'Shouldn't you be writing this down? I didn't give you permission to record anything.'

'I have a good memory,' Seb assured him as a burst of sound came from the television. Up on the screen, Florrie had started nailing together what looked like two pieces of wood from an old packing pallet in order to make a raised vegetable garden.

'And I'm the backup.' Birdie held up her notepad and pen. Then she gave him a wild smile. 'So… about the fan mail. What happens to it if Florrie doesn't see it all?'

'Missy and I go through some, and the rest goes to TBG, the production company behind the show. There's a system for flagging and reporting to the police anything offensive or illegal that we receive, but there are hardly any of those. Florrie sees a selection of the "normal" letters and will reply to them. She'd love to do more, but she'd never leave the office if she did.'

'She's certainly dedicated,' Seb agreed. 'Though I'm curious to know if the police have ever expressed concerns over any mail or messages they've been given?'

'Not that I'm aware.'

'Are there any other kinds of messages you hide from her?' Seb decided to push a bit harder. Brian stiffened before checking the passageways to make sure they were alone.

'Look, this has to stay out of print. But there's only one kind of mail that a celebrity never wants to see.'

'What's that?' Birdie demanded, her eyes bright.

'Audition tapes from young wannabes wanting to get a foot in the door. Who want a chance to replace them. We get them all the time. Through the door, in the post, via email. Once someone slipped me one while I was on the bloody loo, for goodness' sake.' He scowled as his phone rang, and lifted an eyebrow to suggest their time was up.

'Okay, thank you for talking to us,' Seb said.

'No problem. And don't forget we need to approve the final copy and all photographs before you go to print,' Brian said before answering his phone and disappearing from the room.

'That was interesting,' Seb said. 'Especially considering Florrie's comment about there always being someone "young, shiny and new" to replace her.'

'It also explains the all-day spa treatment she had. The woman at the reception said that Florrie goes at least twice a week.'

'Looking for the fountain of youth.' Seb rubbed his chin. 'It's definitely an angle we have to consider.'

'Don't young wannabe stars hang out in fancy night-clubs that don't open until past your bedtime?' Birdie pondered. 'How would you ever get to talk to them?'

'I'm not in a wheelchair yet.'

'Got you again. One day you'll stop biting at my jokes,' she promised, smirking.

'And then what would you do for entertainment?' he asked, which earned him a wide grin.

'We don't have much time, so one of us should go to

the TBG offices and talk to the staff there, and the other stay here to keep interviewing the rest of the team,' Birdie said, her expression now serious. 'Then tonight, we'll go to Florrie's apartment building and talk to the concierge. So far, three letters have been delivered to her apartment, each one arriving mysteriously. What's the betting that Ernie, the concierge, knows more than he let on to Florrie?'

'I agree. Not to mention that the most recent letter didn't give a time or location to deliver the money, which means they'll need to deliver another. Do you want to stay here or go to the production company?' Seb asked as the door opened and a man pushing a food trolley walked in.

The room filled with the scent of garlic and butter.

A second person appeared with another trolley of food. Like the Pied Piper, a number of people materialised, including Tanya, who was having an in-depth conversation with a guy her own age. The chatter increased as they all made a beeline for the trestle table where the food was being set up.

Birdie's stomach rumbled, and she gave him a hopeful smile. 'I suppose I could tough it out here.'

'Well, you do work better on a full stomach. Call me if you find anything, otherwise we'll meet up at Canary Wharf and grab some dinner before speaking to Ernie. That's if you have any room left for a meal.'

'I'll take that as a personal challenge,' Birdie promised before heading over to the table, smiling and chatting to people as she went.

Chapter 11

'It's so pretty here—I didn't realise.'

'I thought you'd like it.' Seb turned to where Birdie was staring ahead across the London skyline as the last of the pink-and-orange sunset faded away and the night took hold. It was seven-thirty in the evening and they were sitting in the small park next to Florrie's apartment building.

Ernie, a well-built man, had appeared at the reception counter half an hour ago, but they'd decided to wait outside and observe him first, hoping to speak with him privately when he had a break. That way, if the place really was being watched, the conversation wouldn't be seen.

'Wait.' Birdie suddenly turned to him. 'Is this part of your cunning ploy to make me fall in love with London and want to move here when Sarah returns from overseas?'

'Yes. I have the power to control the sunsets. It comes in useful from time to time,' he said, which earned him a poke in the arm. He held up his hands. 'And no, it's purely a coincidence that Ernie starts work this time of night.'

'Okay, I believe you,' she said, not looking entirely convinced.

Earlier in the evening, they'd met up at a nearby pub, and over a quick meal had compared notes on what they'd discovered. It wasn't much. Birdie had managed to get a list of all the guest hosts who had come and gone from the show over the last ten years, while Seb had spoken to several people at the production company who backed up what Brian had said about the number of aspiring presenters wanting to get into television. Seb had also tracked down Florrie's estranged father, who was in a rest home with advanced stage dementia so they wouldn't be able to speak to him. Because Florrie had shown no interest in him, Seb wasn't sure whether to mention it. It was something they'd discuss before the case was over.

For now, they needed to find out who delivered the blackmail notes.

There was a constant stream of people coming and going from the apartment building, and it was almost nine before Ernie stood up and walked across the foyer and out of the front doors.

He headed down the side of the building, not giving any sign that he'd noticed them.

Seb got to his feet and Birdie quickly followed. A siren rang out in the distance, drowning out the gentle lapping of the River Thames to their left.

'He must be going for a smoke, like Florrie said,' Birdie commented. 'How do you want to play this?'

'We'll tell him we've been hired by the production company to do an audit on Florrie's security. Then we can ask him directly.'

'Sounds good to me.'

They crossed the small square and headed down the side of the building. A couple of plastic chairs were in one corner as well as several upturned milk crates. Ernie was sitting on one of the chairs, smoking. His phone was turned sideways and the sound of horse racing blared out from it. As they drew closer, the commentator's high-pitched voice increased in speed and volume.

'Come on, come on, come on!' Ernie yelled, and then the noise stopped and he slumped down in the chair, a string of expletives accompanying it.

Birdie raised an eyebrow at Seb as they reached him.

He was about thirty and his skin had a dull pallor, probably from working nights. His movements were sluggish but his dark eyes were bright and alert. Ernie didn't look like a man on a winning streak.

As they drew closer, Birdie's sneaker dislodged a stone, which went ricocheting across the concrete.

'Shit,' she muttered under her breath as Ernie's head snapped up and he scrambled to his feet, the despair that had been surrounding him replaced by suspicion.

'What the hell? Who are you?' He threw his shoulders back to reveal the thick muscles running down from his neck. The way his eyes followed their every movement suggested he'd been in his fair share of fights.

'My name's Clifford. We're here to discuss several letters that have been delivered here for Florrie Hart.'

'What's it to do with you?' Ernie's mouth tightened and he tilted his head to one side, clearly uncomfortable.

'We've been hired by TBG to do a security assessment for Ms Hart, and are following up on unsolicited mail. Is it correct you're meant to get a name and signature for everything that's delivered?'

He was quiet, as if weighing up his options. 'Look, sometimes it gets busy, and things slip through the net. But it was only a couple of letters. It's not like a person wandered in. Mistakes happen.'

'Three times? All on your shift?' Birdie growled at him. 'Yeah, right.'

'Now, we could ask management to look at the CCTV footage, but we thought we'd give you the opportunity of explaining what happened first.' Seb gave him an encouraging smile. 'So, let's start again. What can you tell us about the letter that was delivered last Sunday?'

Irritation rippled across the concierge's face and then he let out a sigh. 'Look, I need this job. Like *really* need it. If I tell you stuff, does that mean I'll get fired?'

'Why? Do you think you deserve to?' Birdie took a step closer.

Ernie's face reddened and he shook his head. 'I swear this isn't what I normally do. But a few weeks ago, I'd had a bad day at the…' He broke off and rubbed his neck. 'It doesn't matter. Anyway, this guy comes in and wants to take a letter up to number 205. That's Florrie's place. I tell him no, but say that I can give it to her once he's signed the book. He had this big story about how it was meant to be a surprise for her birthday and he didn't want to ruin it.'

'And you believed him?' Birdie glared at the man.

Seb didn't bother to stop her since he'd long since learnt how effective that particular glare could be.

'Yeah. I suppose.' Ernie cowered. 'I had a lot going on.'

'What happened next?' Seb prompted, his own voice cool.

'He said he'd give me fifty quid if he could leave it, and not sign the book. I swear I didn't mean any harm. I like Florrie… I mean, Ms Hart. She's one of the decent ones in this place. I was in a fix and he came along at the right time.'

'We know he came back twice more. That means Florrie Hart must have had three birthdays in as many weeks. Didn't that seem odd to you?' Birdie asked.

'Look, I needed the money, okay? Besides, what was in the letters?'

'The content isn't the issue, the lack of security is,' Seb reminded him. 'What was his name?'

'I dunno.'

Birdie narrowed her eyes, and her red hair seemed to bounce with irritation. 'Do you remember what he looked like?'

Ernie seemed to pick up on her annoyance and held up his hands. 'About five foot ten. Not much hair. Hard to say how old he was. Maybe fifty-five or something.'

Birdie's eyes flickered for a moment, and Seb nodded at her. The description sounded a lot like Florrie's agent, Brian. Seb pulled out his phone and did an internet search for Brian Springer and held up the screen.

'Is this him?' he asked.

Ernie squinted and used his fingers to enlarge the photo before shrugging. 'Hard to say. One old guy looks much like the next. So what are you going to do? Are you going to blab to management?'

'It's something we'll need to consider.' Seb straightened to his full height and pressed a business card into Ernie's hand. 'In the meantime, if he comes back, I need you to get a name and call me immediately.' There was every possibility that the blackmailer would be returning tomorrow to deliver another note. Especially if they thought they'd been successful with the first three.

'Sure. I understand.'

'I hope you do,' Seb said, not bothering to add that he and Birdie would be there tomorrow and could hopefully put an end to this whole thing.

Birdie held out her hand for Ernie's phone. 'I'll key in my number, in case you lose the card.'

Ernie opened his mouth and then shut it again as he

passed over the phone. Birdie swiped the screen and punched in her details. A moment later, the burner cell phone they'd bought buzzed. She gave Ernie a wide smile.

'See. Now you won't have any excuses. Isn't that great?'

Ernie didn't answer as he snatched back his own phone and stalked off. Once he was gone, they made their way to the Tube station.

'Great idea with the phone.'

'It's the only way to make sure someone doesn't give you a fake number.' Birdie raised an eyebrow, an amused smile tugging at her mouth. 'Which, of course, you'd know if you ever went out to a club.'

'Duly noted,' he said. 'What's your impression of Ernie?'

'I think he's a piece of work. And he did it for a measly hundred and fifty quid.' Frustration shone from Birdie's eyes. 'Do you think he recognised Brian and didn't want to land himself in more trouble?'

'It's hard to say. Outwardly, the man didn't appear to be lying. But then he's a seasoned gambler who's obviously open to bribes, so he might have a complicated relationship with the truth. And if he believes what he's saying, it's harder to pick up the body-language tells,' Seb admitted.

'But why would Florrie's agent be behind this?' Birdie folded her arms.

'Maybe the negotiations aren't going well, and he knows how desperate Florrie is to hold on to her job? Or perhaps he thinks the golden egg is getting tarnished, and he wants to get as much out of her as he can before her star fades?'

'That's brutal.'

'Agreed, but I don't think we should mention that part to Florrie until we've done a bit more research into Brian. We could be wrong.'

Birdie nodded. 'I'll give Florrie a call, update her on what we now know about Ernie, and let her know we're going to be watching the apartment tomorrow to see who shows up with the letter. Hopefully in twenty-four hours we'll have our blackmailer right where we want him.'

Chapter 12

Seb tugged at his jacket, while next to him Birdie huddled under the cheap umbrella she'd bought on the way from Canary Wharf Tube station, trying to shelter from the rain that had started early that morning. However, it hadn't done a great deal to keep her dry, and her red hair was plastered across her face.

Inside the apartment building, the day concierge had taken over from Ernie, and Birdie used the binoculars to peer inside. She lowered them and scowled.

'It's not fair. Everyone inside the building is dry and we're standing here getting soaking wet. I still don't get why we have to be here the whole day, considering all the other letters were delivered during Ernie's shift.'

They'd arrived at nine in the morning and it had been bucketing down ever since. During the seven hours, they'd taken it in turns, with one watching the entrance, and the other watching the park and walkway to see anyone approaching. The only silver lining was that the dreadful weather had kept most people away, making it easier to monitor.

The previous evening they'd researched further into Brian Springer. As well as his celebrity portfolio, he also owned several properties and ran most of his money through BS Trading Ltd, which, according to Companies House, was in good standing. This meant there wasn't an obvious motive for blackmailing one of his own clients.

'In case the blackmailer decides to change his MO.'

'What if we've missed him?' Birdie held the umbrella to one side so she could shake off the excess moisture. 'We should go inside and ask if anyone's delivered a letter. Or if the concierge has seen anyone matching the description Ernie gave us.'

'We'll give it a little longer.' Seb managed to repress a smile. Birdie wasn't known for her patience even when the weather was nice.

'We should have taken Florrie up on her offer of using her apartment? At least one of us could be having a hot shower and a warm drink instead of both of us suffering.' She gave a wistful shrug.

When Birdie had called Florrie to give her the latest update the previous evening, she was still at the studio. After hearing about what Ernie had done, she decided not to go home and instead booked a room in a nearby hotel for a couple of nights, leaving her apartment empty, which was why she'd offered it to them.

'And if one of us was up there and one down here, how would we manage to liaise, or follow someone at a moment's notice? I'm sorry, Birdie, but this is the only suitable place.'

'Okay, okay. Ignore me. I'm just cold, wet, and grumpy.' Birdie paused for a moment. 'And hungry.'

'Why don't you grab us some food and drinks from over there?' Seb pointed to a newsagent's close by. He wasn't hungry but thought it would ease Birdie's frustration. 'And then—'

He was cut off by Birdie's phone, which she pulled out of her pocket.

'It's Florrie,' she said.

'Put her on speaker.'

'We won't hear her.' Birdie indicated to the rain that was still pounding down all around them. She accepted the call, tilted her head to one side and pulled her umbrella down until it almost touched her. To help her hear, he assumed. Although it meant he couldn't see or hear anything.

After a couple of minutes, Birdie lifted the umbrella, returned the phone to her pocket and turned to him, her face paler than usual.

His spine stiffened. 'What's happened?'

'Florrie's received another note. This time, it was delivered to the studio and left in her dressing room.'

He swore under his breath as they both stepped out from their hiding spot behind a sodden oak tree. In true irony, just at that moment, the rain lessened and the first peek of sunlight pushed its way through the dull skies.

'Did anyone see who left it?' Seb asked.

She shook her head, her wet hair hanging in long clumps. 'Not as far as she knows. I've told her we'll go over there straight away.'

While they headed in the direction of the underground car park, his mind raced. 'The question is, did the person delivering the letter come here first, but saw us watching and therefore changed their mind about leaving it here?'

'Not just that, but also, why was the letter delivered during the day and not the evening like the others had been?' Birdie said, practically jogging to keep up with him. 'Unless Ernie warned the guy that we've been asking questions, so he decided to go to the studio instead… if it was a man delivering it again. It could have been a woman.'

'The other times it was the same man so let's assume it was a man. However, for your scenario to work, Ernie would need a contact number to give them advance warning.'

'True. Maybe the blackmailer knows her schedule and delivered the other letters to the apartment because he knew she was at home. This time he knows she's at the studio and also knows that she's staying in a hotel?' Birdie suggested, panting. 'Can you slow down a bit, I'm knackered.'

'Sorry.' He slowed his gait—no easy task with his long legs. 'The worrying thing about these scenarios is they suggest the blackmailer knows more than we do,' Seb admitted.

'And that's not the worst of it. They want the two hundred thousand pounds delivered in cash on Tuesday morning.'

'I didn't expect to see him,' Birdie whispered when Brian Springer came out of the lift at the studio and headed to the large reception desk to greet them. Despite having security clearance, they were still required to sign in and be accompanied to the studio. 'Do you think he knows we've spent the morning outside Florrie's apartment?'

'Ernie could have called him, assuming that Brian is the culprit, which seems unlikely,' Seb said. 'And leaving the letter here might have been a mistake, because it's harder to get into the studio than it is to leave an envelope with a night concierge who has a gambling habit.'

'So, we're right in focusing on Florrie's colleagues,'

Birdie said as Brian reached them. His gaze swept over them.

'Back for round two, I see. And not looking very dry.'

'We've been taking some location shots, but still need a few more photos of Florrie at work. We hadn't expected to see you here again. Is it usual for agents to spend so much time on set?' Seb asked while they waited for their temporary ID badges.

'Only when they're in the middle of negotiating a new contract.' Brian flashed them a smile, which didn't reach his eyes.

'How's that going?' Birdie asked in a casual voice as they walked back down the long corridor. Some of the props had disappeared and people were coming and going, talking into phones, an air of panic clinging to them like confetti.

Brian raised an eyebrow, as if amused to think he'd answer such a question to a journalist. 'Excellent. We all adore Florrie and want what's best for her career.'

'Hmmm,' Birdie mumbled as a woman balancing a tray of glasses hurried past. 'What's going on here?'

'Freddie, the latest pop sensation, is booked for a live segment in studio three. That kid has star power. I hope his management is making the most of it, because one day those looks will fade.' He came to a halt outside Florrie's dressing room. 'I won't come in. One of my new signings is desperate to meet Freddie, so I'm taking her along. If they started dating... well, it wouldn't be the worst thing that could happen to her singing career. And don't forget, I want to see a copy of the article before it goes to print. We only want good press. Understand?'

'We sure do.' Birdie gave him what Seb recognised as her fake smile. Once Brian was gone, she dropped it and growled. 'Even if he isn't behind this, Florrie needs a new agent. He's a total creep.'

'Maybe that's what makes him good at his job.'

'If you say so.' Birdie knocked on Florrie's dressing room door, which had a *Do Not Disturb* sign dangling off the handle. 'Florrie, it's us. Birdie and Seb. Can we come in?'

There was no reply, but the faint shuffling of feet suggested someone was in there. A moment later, the door handle turned and Florrie appeared in front of them. She was wrapped in an oversized dressing gown, which made her look small and vulnerable despite the flawless makeup.

'Thank you for coming so quickly.' She ushered them in before closing and locking the door. Yesterday's neatness was gone, and the table was littered with foil wrappers and a half-finished mug of coffee. In the middle of the table was what looked like the letter. 'Excuse the mess. Some people turn to alcohol, I go for a coffee and chocolate.' She walked over to the sofa and sat down.

'Sugar can help with the shock,' Birdie said, following her.

'I-I can't believe they came in here,' Florrie stuttered, panic in her eyes. 'This has always been my happy place and now I keep thinking they're going to step out in front of me.'

'Can you tell us exactly what happened?' Birdie sat next to Florrie on the sofa while Seb positioned himself on the other side of the coffee table, both waiting for her to speak.

'We'd finished filming and everyone was in a rush. They all wanted to talk their way into the event with Freddie. You wouldn't think most of us had worked in television for years and have met everyone from royalty to Hollywood stars. But I guess everyone wants a piece of the hot new talent. Anyway, it's not my thing, so I came back here to get changed. I have another fundraising gala tonight—it's for a literacy charity—and I'm meant to be meeting a couple of friends for a drink first. The letter was waiting for me when I walked in. It was on the dressing table.'

'Who has access to your room?'

'Everyone. I mean, it's not usually locked.'

'Did you ask at reception whether it was left there and then someone brought it to you?'

'I called and asked if anyone had left anything for me and they said no.'

'Could it have been given to Lily and she brought it in here?' Seb asked.

'No. She's got a family thing on today and won't be in until later.'

'Is that it?' Seb asked, pointing to the letter on the table.

'Yes. As soon as I saw it, I knew what it was. I brought it over here to read.'

Florrie leaned forward to pick it up, but her oversized sleeve caught on her mug. The china teetered dangerously towards the envelope before Birdie dived forward and caught it, not spilling a drop.

'Howzat,' she automatically said. 'Sorry, once a crick-eter, always a cricketer.'

'Don't apologise.' Florrie shrank back onto the sofa and wrapped her arms around her chest. 'It was lucky you caught it or the note might have been ruined.'

'Do you mind if we read it?'

'Please do.'

Seb pulled on a pair of disposable gloves and picked it up from the table. 'The envelope appears to be the same as the others,' he commented before opening it and extracting a folded piece of paper and a newspaper cutting, dated six months after the first. He flattened out the cutting and Birdie came over and sat beside him, so they could both read it.

Local businessman shuts up shop, a year after being attacked by louts

Respected businessman, Tom Winger, who was attacked in his house twelve months ago by a gang of youths has decided to sell the three supermarkets that have been in his family for three generations. Winger said that the ongoing fear he and his family now feel makes it impossible for them to stay in Peterborough any longer. With a national chain taking over the businesses, staff rationalisation has meant that up to one hundred people may lose their jobs.

The information itself wasn't new—they'd already discovered it during their own research—but the photo in the article was one they hadn't seen before. It was of Katie Wilson and Dean Knowles, and standing between them was Jane. The way Knowles and Katie were looking at her made it appear she was the most important person there.

'I had no idea that photo even existed,' Florrie said in a tiny voice as she fumbled in her pocket and pulled out a chocolate. Her hands shook as she tore off the wrapper and put it in her mouth. 'This photo makes me look like the ringleader. I'll be blamed for the entire thing. No one's interested in the truth these days. They'll build up a story around the crime and the photo. I'm so stupid. I should've known I couldn't outrun the past.'

'What does the note say?' Birdie asked quickly, obviously trying to distract Florrie from her rising hysteria.

Seb picked it up and examined it. Another A4 sheet of paper with a message in the middle, typed in Times New Roman.

Time's up. Take £200,000 in cash to King's Cross Station on Tuesday morning at nine. Leave it behind the counter at the flower shop. I'm watching your every move and if you call the police or tell anyone, then I'll see you at the press conference.

Birdie wrinkled her brow. 'What press conference?'

'It's to announce an upcoming live anniversary special we're doing next month. The show itself is going to be a fundraiser, and we'll be having past presenters there. The press conference is to generate some media coverage.'

Damn. Seb recalled Lily mentioning a press conference as she'd run through Florrie's busy schedule, but he hadn't thought to ask for more details. He had to admit it was a good move. Not only to tie it in with the press conference, but to pick such a busy time at King's Cross Station. Even if they did stake it out, it would be almost impossible to find anyone without the backing of a large police force. It was a well-thought-out plan on the blackmailer's part.

'So, if you don't pay up, the blackmailer will crash the press conference and make sure to tell everyone who you really are,' Birdie said.

Florrie nodded and with a shaking hand reached into her pocket for another chocolate.

'The most obvious way to beat them at their own game is tell them the truth,' Seb suggested, knowing she wouldn't want to hear it but as their client, he owed it to her to be honest. 'You could call a press conference this afternoon, or tomorrow morning.'

Florrie shook her head. 'I can't. Brian's already losing interest in me. We were meant to have a meeting today, but he cancelled because he *had to* take his latest signing to meet Freddie. He'll drop me if my contract negotiation falls through. And if this gets out, that's exactly what will happen. I should start liquidating assets. I could start by selling my jewellery.' Her hands flew to her earlobes, and she touched the diamond studs she was wearing.

'No.' Birdie's eyes glittered with determination. 'You

asked us to stop whoever's behind this, so you need to let us do the job. If you give them the money, they might disappear, and we'll never find them.'

'But—'

'But nothing,' Birdie interrupted. 'Because remember, there's nothing to stop them from asking for more money when the two hundred grand runs out. They have to be stopped, Florrie. It's the only way.'

Florrie sunk back into the sofa, as if the fight had gone out of her. 'What shall we do?' she muttered.

'*You* should do nothing, except carry on as normal,' Seb said. 'This includes meeting your friends for a drink and going to the charity event. The only difference is that we'll be there, too,' Seb said.

Florrie gave him a horrified look. 'Socialising is the last thing I feel like doing. I want to go home.'

'I thought you'd booked into the hotel for a further night?' Birdie said.

'It was noisy and I couldn't sleep, so I cancelled tonight. I'd planned on going out straight from here, so I didn't have to speak to Ernie.'

'Don't worry about him. We don't believe he's involved,' Birdie said, leaning forward and looking directly at Florrie. 'The blackmailer played into our hands by delivering the letter here and saying that he's watching your every move. Because now *we'll* be watching out for him. Do you see?'

Florrie blinked, as if waking up. 'Y-y-you want to see if someone's following me? Will that even work?'

'If our cover had been blown, then he would have said something in the note. And we've both worked undercover before, so it's a viable option,' Seb said.

'Shall I go somewhere quiet, so you can confront them?' Florrie's voice quivered, though some of the fear in her eyes had lessened.

'Definitely not.' He shook his head.

He and Birdie had both worked cases that had involved members of the public as part of the operation, and they'd been fraught with problems. Florrie might be a natural on television and dedicated to her charities, but she didn't have the training to know how to act when under threat.

'Seb's right,' Birdie said. 'Stick to the plans you've made. Meet your friends at the pub and then go to the gala. Will you all be going together?'

'No, my friends aren't attending the gala. I'll be going alone and meeting people there.'

'Okay. Whatever you do, don't look for us, or try to see if anyone's following you. You've got to pretend it's a normal night and be your usual happy self. Okay?'

'You mean fake it like I usually do.' Florrie gave a hollow laugh. 'I hate these events. Everyone's so false and no one ever says what they really think. And let's not even talk about the dress my stylist sent over. It's like a torture device.' She pointed to a long red gown with a narrow waist hanging from the rack.

'Will Brian be there?' Birdie asked.

Seb gave an approving nod. It was a good question.

'You must be kidding. He wouldn't be seen dead at something like that.' Florrie raised her eyes to the ceiling. 'I did invite him, but he said, and I quote, "Reading isn't sexy enough to attract the real movers and shakers." Knowing him, he'll be trying to get invited to the bloody Freddie afterparty. Why do you ask?'

'No reason.' Birdie shook her head, though her mouth was set in a thoughtful line.

Was she thinking the same thing as him? That if Brian was the blackmailer, he would have wanted to keep an eye on her.

'Do you think you'll find who's doing this before Tuesday?' Florrie chewed her lip, clearly still uncertain about it all.

Seb exchanged an uncertain glance with Birdie before turning to their client. 'We'll do our best.'

Chapter 13

'I need to teach you how to flirt,' Birdie said two hours later as she used her elbow to make some space at the crammed bar.

Florrie had neglected to mention that the pub she was going to was an exclusive rooftop bar in Chelsea that had a closed-off VIP area, protected by a thick rope, a large security guard, and a hostess wearing a tight pink dress. And while the woman had barely glanced at Birdie, she'd definitely given Seb the once-over. If only he'd been smart enough to do something with it.

He hadn't, and they'd been turned away and herded into the long strip at the back of the roof, half in the shadows.

Seb, who'd been about to take a sip of his drink, blinked. 'Excuse me?'

'Flirt,' Birdie repeated in a patient voice. 'It's a thing that people do to show they find someone attractive. A little eye contact and some decent banter and we would have been in there.'

'I'm almost ninety-nine per cent sure you're joking.'

Birdie took a sip of her cider. 'Yes. Unfortunately. I don't think anything short of a *Magic Mike* moment would have convinced her to let us through.'

'A *what* moment?' Seb asked, frowning.

'It doesn't matter. At least you're tall enough to see over everyone's heads. Is Florrie still there?'

Without appearing to turn, Seb gave a short nod. 'Yes, she's with her four companions. There are only three other groups in the area and none of them seem to be paying any attention to Florrie or her friends.'

'Unlike this mob.' Birdie did her best to peer around. Despite the magnificent view of so many of the iconic London buildings set against the early-evening sky, most of the crowd were busy glancing at the VIP section. So if the blackmailer was there, it was going to be hard to isolate him.

'At least it's stopped raining,' Seb said, before putting his drink down on the bar. 'They're standing up to leave.'

'Thank goodness.' Birdie winced as someone pushed into her back while trying to get past them. 'If I'm going to get bumped like this, I need to be on a dance floor, and a lot drunker.'

'No comment.' Seb turned and cleared a path through the crowd. Once they'd reached the far side where the lifts were, he slowed down.

Florrie had hired a car to take her directly to the charity event across town in Richmond. The plan was for Seb to leave first, in order to bring his own car around to the front of the building, while Birdie stayed behind to see if anyone was following their client.

It also had the added advantage of letting her take the stairs once Florrie was in the lift. Definitely her preferred option.

Birdie stepped behind a large brazier, which would no

doubt be turned on as the weather got cooler, and watched while Florrie and her friends slowly made their way over.

'Okay, I can see her clearly. You get the car and keep your phone handy.'

'You too, and be careful.'

'Always.' Birdie grinned at him. They were about even in how many times they'd both run into danger. 'Now go.'

Without another word, Seb headed over to the lift and stepped inside before disappearing from sight. Florrie must have been watching him out of the corner of her eye, because when Birdie turned back to her, she was still involved in an elaborate goodbye with someone. Good. It meant she was buying Seb some time.

Birdie studied her phone, like she was casually reading a text message, though her full focus was on Florrie. Despite grumbling about how uncomfortable the red dress would be, she moved easily in it. Her blonde hair had been twisted into loose curls that hung down her back, and Tanya's make-up had taken away the dark shadows and hollowed cheeks, leaving her looking like she'd just returned from a week's holiday in the south of France.

Birdie touched her own hair, which was neatly tied back into a ponytail. She'd purposely worn a pair of plain black trousers and a pale green shirt. Smart enough to get her inside, but not so fancy that it would make her stand out.

Several people in the bar recognised Florrie, and a few shouted her name in excitement. Florrie gave them all warm smiles, and Birdie's spine tensed, alert for danger.

She put her phone away and moved her focus to the rest of the bar, so that she wasn't looking at anything in particular. It was a trick she'd used many times. By widening her visual perception, she'd often managed to pick up anything out of place. Right now, no one stood out.

Was that a good or bad sign?

Florrie and her friends stepped into the lift, and Birdie's breath quickened while she waited for the doors to close. Would someone try to step in after her? Or head to the staircase to follow on foot?

Birdie waited, but no one moved in that direction.

She unlocked her phone and sent Seb a quick text.

She's on her way down.

She waited a while longer, not wanting to risk moving from her spot too quickly. If the blackmailer was there, they could be watching in the same way she was. After counting to sixty, she still couldn't see anyone acting out of place. She sent Seb a second message.

All clear. I'm on my way.

Birdie didn't wait for a reply but instead took the stairs two at a time. During cricket season, she always worked out more, which meant she was barely out of breath by the time she'd reached the bottom. Florrie and her friends were nowhere to be seen, but a recent-model white Range Rover was parked in front of the building. The windows were tinted, making it impossible to see who was in there, but Birdie knew it was the one Florrie had hired for the evening.

Her phone pinged. It was from Seb and would have been sent to both Birdie and Florrie.

I'm around the corner. You can leave now.

On cue, the Range Rover indicated and slid out into traffic. It was a one-way street and Birdie's heart pounded as she scanned the row of parked cars on the far side: a collection of BMWs, Audis and Mercedes. None of them seemed to be occupied, and she was about to message Seb to collect her when a navy Fiesta pulled out from behind a large SUV and crossed lanes until it was four cars behind the Range Rover.

'Crap,' she muttered.

The car was already past her before she could see who was driving, but she quickly held up her phone and took a photo of the registration plate. Then she texted Seb.

Now.

He appeared moments later, stopping only long enough for her to climb into the passenger seat. 'It's the blue Fiesta,' she told him.

'Good work.' His jaw was tight as he expertly merged back into the traffic, adjusting his speed several times so he could keep a safe distance behind it as they drove through South Kensington and onto the A4. The Fiesta was now directly behind Florrie's vehicle and had even run a red light to make sure it stayed that way.

'If this is our blackmailer, then he's clearly not followed many cars before,' Birdie commented as Seb, who had stopped at the light, easily caught up with him. 'Or they'd know that running a red light like that makes it more obvious they're tailing them. If they want her to know, that is.'

'That suggests that they're not a professional criminal, which is to our advantage.'

'Except that's not always good,' Birdie reminded him. 'We could be dealing with someone impulsive and harder to predict.'

'Let's hope not.' Seb frowned as the traffic snaked along.

By the time they'd crossed the Thames, the endless stream of cars had begun to thin out. They'd already put in the address of the old manor house in Richmond where Florrie's charity event was being held, and Birdie let out a breath as a huge sandstone building came into the view.

'That's it. We're almost there.' She leaned forward, her heart pounding as adrenaline flooded through her body.

The Range Rover indicated right and turned into the car park. There was only one entrance and exit, which meant as soon as the Fiesta entered the car park, Seb could block the exit off with his vehicle and they could discover who was behind the blackmail threats.

He slowed his speed and Birdie's excitement increased. When she'd left the force, her biggest fear had been that PI work would be boring, but that was proving to be unfounded. In a few more seconds, they'd—

'Damn. Hold on.' Seb slammed his foot on the brake and spun the steering wheel to the left, as a huge party bus veered into their lane, missing them by inches.

The dramatic swerve had pushed Birdie back into her chair and the seatbelt tightened across her chest like a steel hand. Behind them, a car horn blared out, quickly followed by another one. Whoever was driving the bus didn't bother to stop. Instead, they sped away in the other direction.

She was quiet for several seconds, taking deep breaths, trying to slow her heart rate.

'Are you okay?' Seb asked, his own voice remarkably calm as he turned into the car park and came to a halt. Birdie nodded, her breathing still a little erratic.

'Yes. I'm fine. But what a complete idiot. That driver should be locked up. Imagine how many people would've been injured if you hadn't managed to stop in time?'

'It was a closer call than I would've liked,' he admitted.

'The worst thing is, I don't think the driver even knew what they'd done,' she said before unbuckling her seatbelt and scrambling out of the vehicle. She scanned the car park. It was filled with expensive vehicles, including the Range Rover, which was several rows away from them.

Florrie was carefully climbing out of the back seat, but there was no sign of the Fiesta. 'Oh no. The Fiesta. It's not here. Where the hell is it?'

Seb joined her, scanning the car park before shaking his head. 'Either they knew we were behind them and used the bus as a distraction to shake us, or they had never planned to stay, and just wanted to confirm Florrie was attending the event?'

'I can't believe this. We were so close.'

'Don't let it get to you,' Seb said, obviously reading her mood. 'It's part of the job. You should know that.'

She let out a breath and shook her arms in the hope of getting rid of the adrenaline and frustration that had built up. Her breathing settled and she turned to him. 'Sorry. It's just so bloody frustrating.'

'I agree. And you're right about the bus driver. I've made a note of the company and registration and will be reporting them. It was dangerous driving and could've put a lot of lives at risk.'

'Not to mention letting our best lead get away. Now we'll have to call Rob or Twiggy to find out who owns it, and we can't very well do that on a Saturday night.'

Seb was silent, as if considering something. 'There might be another way. Can I see the photo you took of the Fiesta?'

'Why? We've been following it for almost forty-five minutes so you must have seen it. Don't tell me your memory has finally stopped working?' Birdie's frustration was replaced by confusion, but she still brought up the photograph and handed him her phone.

'My memory's working just fine,' he said, before parroting back the number plate. Then he tapped on the screen to enhance the photo so they could clearly see the back of the car. 'But my vision is a normal twenty-twenty, which means I couldn't read the sticker at the bottom of the rear window.'

Birdie leaned over to study the image. She hadn't bothered to look at the car close up, but now she could clearly see what Seb had been looking at.

'"Alfie's Car Rental",' she read from the sticker. 'They used a hire car. And not a national company by the sound of their name. Well spotted.'

Seb handed her back her phone and quickly used his own to search for an address. 'They're based in Watford and open tomorrow morning at eight.'

'Great. We'll visit them first thing.'

'Text Florrie and give her an update. I suspect now the blackmailer has seen where she is, she'll be safe for the rest of the evening. Their main concern is that she hasn't gone to the police, and from what they would have seen, it looks like she hasn't. Providing she turns up on Tuesday with their money, I doubt they'd want to harm her.'

'I think you're right. So, what now?'

'We'll go back to my flat and start digging into everyone on the production team.'

Chapter 14

'I'm surprised half of these still work,' Birdie said, staring at the forecourt of Alfie's Car Rental the following morning and taking in the pitiful collection of old Fiats and Volkswagens. 'Do you think they picked this place because it was cheap, or because they live nearby?'

'Cheap,' Seb immediately answered. 'While I don't think we're dealing with a professional, they're at least attempting to cover their tracks. Going somewhere out of the way to hire a car was probably part of the plan.'

'Well, it would be very convenient if they returned it right now,' Birdie said, yawning.

'Indeed, it would.'

They'd been up since six, to make sure they missed any early-morning traffic, not that there was much, being a Sunday, and she needed a second coffee if she was going to feel fully awake. Her attention was diverted by a skinny woman in her mid-sixties half-heartedly dragging out a broken signboard announcing they were open.

'Finally, they're opening. Come on, let's go in.'

The entrance was grubby and wind had blown leaves through the open door and onto the tiled floor. A buzzer went as they entered and the same woman appeared from an inner office. Her skin had deep lines from too much sun and cigarettes, and her hair was dyed an inky black.

'Name of booking?' she asked without much interest.

Clearly Birdie wasn't the only one who needed a coffee.

'We don't have a booking. We're looking for information on a person who was driving a blue Fiesta yesterday with your details on it. Are you the manager?'

'I own the place,' the woman said.

'You're Alfie?' Birdie said.

'Do I look like a geezer?' The woman rolled her eyes. 'Alfie was my husband. God rest his soul. Why do you want to know about the Fiesta? If it was involved in an accident, then you need to contact the insurance company.'

'This isn't about an accident. The driver is a person of interest in a case we're investigating.'

The woman stiffened and took a tiny step backwards. 'Are you the police?'

'No, we're not,' Birdie quickly assured her. 'We're private investigators. We have no interest in your business, only the person driving the car.'

'Oh.' Some of the tension left her shoulders and her mouth curled into a sneer. 'In that case, you can piss off.'

Crap. Birdie opened her mouth, but before she could speak, Seb stepped closer to the counter, his full height dwarfing Birdie and the older woman.

'If you prefer, we'll be more than happy *to* take an interest in the business.' He nodded to the forecourt. 'The white Nissan has a tinted windscreen, which is an illegal modification, and on page five of your contract, you disclaim any responsibility for mechanical failures, which violates the Consumer Rights Act of 2015. Plus, Alfie Henderson died two years ago, yet someone is still drawing on his private pension. Want me to go on, Cherry?'

Birdie blinked. Cherry? She had no idea how Seb had figured all that out, but it was impressive. It also had the desired result, and the woman turned to Birdie.

'Is he for real?'

For the first time that morning, Birdie grinned. 'Most definitely. He's got this super memory thing, and trust me when I say that he forgets nothing. He's also a ninja at discovering things you'd rather he hadn't. My guess is that he's only scratched the surface with you… So, let's start again, shall we?'

Cherry gave an exaggerated eye-roll before shrugging her shoulders. 'Fine. We do have a blue Fiesta on our books. What's the registration?'

'Gladly.' Birdie recited the number from her phone and Cherry typed it in. Her acrylic nails tapped against the keyboard as she moved through several pages of the database before she suddenly slammed her palm onto the counter.

'That little shit, Greg. I'm going to kill him.'

'What is it?' Birdie leaned across to see the screen. The booking programme was a basic one and she scanned down to the name and address. 'Oh.' She turned to Seb. 'It's under the name Elvis King. Address, twenty-three Graceland Road. Which means whoever hired the car gave false details. And *Greg* let them.'

'Who's Greg?' Birdie asked.

'My bloody waste-of-space son,' the woman snapped.

'I suspect Greg and Ernie have a similar love of money,' Seb said.

'And I know why,' Cherry said. 'It's his bloody girlfriend. She convinced him he needs pec surgery. I thought he was doing a bit of under-the-table work for a building gang on his days off. But obviously not. He's lucky his dad's passed, because he'd have had his balls on a platter.'

'When was the car picked up and when is it due to be returned?'

'It was collected on the twenty-fifth of August and was due back two days ago. Great. So not only has it been involved in something illegal, it's late, too.' Cherry's eyes glittered in a way that suggested Greg was in for a lot of grief.

Birdie flicked through her notebook. 'Twenty-fifth of August. That ties in with when the first letter was delivered.'

'Yes,' Seb agreed before nodding to the camera pointing out to the forecourt. 'Does the camera work?'

'Yes, but there's no way in hell I'm going to let you—' The woman broke off, as if suddenly managing to join the dots in her mind. 'You said you lot are investigators. If I show you the footage, is there a chance you might find out who this clown is and return my car?'

'It's possible,' Seb answered, his voice non-committal. But it seemed to work and Cherry chewed on her mouth before nodding.

'Okay, but if you find him and my car, I want it back. Deal?'

'We need to see the footage first. Do you know how to access it?' Seb said.

'Yeah. One thing Alfie taught me was to hold on to the video for as long as possible— You never know when you might need it. For leverage and stuff.'

Cherry tapped on the keyboard and then started fast forwarding through frame after frame of people coming and going from the forecourt. The footage was black-and-white with a grainy filter going through it, making it hard to tell if it was day or night. A couple of times, the woman stopped and muttered something under her breath to the ghostly figures on the screen before she finally froze the screen and leaned back.

'There.' She pointed a finger at a man standing next to a Fiesta. He was holding out a bundle of notes to a young guy with a buzz cut. Cherry pressed play again and they watched while the man handed over to the young guy, who was now grinning. No points for guessing which one was Greg.

'Can you find a better frame of him?' Seb asked.

'I'm not a bloody tech genius,' she mumbled, but all the same continued stopping and starting the video, bringing up each photo, making it bigger and then reducing it back to size.

Finally, they came to one of the man holding up the keys, his face turned in the direction of the camera. He was in his mid-fifties and of average height with thinning hair. He was wearing a pair of tight ripped jeans that made him look like he was trying too hard.

'There goes our theory about Brian,' Seb muttered.

He was right. While the man was definitely similar in age and build, he wasn't Brian Springer. Though Birdie would pay a lot of money to see the smug agent wearing a pair of ripped up high-street jeans.

'Does that mean you can't find out who he is?' Cherry glared at them.

'No, it doesn't mean that all,' Birdie retorted as she reached into her bag for a memory stick. 'Print us off a copy and save the footage on this, please.'

The woman opened her mouth as if to protest, but

then thought better of it. 'Fine. But I meant what I said about the car. I want it back if you find it.'

'We don't go back on our word,' Birdie said in a tight voice as the woman stood up and walked over to the printer.

Seb sat down behind the computer, and she passed him the stick. Good move because Birdie didn't trust Cherry to download it properly for them.

By the time Cherry had returned from the photocopier, Seb had finished and Birdie had returned the memory stick to her bag.

'Thank you for your help. We'll be in touch if we find the car,' Seb said, but the woman only grunted in reply.

'That was some trick in there,' Birdie told him as they walked across the forecourt to their own vehicle. 'How on earth did you know she was still claiming his pension?'

'It was an educated guess.' He unlocked the car, and they both climbed in. 'While I was waiting for you to get ready this morning, I did a quick search on the business. Alfie Henderson registered it in the eighties and then, two years ago, it was transferred over to Cherry. Private pension fraud is surprisingly common these days. And well… Cherry gave me a vibe.'

Birdie raised an eyebrow. 'A vibe? You don't have vibes.'

'Well, I did this time. Do you recall seeing the man on the footage when we were at the studio yesterday?' He started the engine and joined the slow-moving stream of traffic heading into London.

'No, but they do use a lot of contractors so he could have blended in. Fingers crossed it's someone Florrie recognises.'

'Email it through to her.'

Birdie shook her head. 'She's already on edge. I'd rather be with her when she sees the image. Or, better still, let's see if we can match a name to the face before she sees it. While we're stuck in traffic, I'll go through some networking sites and look for photos of people working for the studio. Any names I find with no photo can be cross-checked against other social media platforms, and, just maybe, we can put a name to a face.'

Chapter 15

'At least Elsa's enjoying herself.' Birdie shifted her position on the park bench as they watched the excited Labrador race through a pile of brown and golden leaves, her tail wagging in delight as the leaves flew up into the air before scattering around her.

'I'm not sure the gardener will be happy,' Seb said.

'It wasn't like he'd raked them up. Plus, look how cute Elsa is.' Birdie held up her phone and took a photo as a leaf settled on the dog's nose. She'd have to show Lacey when she got back home. Her aunt's young foster daughter was currently obsessed with dogs and loved seeing photos of Elsa.

They'd arrived back in Central London an hour ago but because Florrie was still too nervous to meet them at her apartment, they'd settled on a park in Paddington, a thirty-minute walk from Seb's flat. That had been fifty minutes ago, and there was still no sign of the woman.

Birdie swung her foot impatiently in the air and then picked up her phone from the bench. 'This is ridiculous. I'll give her another call.'

'No need.' Seb nodded to where a small woman wearing a cream trench coat, a dark brown knitted hat, and sunglasses was heading in their direction.

'Finally.' Birdie put her phone down and ignored Seb's smile. Yes, she knew it was ironic to get mad at someone else's timekeeping, but considering it was already lunchtime, their Tuesday-morning deadline was getting far too close. 'Let's hope she recognises him. If not, you can ask Rob to run a facial recognition scan. He might be in the system.'

'And he might not be. I'm wary about asking Rob for too much help. Especially since it's all monitored.' Seb stood up and retrieved Elsa. The dog gave him a mournful look as he clipped on the lead.

Birdie gave Elsa a rub. 'Sorry, girl. We know you're lovely, but Florrie didn't seem too comfortable around you the last time.' Elsa snuggled into her leg, as if to say she understood. The dog was a genius.

'Sorry I'm late.' Florrie was puffing as she reached them. 'Brian called as I was about to leave. He wanted to discuss why it might be good for my career to start doing voiceovers. Can you believe it?'

Birdie exchanged a look with Seb. 'What's wrong with that?'

Florrie sighed. 'I keep forgetting you two aren't part of this industry. It's basically saying that he thinks I look too old for television.'

'Wanker,' Birdie blurted out before she could stop herself. Seb raised an eyebrow, and she held up her hands. One thing she had to work on was making sure that she didn't let her personal feelings affect her job. And while she might think Brian Springer was an arse, it wasn't her place to tell Florrie that. Unfortunately. 'Sorry, Florrie. I didn't mean that.'

'Don't apologise. I agree, he's the worst. But right now, he's all I've got.' Florrie settled herself on the far side of Birdie, though she did glance over at Elsa and give her a shy smile. Was she getting more comfortable around her?

'How are you?' Seb asked.

'Okay... I think. I can't believe someone really followed us to Richmond last night. I'd sort of thought it was an idle threat. But what do I know? Did you find out who hired the car?'

'Not exactly,' Birdie admitted. 'They used a false name and bribed the guy working there. The car was due back two days ago but hasn't been returned. The good news is their image was captured on CCTV. Do you recognise this man?'

Birdie passed her the grainy photo that Cherry had printed. Florrie dragged the enormous sunglasses off the bridge of her nose and studied the image. Then she held it further back, tilted her head to one side and squinted.

'No. The more I look, the less I can see.'

'That's okay. We do have it on video as well. You might find it easier.' Seb held up the tablet they'd brought with them and passed it across to her.

Florrie let it run through to the end, and then started it again, this time slowing down the frames. Her mouth was drawn together in concentration as she kept going forwards and backwards. Finally, she came to one frame and let out a tiny gasp. 'Oh my goodness. Yes. I *do* know him. There was a camera operator working on the show, and—' She broke off as her hand flew up to her mouth.

'What is it? Tell us.' Birdie's skin prickled with excitement, the way it did whenever they made a breakthrough.

'Last year, we were filming a segment on location in Blackpool featuring a popular children's comedian who was starring in pantomime. We wanted to do it in a nearby studio, but he insisted we went to the pier. Something about wanting to keep it real. But it was December and freezing cold and the whole interview was a disaster. He wouldn't answer any of my questions and kept making smutty jokes. After we finished, he went back to the hospitality tent to drink mulled wine with our director, while I stayed to film some continuity shots before we lost the light. By the time we finished, my feet were so cold that I tripped and twisted my ankle. I couldn't stand and the cameraman rushed over to help me up. I moaned about the awful weather and how we were the only ones left outside. He then sounded off about bloody prima donnas and how he wasn't even funny. The trouble was, even though we'd finished, my mic was still on and—'

'Let me guess. The comic heard?' Birdie interrupted.

'I'm afraid so. The comedian, director and crew overheard the whole thing.'

'Was it a live broadcast?' Seb asked.

Florrie shook her head. 'No, thank God. But it was still hugely embarrassing for the studio. As soon as Brian heard about it, he insisted the guy was fired. Well… I'm not sure fired is the right word. He was a contractor, so I guess they didn't rehire him for any other jobs.'

Birdie glanced across at Seb.

Loss of income and humiliation. Was that sufficient motivation to blackmail her?

'And did the cameraman speak to you about it?' Birdie asked.

'Yes. He begged me to put in a good word for him and I told him that it would be a waste of time because once Brian had made up his mind, that was it.' She paused a moment, biting down on her bottom lip. 'I probably should have at least tried, but it would have been pointless.'

'Do you remember his name?' Seb asked.

'It was something like Harrison… no, Harris.' She paused and rubbed the bridge of her nose. 'Norman. That's it. Norman Harris.'

'Excellent.' Birdie tapped his name into her phone. There was no sign of him on the networking site she'd checked, which is why he hadn't come up in her previous search, but after continuing to scroll she finally found him listed on a message board for freelancers advertising their services. 'Got him.'

'Already?' Florrie blinked.

'Birdie knows her way around a search engine,' Seb said. 'What have you found?'

'Not much, other than he's forty-four and was born in London. He graduated with one A level and worked on a few independent movies before doing *Hands On*. According to his credits, since then he's only done a bit of freelance work for a now-defunct cooking channel.'

'Do you think he blames me for what happened?' Florrie's face was pale.

'It's possible,' Birdie said. 'Have you had any contact with him since then?'

'Nothing at all. It's probably why the incident had slipped my mind. Now that we know it might be him, shall I contact him and explain that it wasn't my fault? I'm sure he'll see reason, and he can keep the money I've already given him.'

Birdie exchanged a glance with Seb. Was Florrie for real? Surely, she didn't believe that it could be over just like that.

'Why do you think that will work?' Birdie asked.

'If we promise not to tell the police what he's done, surely that could…?' Florrie paused. 'I'm being stupid, aren't I?'

'Not stupid, but naïve. Because you paid him before, he

thinks you'll do anything to stop your past life becoming public knowledge. And that includes not going to the police.'

'Oh.' Florrie's face crumpled and she leaned back against the bench. 'What happens now? Will you try and find him?'

'Yes. If he's listed on a website, we'll contact him via that and pretend we're interested in hiring him.' Seb got to his feet, and Elsa, who'd been napping, opened up her large brown eyes and yawned. 'We'll call you as soon as we know more. In the meantime, try not to worry. If Harris is behind it, there's no reason for him to do anything rash, because he'll still be hoping for his payout.'

'Not that that's going to happen,' Birdie quickly added. 'Trust that we're doing everything we can to get to the truth.'

'I understand. And thank you. I don't know what I would have done without you both.' Florrie put on her sunglasses and made her way back to the path.

Once she was gone, Birdie turned to Seb. 'Is Harris our guy?'

'It seems likely. We've connected him to the rental car, and he has a grievance against Florrie because he's no longer employed by the TV studio.'

'Don't forget the lack of jobs he's had since then. He probably blames Florrie for that, too.' Birdie patted Elsa on the head before they left the park and began walking to Seb's flat.

'Agreed,' Seb said, nodding.

'I'll do some more digging once we get back. We need to arrange a meeting with him, pronto. I've always wondered what it would be like to work in TV and now we're about to find out.'

Chapter 16

Norman Harris was a man who'd seen better days. His leathery skin was lined and his thin hair was receding, leaving behind a patch of sunspots that made him look at least ten years older than his real age.

He was sitting in the corner of an old-fashioned café, just off Streatham High Road. The other tables were filled with a combination of secondary-school kids and old-aged pensioners, who seemed indifferent to the fading wallpaper and dirty smudges on most of the glass food cabinets.

It was Seb's own fault for letting Harris pick the location. But while he'd been on the call, all he could think was that it might give them a better idea of what suburb Harris lived in, and how his finances were. And to be fair, that's exactly what they now had, because if the man's tired face and the dirty café said anything, it was that Norman Harris was broke.

'What a dump,' Birdie murmured as they made their way through to the rear of the café. 'I hope it's one of those places where the food is better than the décor.'

'I'm sure that wouldn't be too hard.' Seb grimaced.

'Though if you don't want to risk salmonella poisoning, we can always pick up something on the way back.'

'Which is code for you not wanting to stay here too long.' She flashed him a quick grin. It was alarming how well she knew him. Because she was right. It had been a long day and he was concerned about Florrie. Despite her promise to not release funds to pay the blackmailer on Tuesday morning, her nerves might get the better of her. And, if Norman Harris did prove to be the blackmailer, they'd still need to work out a way to convince him to back down.

'I don't think we should drag it out.'

'I agree,' Birdie said. 'Now, remember, use your posh voice. It can be very intimidating.'

'Do you mean I should speak normally?' He raised an eyebrow but was saved from a reply as they'd reached the table. Harris scrambled to his feet, his narrow eyes sweeping over them, as if calculating what he might get from them.

'Are you the people making a documentary about women's cricket?' he asked, his cockney accent mashing the words together. His chest was puffed out and his stance was aggressive. 'Because I've never heard of a company called Clifford and Bird before.'

'I see no reason why you should have.' Seb cleared his throat, much like his own father had done numerous times over the years. It seemed to work and Harris' jaw went slack.

'W-w-what I mean is that I've been in this business for some time. Seems weird that I know nothing about you,' Harris explained, though his initial swagger had gone.

'If you say so.' Seb lowered himself in the chair as Birdie gave him an encouraging nod. He'd obviously sounded 'posh' enough for her.

'We both prefer to let the cast and crew take the recognition,' Birdie explained before claiming the chair closest to Harris. It was her role to be the friendly one. Hoping that the good producer, bad producer routine might work on him.

'Yeah, well you'd be the only one,' Harris retorted, before suddenly seeming to recall why they were there. 'Sorry. I shouldn't tar everyone with the same brush.'

Before Seb could answer, a waitress came along, pad already out. 'Whatcha having?'

'Yorkshire tea for me,' he said.

'Make that two,' Birdie added before looking at Harris, who was suddenly studying his dirty fingernails. 'I'm still full from lunch, but Norman, please, if you'd like anything, it's on us. It's the least we can do for you agreeing to meet us at the last minute.'

At the mention of free food, Harris glanced up, his eyes grateful. Clearly money was tight. And it was a good idea of Birdie's. Hopefully he'd be more forthcoming with a full stomach.

'Well, if you insist. I'll have an all-day breakfast with a cup of tea, and an extra round of toast.' Once the waitress had gone, he shrugged. 'I've got a night shoot coming up, so probably won't get a chance to eat later. How did you hear about me?'

'It was from Eugene Lewis, the TV producer. He's a good friend, and said you did good work for him in the past.'

It was a lie, of course. Seb had never met Eugene Lewis, but the man had gone to university with Seb's older brother, Hubert. After going through Norman's patchy list of credits, Eugene had seemed like the best connection.

'That was decent of him.' Harris nodded, the wariness leaving his eyes. 'Tell me more about your project and when you're going into production. I've got a full calendar with very little space.'

Next to him, Birdie bristled slightly. Seb ignored her and narrowed his gaze on Harris.

'We plan to start in a week. Full disclosure, our original camera operator broke his leg, which is why it's such short notice. Is that a problem?'

'Depends on the money?'

'I think you'll find us more than fair. Because of the short notice, we'll pay twenty per cent over standard rates.'

'Then I'm interested. So, what now?' He leaned back in his chair.

'We have a few questions. Do you have a clean driver's licence?'

'Yes. Not even a parking ticket,' Harris said immediately.

'Great.' Birdie beamed, making a show of writing something down. 'And what about transport? Do you have your own vehicle? We do have some very early starts.'

This time, he did pause, eyes flickering with indecision. Then he gave them an apologetic smile. 'Sorry, you've got me with that one. I sold the car a few months ago. It failed the MOT and I got sick of throwing good money after bad. You know what it's like.'

'Sure do—my car's exactly the same. It's not a deal breaker,' Birdie assured him, before nodding to Seb to ask the next question.

'It's important to have a good team who work well together and have a broad range of skills.' Seb flicked through the pages they'd printed out from Harris' profile, as if he was reading off the different jobs. Since he already knew them, it was more for Harris' sake. 'I see you've done children's television. Can you tell us more about that?'

'Sure. I worked on *Hands On* for a while. Though it was

more like "hands off" for most of them. People were always pulling a sickie, and I ended up doing way more than I was meant to. Pretty much did all the lighting and miking up, on top of the camera.'

Somehow Seb doubted the unions would have allowed that, but the fact he was bragging meant he might let something slip.

'That must have been challenging. Do you think it was a culture problem?'

Harris snorted. 'Not a culture problem. A Florrie Hart problem. She might be all apple pie and "Hello kids!" on the television, but in real life, she's a monster. I think that's why so many of the team were always off sick.'

Seb was a patient man, but Harris was definitely pushing it. And if they really were interviewing for a position, he'd never consider hiring anyone who could be so critical of their previous employer. Thankfully, Birdie seemed happy to stay in character, and she leaned forward, her eyes as wide as saucers.

'No way. I loved Florrie when I was young. I never would've pictured her as a tyrant.'

'Trust me, she is a total nightmare.' Harris puffed his chest out and there was a cocky air to his voice. 'She even blamed me when she was caught bad-mouthing one of her guests. He was a well-known comedian who couldn't believe he'd been treated so badly. He told me he'd never worked with someone so unprofessional in his entire life. And that included doing a stint as a school clown.'

'Is that why you left that job?' Seb asked.

'What? Oh no, I didn't leave. That bloody—' Harris broke off and blinked. Once again, seeming to remember where he was. 'I mean, yeah. You've got to have standards, right?'

'Indeed,' Seb said as the waitress appeared with the

man's breakfast and their teas. 'It must have been frustrating to *leave* a job because of one person. Did the studio know all about this?'

Harris picked up his fork and began to shovel beans onto it. 'Of course they did. Everyone knew what she was like. But they were worried she'd turn on them and drag the show through the mud. So, I was caught between a rock and a hard place.'

'Have you seen Florrie Hart since?' Birdie asked.

'You mean, on television? God no. I can't stand that show.'

'No, I wondered if you'd seen her around while you're doing other jobs. At the studio? Or around London?' Birdie picked up her cup of tea, though her gaze was fixed on Harris, who was now busy studying his food.

'Why are you asking?'

'I thought it might have been awkward for you, that's all.'

'No, I haven't seen her. My time's been spent on projects with a bit more stretch in them. I like to be challenged. Which reminds me, about these women cricketers? What else can you tell me? Any bikini scenes?'

Birdie coughed, nearly spitting out her tea all over the table, but before she could say anything, Seb got to his feet.

'Unfortunately, until contracts have been signed, we can't discuss it any further. What's your address, so our legal team can start drawing up the documentation?'

'Oh.' Harris blinked, and rattled off an address before he seemed to realise he was doing it. 'Does that mean I've got the job?'

'All being well, once the paperwork's completed. But we do need someone to be at home to receive it. Will you be available Tuesday morning, at nine?'

'Yeah… I mean, no. Shit. I have a thing on, but they

can always leave it with Dunc. He's been staying in my spare room while he's between places. He's a bit of a stoner, but pays half the rent and doesn't mind sharing his gear.'

'I see. We'll get them delivered as soon as we can and then be in touch,' Birdie said, her fists clenched by her sides.

Seb peeled some notes out of his wallet, before dropping them onto the table. 'This should cover the meal and drinks.'

'Thanks,' Harris mumbled, his mouth full of food as they left the café.

'Bikini shots?!' Birdie exploded as soon as they were outside. 'Usually I feel bad if we have to go undercover like that, but I almost wish it was a real job so that we could fire him from it. No wonder he's hardly worked since *Hands On.*'

'That aside, is he capable of blackmailing Florrie?'

'One hundred per cent. He's petty, broke, and seems to think the world owes him a living.' Birdie gave an emphatic nod.

Part of what made her such an excellent investigator was that she was happy to follow her instincts, but not let it override what the evidence told her.

'He also said he had something on Tuesday morning. King's Cross Station, maybe?'

'I agree, but we need proof.' Birdie scanned the parked cars on either side of the road. 'We know he hired the car and that someone was driving it last night. If it was Harris, there's a chance that he drove here today.'

'If we find the car, then we can wait until he returns to it,' Seb agreed as they walked back down the road. The wind had picked up, and litter and stray leaves skipped and skittered around them. But there was no sign of the Fiesta.

'It was always a long shot,' Birdie conceded as they climbed into Seb's car. 'He might have it stashed in a garage somewhere. After all, it was due back a couple of days ago, so he might be worried that Cherry has notified the police.'

'Car aside, there's another question we don't have an answer to. How did he know about Florrie's other life?'

'That's what's been troubling me. She's had twenty years in the public eye without any of the tabloids running the story. All I can think of is that he was so angry about being fired, he started digging into her past to see what he could find.'

'Which means we need to dig into *his* past.' Birdie already had her phone out, her fingers flying across the screen as she brought up a search engine. She chewed on her lip as she brought up a second screen, and then a third before wrinkling her nose. 'Yuck.'

'What have you found?'

'Photos of Harris' drunken trip to Ibiza three years ago.' Birdie lifted her head and dropped her phone onto her lap. 'The problem with people posting their entire lives online is there's so much to wade through, especially if you have no idea what you're looking for. The words *needle* and *haystack* spring to mind.'

'We'll continue searching later,' Seb said as he started the engine. 'In the meantime, we do have his address. Let's go there now before he heads home. If the lodger's there, we can pretend that we have something to drop off for Harris and take a look around.'

'But we don't have anything. Plus he'll tell Harris when he gets home and he'll know we're on to him.'

'We can improvise. I've got a blank contract in the glove compartment. We can use it.'

'With our company name on it? Won't that be a giveaway?'

'I won't use the top page which has the name in full. The rest has *CIS* as the header, so I doubt the lodger will notice. It's worth the risk.'

'But when Harris gets back, he'll know it's fake.'

'We'll work something out.'

'Okay, if you think we can get it to work, although you're sounding a lot more like me than your usual self.' Birdie grinned in his direction and keyed something into her phone. 'I've just checked his address and it's a thirty-minute walk from here. If Harris really is as skint as he appears, he won't want to pay for a bus ride so we have some time. What's the name of his lodger?'

'Dunc the stoner,' Seb automatically answered. 'On the way back, we'll visit Ernie and show him Harris' photograph. If we can get a positive ID, then at least we know we're heading in the right direction.'

Chapter 17

Harris' flat was in a four-storey red-brick Victorian building next to a neglected park with a few rundown graffiti-covered swings and slides. A tall brick fence ran down one side, with barbed wire running along the top of it to discourage anyone from climbing over. The place had a general air of neglect, and it confirmed Seb's suspicion that the camera operator had fallen on hard times. But was it sufficient motive?

Birdie had gone around to the rear of the property to check if there were any car parks or garages, and Seb was standing at the top of the tiled stairs, which led to the floor on which Harris had his flat. He was holding an A4 envelope with the blank contract inside.

Harris lived at number eight but, while Seb waited for Birdie, he decided it might be beneficial to see if a neighbour would talk to them first. He tried number seven.

'What?' a woman with a shrill voice demanded from down a tinny intercom.

'Good afternoon. I'm looking for Norman Harris,' Seb said, deciding to continue his new undercover profession as a documentary producer. 'I'm delivering a contract.'

'Good luck. He's in number eight.' The woman snorted and the intercom stopped hissing. He could only assume she wasn't a fan.

He pressed number eight just as Birdie reappeared. She gave a quick shake of her head, letting him know she hadn't found anything worth reporting.

The intercom made another hiss, and Seb straightened up to his full height.

'Friend or foe?' The voice was male and was gravelly, like he'd been rubbing sandpaper against his throat; not uncommon when someone smoked too much cannabis.

'A friend, hopefully. Is Norman there?'

'He's out.'

'He was with me earlier. I thought he might be back by now. My name's Sebastian Clifford. I have some papers of a sensitive nature and someone needs to sign for it. I'd prefer to come up. Is that okay?'

'Yeah, man,' the voice, presumably Dunc, said as the door made a clicking noise. 'Second floor.'

'Thank you.' Seb pushed it open before the timer could lock them out.

'That was too easy,' Birdie whispered as they stepped inside. A staircase ran along one side of the carpet-less hallway.

'We still need him to let us in to the apartment,' Seb reminded her as they took the stairs two at a time. 'And make sure we're gone before Harris returns.'

There was a small landing on the first floor with four doors running off it, and at the end was a narrow window facing the busy street below.

'I'll stay here and watch out for Harris?' Birdie suggested.

'Okay. Call me if you see him.' Seb climbed the next flight of stairs to where he was met by a skinny guy with pockmarked skin. His bloodshot eyes swept over Seb's suit and then zeroed in on the envelope in his hand.

'Looks pretty official. Is it for a film?'

'Something like that,' Seb agreed, holding up the envelope as proof. It was almost as effective as a clipboard and hi-vis vest. 'I've learnt the hard way not to trust couriers to deliver important documents. Now, if you have a flat surface, I'll need you to sign for it.'

'Cool. Come in.' Dunc stepped to one side and ushered Seb inside.

The flat had a narrow hallway, and Seb followed the man past a collection of muddy shoes that littered the floor until they reached the main living area. An overwhelming stench of stale alcohol, damp towels and neglect hit him. He fought the urge to gag, but Dunc, who was obviously made of stronger stuff, didn't seem to notice.

'Leave it there.' Dunc pointed to a large dining-room table that was home to several computer screens and a collection of unwashed plates and empty beer bottles.

Seb walked past a large shelving unit that housed a multitude of cameras. Next to it was a wooden cabinet with a bowl of random keys and two framed photographs covered in a layer of dust. One was of Harris wearing a gorilla costume without the head, and the other was of an older woman, possibly his sister, judging by the jawline. She had her arm around a man with a beard and they both looked to be in their fifties.

Seb placed the envelope on the table and retrieved the last page of the contract from it. He pointed to the signature line and handed Dunc a pen. Once he'd completed an elaborate scrawl and added in a phone number and date,

Seb picked it up and read it. He raised an eyebrow at his full name.

'Duncan Tarquin Wilde?'

'Yeah, it's a mouthful. But Wilde by name, wild by nature. So, tell me more about this film.' Dunc gave him a smile that revealed several chipped teeth. Seb was saved from answering by a jolting clang of heavy metal music blasting from Dunc's pocket. He fumbled around for his phone. 'Oh... I've got to get this. Hey, Rick...' Dunc wandered back into the hallway, talking loudly.

Seb didn't waste any time and pulled out his own phone so he could get a photo of the woman who looked like Harris. Then he crossed over to the bookshelves, where he found a stack of *Playboy* magazines and a collection of parking tickets from a year ago, along with a letter to say his licence had been cancelled.

Seb raised an eyebrow. So much for Harris' boast about having a clean record.

It also explained why he'd had to use bribery to hire the Fiesta.

Seb headed back to the table and picked up the envelope, just as Dunc returned to the room.

'A little bit of business I had to take care of,' Dunc confided.

'No problem.' He held up the envelope. 'I've just checked and my partner's given me the wrong contract. This is for someone else.' He shook his head and rolled his eyes for good measure. 'Sorry, I'll have to come back another time, hopefully when Norman's here.'

'It's all good, man. But hey, not sure if Norm mentioned, but I'm an actor, so if you want, I can send you a reel...' He nodded his head encouragingly.

'I'll ask my casting director to contact you, and we can take it from there?'

'Really? That's bloody brilliant. Thanks, mate.'

'You're welcome.'

'Do you know when they'll be in touch? You know, so I can make sure to have everything they'll want to see.'

'We're on a tight schedule at the moment, so it might be a while, but as soon as there's some slack, then you'll hear something.'

'Just so you know, I've worked as an extra on two soaps, and had a speaking part in a film… Well, not actual words, but I had to shout and scream in a fight scene. And—'

Seb held up his hand to silence him. 'Thank you, Dunc. I'll make sure to pass all this on. Now, I really must go. The people I'm meeting next don't like being kept waiting.'

'Is it with someone famous? I suppose you know everyone, don't you? Norm's so lucky. I'm thinking of training on cameras… You know, just as a stopgap. Acting's my thing, really.'

'I'm sure you appreciate that I can't tell you who I'm seeing. Thanks again for your help.'

Seb hurried out of the door before the man could detain him any longer. They now had something to work with and time was of the essence.

Chapter 18

Seb headed down the stairs and met Birdie on the landing below, but they didn't speak until they were in the safety of the car.

'Well? What have you found out?' she asked.

'There was very little of interest in the lounge apart from two framed photographs, one of Harris and the other of a woman standing with a man.' He opened up his phone and forwarded the images to her and then started the engine. 'She could be Harris' sister. There's a definite likeness. And if she is, it might speed up our research into Harris' past. I'll send it to you.'

'Excellent.' Birdie's phone dinged, and she studied the photograph as Seb pulled out into the traffic. 'Yes, I see what you mean. I'll check Harris' social media accounts to see if she's on there.'

The journey across town was tediously slow and Seb regretted taking the car. At least he knew that Jill would have taken Elsa out for an extra walk. He flashed his lights to let a car in from a side street and then merged into the far lane to make their exit and head for Canary Wharf to talk to Ernie and show him the photo of Harris.

It would have been quicker to phone, but Seb didn't trust the concierge to tell them the truth. The traffic finally started to move as a sharp horn blasted out from somewhere behind them, followed by a second, deeper honk. In his rear-view mirror, Seb observed a black Vauxhall cutting across several lanes to reach the exit.

'Someone's in a hurry.' Birdie peered into the wing mirror before once again focusing on her phone, trying to identify who was in the photo.

'Traffic brings out all kinds of craziness.'

He took the second exit off the roundabout and the black car forced itself into the inside lane and did the same. Seb frowned. Were they being followed?

Probably not. This was London. Traffic was heavy and the chance that some of them were heading in the same direction was high. But it didn't hurt to be cautious.

He looked in his rear-view mirror again and made a note of the registration plate. The driver was a man with a thick neck and a shock of blond hair. There was a second person in the passenger seat, but they were buried under a giant hoodie, making it difficult to see any distinguishing features.

'Yes.' Birdie whooped with excitement. 'I've got a name. Ingrid Glover, and the man is her husband, William. Hang on, let me see what else I can find... Oh, you were right. Ingrid is Harris' sister. In 2005, she married William Glover, and in 2006 they took over a betting shop. They've run it ever since.'

'Excellent work. Find out if the betting shop is connected to Ernie. They might be working in cahoots.'

'Cahoots? Really? Actually, never mind.' She waved a

hand at him and twisted in her seat, so she was facing him. 'No. Ernie and Ingrid Glover aren't in *cahoots*. But...' She paused, most likely for effect. 'The betting shop is in Peterborough. The exact address is twenty-two Arbour Lane, which puts them...?'

'Right next to Dean Knowles' pawnshop,' Seb said, the familiar sense of satisfaction he got when he was getting somewhere with a case rushing through him.

'Do you have any paper?' she asked.

'Under the passenger seat there's a sketch pad.'

'Cool. You know I always think better if I write everything down.' Birdie reached for the pad and pulled out a marker pen from her bag. In the middle of the page she wrote *Florrie Hart/Jane Smith*, then *Norman Harris*, and drew a line between them before looking over at him. 'Right, let's make sure we've got everything. Norman Harris is pissed off after getting fired from *Hands On* last year and, rightly or wrongly, he blames Florrie Hart. What happens next?'

Seb took a quick look at the paper in her lap. 'One scenario could be that when he couldn't get another job, he decided to go to Peterborough to be with his sister and lick his wounds, and in the process of complaining about how Florrie Hart had ruined his life, his sister made the connection?'

'Hmmm,' Birdie muttered. 'But *how* did she connect them? Because if Ingrid knew Florrie's real identity, then she could only have found out from Dean Knowles.'

Seb drummed his fingers on the steering wheel. 'If that was the case, then he hid very well his knowledge that Florrie was really Jane. Neither of us believed that he was lying.'

'Okay, so let's put a question mark there.' Birdie

chewed on her lower lip. 'If only we'd known about this when we were up there talking to Knowles. We could have easily paid a visit to the betting shop next door and killed two birds, so to speak.'

'We might not need to.' Seb slowed as he drove past Florrie's apartment building, looking for somewhere to park. He checked in the mirror, but there was no sign of the black Vauxhall. 'If Ernie confirms it was Harris who delivered the threats, we have enough to go back and press him further. He didn't strike me as someone with much backbone.'

'He's practically an invertebrate,' Birdie agreed.

Seb raised an eyebrow. 'I didn't know you had an interest in biology?'

'More like an interest in a biologist. We dated for a few months before she got a job on some tiny Pacific Island and we figured long distance wouldn't work.'

'Sorry to hear that,' Seb said truthfully. Despite being so forthright when it came to her work, Birdie had a layer of reserve around her when it came to her personal life. He'd sometimes wondered if it originated from the fact she was adopted. Not that he was much better, though his reasons were different. Growing up as the second son to a viscount meant he hadn't received quite so much pressure regarding not tarnishing the family line as his older brother Hubert, but it was still there, in the small sighs and disappointed glances when he spent time with the family.

'Yeah, well, there's plenty more fish in the sea. Or, should I say squids and lobsters?' Birdie quipped. 'Look, there are some parking spaces available in there,' she said, pointing over the road to the underground car park.

Seb drove down the ramp and parked the car. Florrie's apartment was two streets away and while the sun hadn't quite set, the sky was grey and a cool breeze rippled up from the Thames. There was no sign of Ernie at the reception, but they had better luck at the back of the building, where they'd last spoken with him; once again he was hunched over his phone as the fast-paced commentary of a horse race blared out.

Birdie coughed and Ernie's face darkened at the sight of them. He jumped up, sending the rickety chair falling backwards. 'What's going on? Why are you back? Because if you're going to tell my manager, then—'

'Tell your manager what?' Birdie walked over and stood to one side of him. Her eyes were wide and curious, which had the effect of making Ernie sweat. 'Have you done something else that he needs to know about?'

'No. I swear. Look, I don't even have a bet on this race.' He held out his phone, as if it somehow erased what he'd done. Then he frowned. 'If you're not here to drop me in it, then what do you want?'

'We require a simple yes or no.' Seb stood on the other side of the man and held out his phone to display a photo of Norman Harris, taken from the recruitment website where they'd first found his details. 'Is this the man who paid you to give Florrie the letters?'

Ernie studied the screen and then rolled his shoulders, as if trying to decide what to do. Seb coughed and Ernie groaned. 'Yes. Okay. That's him.'

'You're one hundred per cent certain?' Seb pushed. 'Are you willing to risk your job on it?'

'Yes,' he snapped, his tone almost belligerent. Though it was the confirmation they needed. Ernie was obviously more concerned about what they might do if he was lying, than whether Norman Harris might come for him. 'Now, if that's it, I need to get back to my shift.'

'Go.' Seb nodded. Ernie didn't need to be told twice, and he hurried back around the building, leaving them alone.

'I hate that we're letting him get away with it,' Birdie said, frustration in her voice. 'What's to stop him from doing something like that again? And it could be worse.'

'We'll hope that we've scared him enough to not cross the line again. You know as well as I do, that no matter how much we want it, justice isn't always served. Now, I think we need to pay Harris another visit.'

'First, we should give Florrie an update.' Birdie craned her neck, her gaze taking in the multistorey building. 'I wonder if she's home? If she doesn't want us to go up, she might agree to come downstairs? We could go somewhere and grab dinner. I'm starving, since we didn't have time to stop for something to eat, and you didn't want me to eat in the café where we met Harris.'

'Considering what his meal looked like, I did you a favour,' Seb reminded her. 'But food would be good. Shall we try the Indian restaurant around the corner?'

'That works for me.' Birdie brought up Florrie's number on her phone. It rang four times before Florrie answered.

'Is everything okay?' Her voice was shaky. 'Has something happened?'

'Nothing bad,' Birdie said, holding her phone in front of her. 'Seb's here and you're on speaker. We're outside your apartment building. Is it possible we could meet up at a nearby restaurant to give you an update?'

Florrie swore. 'I'm stuck at an art exhibition in Aldgate East. I promised a friend's husband that I'd turn up for opening night. Can you give me a quick update now, on the phone?'

'First of all, we've had a friendly chat with Ernie, who's

confirmed it was Harris who delivered the letters. And second, it turns out that Norman Harris' sister owns a betting shop next door to Dean Knowles' pawnbrokers in Peterborough. That means there's a connection with your past, but we don't yet know exactly how he put two and two together. We'll find that out.'

There was silence down the other end of the line, before Florrie let out a soft moan.

'I think I know how he did it. One time on set, he mentioned going to Peterborough to see his sister and that she had a betting shop in Arbor Road. Without thinking, I asked if it was next to the pawnbrokers. But before he had time to answer, we started filming. That's it, isn't it? He knew my connection to Peterborough and Dean's shop. I totally forgot about it until now. But I still can't believe he'd do something like that to me. Was it just for revenge?'

'That appears to be the most likely motive,' Seb said. 'He's out of work and his living conditions are poor.'

'Poverty makes people do strange things,' Florrie said, almost sounding wistful. 'I can't believe it's over.'

'It isn't, yet,' Seb reminded her. 'Without taking this to the police, we still need to confront him and convince him to back down and not go to the press.'

'Of course,' Florrie said in a rush. 'But I'm sure he'll see reason. What if I come along with you? And explain everything to him?'

'I don't think that's a good idea,' Birdie said. 'If he is out for revenge, there's no telling what might set him off. We'll visit him first and get back to you as soon as we can.'

'Are you going tonight?'

Seb exchanged a glance with Birdie. It was after eight and neither of them had eaten, not to mention that Elsa was still with Jill. Birdie shook her head, as if they'd discussed it out loud.

'No, we'll go first thing tomorrow morning. In the meantime, do you have somewhere else you can stay, until this whole thing is over?'

'W-w-why? Do you think he might come after me?'

'No,' Seb quickly assured her. 'It's a precaution. It will make us feel better if you do.'

More silence and Florrie finally sighed. 'I'll ask my friends running the exhibition. They have a huge guest room that I've stayed in before. I'm sure they won't mind. But in return, you need to call me as soon as you've spoken to him. Please, you have to promise.'

'We promise.' Birdie ended the call and they started walking back towards the car park. The traffic had died down and the restaurants and bars were filling up. Seb increased his pace as he scanned the street, but there was no sign of the other car.

Birdie came to a halt and folded her arms. 'Okay, spill. What's going on? Why do you keep looking around? You were doing it in the car, too.'

Seb should've known he couldn't get anything past her. He held up his hands to admit his guilt.

'Remember the black car that crossed over two lanes when we were on our way here? It was behind us for most of the way, but I haven't seen it since we parked. I'm being cautious, that's all.'

'Why didn't you tell me? I could have called Rob and asked him to run the plates. Or Twiggy.'

At the mention of her ex-partner's name, Seb raised an eyebrow. 'I doubt Twiggy would still be in the office. It's almost seven at night.'

'He'll be there if he's needed on a job,' Birdie defended. 'And stop changing the subject. You should have told me.'

'I would have as soon as I—' He broke off as a black Vauxhall turned onto the street. 'Quick.' He grabbed Birdie's hand and dragged her down behind a Range Rover that was illegally parked in a loading bay. He peered over the bonnet as the Vauxhall slowly drove past, giving Seb enough time to see the registration plate. It was a match. He turned to Birdie. 'Okay, scrap that, it looks like that Vauxhall is following us.'

'Right. Okay. Well, we either go back to your car and risk them following us, or leave it there overnight and catch a Tube back to your place. Though that will cost a bomb in parking.'

'Maybe, but I think it's safer than driving back. They could be waiting down a side street. We'll catch the Tube halfway and then call an Uber. Mix it up a bit, if they are trying to follow us. We'll return for the car first thing in the morning.'

'But who are they?' Birdie frowned. 'Do you think it's Harris? Or Dunc? Maybe they're in it together and when Dunc told him about our visit, he got suspicious.' She paused. 'But how could they have followed us so quickly? Harris hadn't got home yet when we left, so he had no idea that we'd been there. None of this makes sense.'

'I agree.'

'And if it was them, why not use the Fiesta?'

'We don't know where the Fiesta is. Maybe they had to hire another car?' Seb suggested.

'Or they could have stolen it. I didn't catch the registration number, but I assume you did. There are plenty of websites that will tell us who owns the car. Even if we don't get the info we'd get from police records, it will help and save us from having to wait for Rob or Twiggy.'

'It's better than nothing.' Seb rattled off the registration number and Birdie keyed it into the app.

She watched the screen for several minutes before shaking her head.

'It's not stolen. But tomorrow morning we should call Rob for more info. This is getting really weird. Hopefully tomorrow, Harris will spill the beans and we'll know the whole story.'

Chapter 19

Birdie scanned the street as Seb reversed his car into the parking space they'd finally found after going around the block three times. Ever since they'd caught an Uber back to the underground car park that morning, she'd been hypervigilant, searching everywhere for the black Vauxhall that had followed them the previous evening.

Seb had called Rob earlier to ask him to check on the car but he hadn't replied. Nor had Twiggy when she'd called. It was probably too early. In the end, Seb had left a message for Rob and emailed the car's details. Hopefully he'd check when he arrived at work.

Harris' building was even more unappealing in the gloom of the early morning, and Birdie's skin prickled; a physical reminder that she needed to be aware of her surroundings. Next to her, Seb's back was straight as he coolly surveyed the street. Then, he strode up the stairs and pressed the buzzer. But there was no answer. He tried several more times before turning to her, eyebrows raised.

'I'll phone him.' Birdie hit Harris' number, but it went straight through to voicemail. She then tried Dunc's number, which Seb had been clever enough to get yesterday. But there was no answer either. Were they both still asleep? It wasn't even eight, so quite likely.

She let out a groan. If they couldn't manage to wake up Harris, they'd have to watch the place until they could speak to him.

'We'll try around the back,' Seb said, turning to head down the gravelled driveway leading to the rear of the building. There was only space for four cars and when Birdie had been there yesterday, it was empty. But now all the bays were full. Including at the far end.

'Look, over there,' she said, her heart pounding. 'A dark blue Fiesta. It's got to be the one from the car hire place. So where was it yesterday?'

'He might have been driving it when we met him,' Seb said.

'In which case we were bloody lucky that he didn't catch us here with Dunc. But if he was driving it, then we still don't know about the Vauxhall.'

They walked over to inspect the car. There was a long scratch down one side.

'That damage is new,' Seb said. 'There are still flakes of paint coming off it. And look at these other scratches and the wing mirror. It's been in some sort of accident.'

'He's not worried about his deposit then,' Birdie joked.

She pulled on some disposable gloves and tried the handle, but the car was locked. Instead, she peered through the window. The backseat was covered in empty drinks cans and fast-food wrappers as well as a couple of tatty jumpers and several newspapers. Holding up her phone to the window, she took several photos.

'It's as dirty as his flat,' Seb said, stepping away from the car and heading towards the back of the building. 'There's a door; we might be able to get in that way.'

Birdie hurried over. A small set of steps led up to a back door, and next to it was a dirt-smeared window. It was too high from the ground to see into, but it did appear to be a laundry, judging by the collection of cleaning products that were visible through the glass.

If they dragged over one of the rubbish bins, they could probably reach it, and then try to jam the window open. It wasn't ideal. Especially, if they were caught, but—

'Looks like someone forgot to lock it,' Seb said as the back door swung open.

Birdie blinked. Okay, scrap the elaborate break-in scheme. An unlocked door was always the safest bet. She pocketed her phone and they both carefully stepped inside.

A narrow hallway led to the front of the building and the staircase. At that moment, the front door opened and a couple of older-looking women stumbled in, clearly returning from the night before. One of them giggled as she tried to close the door while juggling a half-eaten kebab. Birdie stiffened, but the women didn't seem to notice them as they stumbled past. They stank of perfume and wine, and Birdie held her breath until they'd reached a ground-floor flat, unlocked the door, and fallen inside.

They didn't want to risk bumping into anyone else so Seb and Birdie climbed the stairs as quickly and quietly as they could, while still being vigilant.

No noise was coming from Harris' apartment, though a faint light glowed from under the front door. Birdie reached for the door handle while Seb stood with his fists clenched to the side in case there was trouble.

Her fingers tightened around the handle and twisted it, half expecting it not to budge. But instead, it clicked and the door creaked open.

'One unlocked door is a coincidence, but two...' She let the words trail off. She wasn't exactly superstitious, but at the same time, she didn't want to go asking for trouble. And while she might not have liked Harris, she was hoping they'd go in and find him passed out on his sofa, too drunk or stoned to have remembered to lock his door.

Seb didn't answer, but the grim set of his mouth showed his concern. Not just for Harris' safety, but for theirs as well. He gave a sharp nod and stepped into the apartment. The passage was long and narrow and he moved down it so that Birdie could slip in and close the door behind them.

Outside, the sound of cars and buses filtered in, but the flat itself was quiet. Seb nodded to the closed bedroom doors and he headed towards them, while Birdie made her way through to the lounge and kitchen.

It was exactly as Seb had described it to her yesterday. The faint stench of weed and alcohol hung in the air, and the room was filled with computers and camera equipment, but there was no sign of Harris or his lodger.

'All clear my end.' She walked back to Seb, who was standing outside what appeared to be the bathroom. His face was pale and his mouth was pressed together. Something was wrong. 'What is it?'

'Harris is dead.'

'You're kidding.' The words tore out of her throat and her stomach churned, but she focused on her breathing, counting to five for the in-breath and six for the exhale. She'd never been squeamish, but she knew as well as most detectives that each death was different. She repeated her breathing exercises until her heart rate had slowed down, then joined him on the threshold.

Harris was in the bathtub, his naked body half submerged beneath the water, which was a muddy red colour. One arm was hanging over the side, an angry red slash running up the vein.

Birdie stiffened, concentrating on her breathing as she took in the rest of the scene. His lips were purple and his eyes wide, staring blankly up to the ceiling. Steam still clung to the mirrors, which meant that whatever happened was recent.

'Suicide?' she asked.

'Why? Tomorrow's Tuesday. It would have been his payday. And even if he did suspect we were working for Florrie, would he have risked not turning up at King's Cross Station?' He pulled out his phone and took a couple of photos before bringing them up on the screen and zooming in. 'Here, look at this.'

Birdie leaned over. There were faint bruises on his face, as if a hand had held him under the water and kept him there. It made more sense. The man they'd met yesterday had been smug. Unless something had drastically changed, then Seb was right.

She pressed the bridge of her nose. 'Did you check the bedrooms? Where's Dunc?'

'Both rooms were empty and neither bed slept in.'

'Do you think Dunc was a part of this?'

'I've no idea. But one of us had better call it in.'

'We need to decide how we're going to play this. If Harris has been murdered, then this is a crime scene and we mustn't contaminate it.'

'It also puts Florrie in a damning position. If the police discover Harris was blackmailing her, she has a motive for wanting him dead.' Seb ran a hand through his dark hair, as if it would help him tease out a solution. 'I'll call the police while you do a quick check of the flat. Don't move anything. If you see evidence that Harris was the blackmailer, photograph it.'

'This whole thing might not even be related to Florrie. He did seem to be a bridge burner. Who knows how many other people he's pissed off,' Birdie suggested, though she was only playing devil's advocate.

Seb nodded but didn't answer as he held up his phone and dialled 999.

Birdie returned to the lounge, pulling on a pair of disposal gloves as she did so. This was now a murder scene and the police weren't going to be happy with them being there. It was the first time she'd been on the other side of the fence. What were officers going to say about their involvement?

But she couldn't just walk away. She owed Florrie her loyalty, and while she wouldn't do anything illegal, she was starting to see how challenging her new career could be.

She headed over to the two old computers. She flicked one on but it was password protected. Swearing softly, she tried the next one, but it was the same. IT wasn't her forte so she reluctantly moved on. She lifted up the tangles of wires and unpaid bills with a pen in search of a phone or memory stick, but there was nothing but food crumbs and dust.

Damn. A stack of magazines were on a shelf and she picked them up one by one, giving them a shake in case anything had been hidden there, before returning them to where she found them. Still nothing. It was the same with the kitchen, where all she discovered was a sink full of dirty dishes and a couple of old saucepans that had seen better days.

Seb was still on the phone when she moved on to the bedrooms. Harris' bedroom consisted of a single bed and a small collection of awards and certificates propped up against a dresser. Most of them were dated from around 2005, which seemed to suggest his career had been on the slide for quite some time. Birdie opened the drawers and forced herself to sort through the array of tattered boxers and socks.

She'd thought her brothers were bad, but they had nothing on Harris. She was about to shut the last drawer when her fingers slid across a slight bump underneath the drawer liner that had been cut from old wallpaper. Her heart rate increased as she pushed the socks away and lifted up the liner to discover an envelope.

'Police will be here in five minutes.' Seb appeared in the doorway, his focus zeroing in on the envelope. He didn't bother to ask questions as he joined her, patiently waiting while she eased back the flap.

Inside was a collection of photocopied newspaper cuttings that were all too familiar. *Five in Jail after a Burglary Went Very Wrong. Local Businessman Shuts up Shop, a Year After Being Attacked by Louts.* And there were more of them. It appeared that Harris had a copy of every article that had ever been written about the crime Florrie had been involved with.

She turned to Seb. 'It's pretty damning evidence. So what do you think happened? Harris blamed Florrie for getting him fired and somehow found out about her past and decided to blackmail her? Or... someone planted all of this evidence to make Harris look guilty?'

Seb rubbed his chin and then shook his head. 'Occam's razor.'

'You what?' She was used to him spouting random Latin from time to time, but couldn't work out where this fitted in.

'Sorry. It means the more obvious solution is usually the right one. Your first theory seems closer to the truth. At least for where the evidence is pointing.'

'And that's your fancy way of telling me I'm right, is it?' Birdie raised an eyebrow at him.

'It is,' he agreed. 'Though we still need to work out who killed Harris. Was he working with someone and they double-crossed him?'

'Dunc seems like the most likely candidate. He's an out-of-work actor with a drug habit, and also seemed like an opportunist, the way he was trying to creep round you to get a job.'

'So, Harris asks his lodger to help out with the blackmail, and they both follow us in the black Vauxhall last night…'

'If it was them. Because as we've already established, it wouldn't have been easy in the time frame.'

'Well, let's assume they managed it,' Seb said. 'What happened then? Did they have a fight and Dunc killed Harris? It would explain why he's not here. Maybe he's gone on the run and is lying low until the press conference tomorrow?'

'But why leave behind all the newspaper cuttings? They're his collateral.' Birdie frowned, turning her attention back to the pile of articles, which were at the heart of the case.

'When I met Wilde yesterday, he didn't appear to be the violent type. If he did kill Harris, then it could have been on the spur of the moment, or an argument gone wrong. In that case, he might have panicked and fled without thinking it through,' Seb pondered, but Birdie was saved from answering by the all-too-familiar sound of a police siren.

She quickly returned everything to the envelope and slid it under the drawer liner. 'We can't remove these from the scene, but if we leave them, it might not look good for Florrie.'

'Only if they connect Jane Smith to Florrie Hart,' Seb reminded her. 'And who's to say that they'll do such a thorough search? Putting them back was the correct thing to do. We'll have to see how it plays out. In the meantime, we need to find Dunc.'

Birdie reluctantly agreed. She shut the drawer and shoved her disposable gloves into her pocket and dialled Florrie's number on her phone as the intercom rang from downstairs. Seb crossed back into the hallway and answered it. Two police officers identified themselves and Seb buzzed them up.

Birdie's pulse quickened as the ring continued. She had to let their client know that the case wasn't closed, but why wasn't she answering? They needed to find Dunc and make sure he was arrested before the press conference.

There was no answer. Crap.

In the hallway, Seb had let the first responders into the apartment and it was soon filled with the thump of feet and chatter of voices. She was probably filming and didn't have her phone. She'd try Florrie again as soon as they were free to go.

Chapter 20

'Who's the detective in charge?' Seb asked the young constable who was standing next to them in the car park of Norman Harris' building.

'DS Fiona Johns.' The officer pointed out a tall woman in her mid-forties standing by the back entrance, talking on her phone.

Next to him, Birdie groaned. Seb could appreciate her frustration. It was almost ten in the morning and they'd already given a statement to the officer who was first on the scene, after which they'd been sent outside and told to wait until the detective handling the case could speak to them. Seb understood—he'd do the same—but these were unusual circumstances.

They weren't alone in the car park. The police had insisted several neighbours leave the building, too. They'd all been happy to talk about Harris and Wilde amongst themselves until Birdie had tried to question them, and then they clammed up as if worried they'd be implicated. Not that what they'd said amounted to much more than speculation and gossip.

They were wasting time being stuck there. With Harris dead, Wilde was the most obvious suspect. Seb had tried calling him several times, but there was no answer, and the longer they were delayed, the more time the man had to disappear.

The DS finished the call and beckoned them over.

'I understand you're both private investigators who happened to break in and discover a suicide.'

It wasn't exactly an allegation, but it wasn't pleasant either. Next to him, Birdie bristled, but he trusted her not to say anything rash. No matter what she was thinking.

'We didn't break in—the door was unlocked,' Seb corrected. 'Nor do we believe that Norman Harris took his own life. The bruising on his face suggests that he was held under the water and then it was made to look like he'd taken his own life. Has anyone found the lodger yet? Duncan Wilde. We have reason to believe he's connected to this.'

'Until we hear back from the pathologist, this isn't a murder investigation.' DS Johns gave him a sharp frown. 'But I am curious about why you were here so early in the morning? One of the neighbours reported seeing you here yesterday as well. She said you rang the intercom to her apartment and she spoke to you.'

'We had been questioning the deceased in relation to a current investigation. We met him yesterday in a nearby café and then visited his apartment, at which time I spoke to Wilde. My colleague and I returned at seven this morning to question Harris further, but no one answered the intercom or picked up any of our phone calls. The back door to the building was open and so we went inside to Harris' flat. His door was open, as well.'

'Why did you want to speak to him?' The DS looked

up from her notebook. It was a good question, but not one Seb was prepared to answer.

'It's a private matter that I'm not at liberty to discuss right now.'

'Oh, really? Would a trip to the station make you change your mind?'

'Why? Do you believe that it *is* a murder investigation now?'

The detective stiffened as her angry gaze swept over them.

Now who was being the rash one?

Seb seldom lost his temper, but he hated wasting time when the murderer was still out there. He was about to apologise but before he could, Birdie patted his arm and smiled at DS Johns.

'What Clifford meant to say was that while we can't discuss our client, we wanted to talk to Harris about a rental car. There's a navy Fiesta at the far end of the car park. It was hired from Alfie's Car Rental in Watford. We have reason to believe Harris hired it using a fake ID.'

The DS was quiet for a moment as she digested the information and then the frostiness left her eyes. 'Okay. Thanks for the tip. And for the heads up about the body.'

'It's been a tricky case and we're not out of the woods yet. But we'd be happy to come down to the station and discuss it further as soon as we've wrapped it up. Here's my card.' Seb handed it over. 'My ex-colleague DI Rob Lawson can vouch for me.'

At the mention of Rob's name, DS Johns' face paled. 'You worked at the Met?'

'I did,' he confirmed before turning to Birdie. 'And my partner was on the force in Market Harborough. We've only recently set up our investigation company.'

'That explains why my crime scene doesn't appear

contaminated.' DS Johns glanced at the back door where a man in white coveralls was gesturing for her to go over. 'Ah. The forensic pathologist wants me.' She pressed her lips together, as if considering something, then dug out her own card from underneath her protective gear. She held it out. 'Okay. You can go for now, but call me if you discover anything relating to this death.'

'Thank you. If you do find Duncan Wilde, we'd appreciate you letting us know so we can stop looking for him.'

'If it is murder, as you believe, then he's our prime suspect. Contact us if you find out where he is. You're not to apprehend him.' The officer turned and headed to the pathologist, and they quickly left the car park and returned to the front of building where they'd parked the car.

The sun was bright and a few groups of curious onlookers were staring at the building and the scatter of police vehicles and ambulances that had double parked along the street.

Seb turned to Birdie, who was staring at him.

'We're lucky she didn't have us both arrested and hauled off to the station for questioning. Talk about getting on the wrong side of DS Johns.' Birdie shook her head, red hair bouncing everywhere.

Seb couldn't blame Birdie for being annoyed; he prided himself on always being professional. He rubbed the back of his neck, trying to loosen the growing tension. 'I'm not sure what came over me,' he admitted, which seemed to appease her. 'But thanks for stepping in like that. It was good work—nice to know you have my back.'

'You've bailed me out enough times,' she confessed, before giving him a reluctant smile. 'Plus, if you did get arrested, I would've owed Twiggy twenty quid. He's convinced you're going to lead me astray.'

Seb was 99 per cent sure she was joking, but sometimes it was hard to tell.

'I'm pleased you're not out of pocket on my behalf. But we have a serious problem. It's only a matter of time before this officially becomes a murder investigation and as soon as they discover Harris has been blackmailing Florrie, she'll become a suspect. We need to convince her to talk to the police first. At least it will put an end to any blackmail attempts Duncan Wilde—or whoever the killer is—might still have in mind.'

'I agree. But Florrie's still not answering her phone or returning any of my messages. And we need to find Wilde before the trail goes cold.' Birdie tapped her phone against her palm, her brow puckered into tiny lines of frustration.

'Call Tanya, her make-up artist, and I'll see if any of the neighbours might know where Wilde could be. Yesterday he had a phone call with his dealer. A guy named Rick. Someone might know who he is.'

'Okay.'

Seb left Birdie holding her phone to her ear and walked around to the back of the building. Several of the neighbours were still standing there. The PC raised an eyebrow but didn't stop Seb from going up to the group.

'When was the last time any of you saw Duncan Wilde?' he asked when he reached them.

A woman in her sixties folded her arms across her chest and narrowed her eyes. 'Are you the police?'

Seb's mouth twitched with impatience. 'No. I'd like to ask him some questions. He mentioned a friend… Rick?'

'Rick Green. His dealer,' a second woman said, which earned her a deep scowl from the first one. 'What? If that lot were banged up, it would be doing us all a favour. I'll tell you what, love. Go to the White Hart. He's always there, sitting at the far table by the fruit machines. If anyone knows where Dunc is, it'll be him.'

Seb looked at his watch. 'Surely he won't be there yet?'

'It's his base. The moment the pub doors open, he's there. Trust me.'

'Thank you.' Seb handed her a card. 'And if Dunc does come back to the building, please call me?'

'My phone's out of credit,' the woman said immediately, her eyes glimmering with opportunity. Seb took out his wallet and extracted a ten-pound note.

'Here. This might help.'

'Sure it will, love.' The woman snatched it out of his hands and grinned at her friend.

Seb returned to the front of the building where Birdie was talking to an onlooker. At the sight of him, she finished her conversation and joined him.

'I spoke to Tanya and you were right. Florrie's been at the studio since seven and will be filming until at least one. She has a script run through this afternoon and then a meeting concerning the press conference tomorrow. It explains why she hasn't been answering her phone. Tanya's promised to ask Florrie to call me as soon as she can. How did you get on?'

'Wilde's dealer, Rick Green, operates out of a local pub called the White Hart. I've also arranged with one of the neighbours to call me if Wilde comes back here. Though I did have to give her ten pounds to pay for her phone credit.'

'You really think that will convince her?' Birdie raised an eyebrow. 'Because I've been trying to talk to some of the residents and I can't get a word out of them. And why would he return if he did it?'

'If he doesn't know the police have discovered the body and he'd left something behind?'

'True, but then if he does come back, guilty or otherwise, he's not going to hang around if the police are all over the place. It seems to me that you've wasted ten quid.'

'Maybe, but it's still worth it, just in case. For now, we'll go to the pub to speak to Rick Green. Allegedly, he's there from opening time.'

'That might cost more than a tenner. I'll check where the pub is.' Birdie tapped the name into her phone. A moment later, she pointed to the end of the street. 'It's around the corner, so we might as well walk. After seeing Harris, I could use the fresh air.'

'Viewing dead bodies never gets any easier.' Seb put his hands in his pockets as they made their way to the pub.

'Not really.' Birdie shook her head. 'But you do learn to deal with it better.'

'True.'

They walked in silence to the pub, both deep in thought.

The pub was on a corner and the outside walls that had once been white were now covered in a grey film of soot and dust, while the hanging baskets were filled with dead flowers. A huddle of men was sitting at an outside table vaping.

'Right. Let's get this over and done with.' Birdie's voice was calm and there was no sign of tension in her shoulders, but her eyes were alert and her hands rested casually on her hips, letting Seb know she was ready for danger.

The interior held no surprises, with its dull lighting and patterned carpet. A man behind the bar with a tea towel in his hand was cleaning glasses, but Seb ignored him and headed to the rear of the pub where the fruit machines stood.

Seb nodded to the far wall where a small table was situated to the left of the two brightly lit machines. A man in his sixties was sitting there staring at his phone, a mug of coffee in front of him on the table, while a couple of younger men hovered close by. As Seb and Birdie drew closer, the younger men both looked up, their faces set hard, as if hoping for a fight. But the older man waved them down. He then fixed Seb with a curious gaze.

'You look a little lost, Detective.'

'I'm not a detective,' Seb assured him as Birdie reached his side, not taking his eyes off the two bodyguards.

He'd never met Green before, but clearly the drug dealer had spent enough time evading the authorities to recognise someone from the police… or who used to be. 'Well, not anymore. My name's Sebastian Clifford. I'm a private investigator. We're looking for Duncan Wilde.'

'Why would I know where he is?'

'I was at the flat yesterday when you phoned him and he mentioned you were doing business together.'

'Did he say what business?'

'No.'

'Good. Let's keep it this way. Why do you want to find him?'

'He shares a flat with Norman Harris who's a person of interest in a private case we're working on.'

Green nodded to the chair opposite, and Seb lowered his long legs into it while Birdie remained standing. It seemed to amuse Green, who shrugged his shoulders.

'Don't you mean *was* a person of interest.' Green gave a hollow laugh. 'I heard about his unfortunate accident.'

News travelled fast.

Unless he knew something about it.

'Yes, that's correct. We spoke to both men yesterday and had some follow-up questions. Now Harris is dead, we'd still like to speak to Wilde. Have you seen him?' Seb asked.

Green drummed his fingers on the table, staring directly at Seb before finally answering. 'I haven't seen Dunc for a while because he's been keeping out of my way. But I did speak to him on the phone yesterday. He made up some story saying he was going to be rich and that he'd pay me back the ten grand he owes me on Tuesday.'

Tuesday. The day the blackmail payment was due.

'And you believed him?'

'What do you think? The man's got a bigger mouth than the Thames Tunnel and all that comes out of it is shit. I told him his time's up. I'm not a fucking bank.'

'What does he owe you ten grand for?' Birdie asked, stepping closer and resting her hand on the back of the empty chair.

'It's nothing to do with you, young lady.'

Seb glanced at Birdie, who was holding the chair so tightly her knuckles had gone white. If there was one thing that wound her up, it was being referred to as *young lady*.

'It's a lot of money for him to suddenly find. Weren't you curious where it was coming from? Especially if he said he'd be rich. I'd have thought you'd have wanted in on any action if it netted you a lot of cash,' Birdie said.

'Well, you thought wrong, didn't you? Wilde is a no-good waste of space and I'm done discussing him with you. I've got more important things to do.'

'Do you own a black Vauxhall?' Birdie asked.

Green appeared puzzled. 'Why?'

'I'm curious.'

'You're the PIs, so do your job and find out. Now fuck off before I ask my boys to *assist* you out of here.'

Seb glanced to the side, as one of the bodyguards took a step towards Birdie.

'Okay, we're going,' Seb said, holding up his hands.

Seb got to his feet and nodded for Birdie to go. She glared at the two bodyguards before sweeping out of the pub, Seb following in her wake.

'What a scumbag,' Birdie said, once they were away from the pub. 'Do you think he knows more about Wilde than he's letting on? He could be involved in the whole thing. He didn't deny having a black Vauxhall.'

'His body language told me otherwise. When you asked about the car, he was surprised.'

'Yeah, I did actually think that, too. I think I'm clutching at straws. But Wilde did mention being rich on Tuesday and that definitely links with the blackmail. The rest of it doesn't make sense. If Wilde was the passenger in the car following us, that means he must have known who you were when you went to the flat. You were there; what do you think?' A look of helplessness crossed Birdie's face.

'He could already have known who we were, because we've been seen with Florrie. But Harris definitely didn't know. When we met with him, he was keen to get the job.'

'It could also have been an act, especially if he thought he'd be getting two hundred grand. Because why would he want our job if he was going to get a big payout?'

'Two hundred thousand doesn't last long if it has to be shared,' Seb said.

'True. What about if Wilde already knew who you were and was pretending to act like he was out of it and stupid. Especially if he'd already decided to double-cross Harris with the blond guy from the Vauxhall. It would mean one hundred grand each instead of sixty-six ... assuming Blondie was already involved.'

'In that case, did Wilde and *Blondie*, as you've named him, kill Harris together, and if so, why?'

'To stop him from going to the police if he'd suddenly caught a guilty conscience and wanted to back out of it? But then why would he go to the police? He could just have walked away.' Birdie gave a frustrated sigh. 'See what I mean? Nothing adds up.'

'I know, but for now we have to assume that Wilde still intends to turn up at King's Cross Station to claim the two hundred thousand pounds.'

'Unless we find him first,' Birdie said when they reached Seb's car. 'We need to get hold of Florrie and persuade her to talk to the police.'

'Yes, and I'll call Rob to ask him to do a search on Duncan Wilde. Although, I have a feeling that this time he'll insist on knowing exactly what's going on.'

Chapter 21

'Well, I'll be damned. I'd never have guessed that your mysterious Jane Smith was the illustrious Florrie Hart.' Rob let out a long whistle from the other end of the phone after Seb finished explaining everything to him through the Bluetooth speakers in the car.

'I didn't have you pegged as a *Hands On* fan, Rob,' Birdie said. 'Who's your favourite presenter?'

'We all have our secrets, Birdie, and I'll reserve judgement on who's the best,' the officer said before his tone turned serious. 'But I don't like this. I understand why Florrie doesn't want to go to the police, but if it's now a murder investigation, she won't have a choice. And if she voluntarily contacts the officer in charge, it will look a lot better.'

'I agree. We're on our way to the studio to talk to her now. In the meantime, we need to know as much as we can about Duncan Wilde, Norman Harris, and Rick Green.'

Birdie frowned in his direction. What was he thinking?

'Why Green? I thought we'd eliminated him from this.'

'I want to cover all bases. If you don't mind, Rob.'

'Is there any chance you can find out whether Harris' death has now been classified as murder?' Birdie added as she refreshed her phone screen yet again. 'I've been checking for updates ever since leaving the scene but, so far, no official statements have hit the media.'

'You do know I have other work to do, don't you? Shall I send an invoice for my services?' Rob gave a deep laugh.

'You know we love you really,' Birdie said, making a mental note that they should be mindful of asking Rob for too much help. They didn't want him to cross the line on their behalf.

'And that's the only reason I'm doing it. Give me a moment and I'll see what I can dig up.'

'Thanks. The next time we see you in person, the drinks are on us... well, Seb,' she added, grinning at her partner.

The tap, tap, tap sound of fingers hitting a keyboard let them know Rob was doing a search. The wait was agonising.

'There's nothing showing up yet about Harris' cause of death, but I've got a list of previous charges against Duncan Wilde. Mainly drunk and disorderly, possession of illegal substances, and destruction of property. But there's nothing outstanding.'

'What about Green?' Seb asked.

'If you don't think he's involved, then keep well away.'

'Thanks for the warning. Are there any other addresses or known associates for Wilde?'

There was more tapping and then a sigh. 'No. But let me keep digging and I'll get back to you as soon as I can. And the pair of you, be careful. This seems like it's turning into something nasty.'

The call finished and Birdie clutched at her phone, fiddling with the cover. 'I don't like this. It feels like we're starting all over again but the stakes are higher. If Wilde did kill Harris, what's to say he won't do something to Florrie as well, especially if there's no money?'

'That thought had entered my head, too,' Seb said while turning the car into the TV-station car park. 'That's why it's important to explain to Florrie face to face how dangerous the situation has become.'

~

'Sorry, I can't let you through.' A bored girl at the reception desk peered up from her phone. 'Your passes have expired.'

Seb tried to hide his impatience. They'd already explained about the passes being expired and asked if one of the production team could meet them at the reception. But that had apparently fallen on deaf ears.

'Could you at least let Florrie know we're here? We need to speak to her urgently.' Seb gave a slight nod of his head, hoping it would convince the girl. It didn't.

'Sorry. No can do. Your passes have expired.'

Seb sighed and walked back to where Birdie was waiting on one of the long red couches next to the wall.

'I've tried calling Tanya and Brian,' Birdie said. 'But neither of them answered. I take it you couldn't charm your way in?'

'Apparently not.' He shook his head before catching sight of an agitated girl balancing a tray of coffees in one hand, and several mobile phones in the other. It was the production assistant they'd spoken with the other day.

Birdie saw her at the same time and quickly stood up. 'It's Lily. Here, let me talk to her.'

'Are you doubting my charm?'

She gave him a cheeky grin. 'It's nothing to do with

charm. Her sister plays cricket for Essex and is brilliant. We chatted about it on Saturday when I interviewed her. Lily, hey.'

At the mention of her name, Lily turned around. Her expression was blank as she looked at Seb, but as soon as her gaze settled on Birdie, she grinned. 'You're from the magazine. Are you here for more photos?'

'Something like that,' Birdie agreed, her concern hidden behind a friendly smile. 'We need a quick word with Florrie before we submit the final article, but she's not answering her phone, and the girl on the desk won't send a message, or let us through.'

'Their passes have expired,' the girl called out, still managing to maintain her bored tone. Lily rolled her eyes towards the ceiling.

'Give me strength. She's worked here all of four weeks and the power's already gone to her head. The good news is that I can sign you in, but the bad news is that Florrie isn't here.'

Seb's mouth went dry, and next to him Birdie's smile became strained. 'Are you sure? I spoke to Tanya earlier and she told me that Florrie was filming.'

'That's right. She came in early for a morning shoot, but there was a problem with the sound and we had to stop. I haven't seen Florrie since.'

'What time was that?'

The girl shrugged. 'Maybe eleven, or twelve? I'm not totally sure. Sorry, I can't stop. I've been sent out for drinks. I'd better get going before they go cold.'

'Did Florrie say where she was going?' Seb asked.

Lily shook her head. 'No. But that's not a surprise. She doesn't really talk much about her private life. They're meant to be doing a script run through this afternoon at two-thirty, so she'll be back by then. Shall I tell her you called to see her?'

'Yes, please.' Birdie handed over a business card. 'And if you do hear from her, could you also text to let me know? It's really important.'

'Sure. It's cool how committed you both are to making sure the article is perfect.' Lily smiled and headed off.

'Well, that was a waste of time,' Birdie said as they left the building. 'If I wasn't so worried, I could happily strangle Florrie for taking off without telling us.'

'I think we should go to Canary Wharf.' Seb increased his pace as they hurried back to the car. Birdie matched him stride for stride, for once not complaining.

He turned on the engine and was about to reverse out when the burner phone rang. The computer display on his dashboard flashed up with a number that he didn't recognise. He pressed the answer key on his steering wheel and the line came to life.

'This is Sebastian Clifford. How may I help?'

'Oh... so you weren't putting on the fancy accent,' a voice said through the speakers.

Birdie turned to him and shrugged.

He returned the gesture because he had no idea who it was either. He might never forget a thing he read, but it didn't mean he could recognise voices any better than the next person.

'Who is this?'

'Never you mind,' the voice said before stopping. 'Actually, you should mind. It's Tessa. Tessa Perkins. I live at number five. You wanted me to call if I had any news.'

That got his attention. 'And have you?'

'Depends what it's worth to you...'

'He's already given you ten quid and no matter what you have, it's nothing that won't be on social media in a few minutes,' Birdie retorted, clearly annoyed with so many people trying to strike deals. Seb glared at her. 'Sorry. Ignore me.'

'Gladly,' Tessa retorted. 'This has to be worth at least twenty quid.'

'Tell me what you know and we'll see,' Seb snapped.

Like Birdie, his patience was starting to wear thin. There was a pause at the other end and some whispering before Tessa coughed.

'Fine. About fifteen minutes ago, after they finally let us back into our flats, Sandra Bingham in number two came up and told us that Duncan Wilde had been found tied up at Mitcham Common.'

'Is he alive?' Birdie leaned forward, her voice urgent.

'Course he's alive. Though he was beaten up pretty badly when the cops found him. I reckon he was relieved they were giving him an escort to the hospital. Stop Rick Green and his goons from finishing the job. If it was them. And I'm not saying it was, mind. Because… well, you know. Anyway, they're going to lock Dunc up for murdering Norman, so I don't think he'll be coming back here any time soon. And good riddance to him. Now, about my money—'

'If what you're saying is true, he'll double it,' Birdie cut in before ending the call. 'If Green found Wilde and the police now have him in custody, that means it's over.'

'It appears to be. But…' Seb frowned.

'What is it?' Birdie asked.

'It's not sitting right. We'd better ring Rob first, or DS Johns, to get confirmation.'

'I'll do that while you drive.' Birdie frowned, her fingers almost white as she clutched at her phone. She turned and studied him. 'You know, the more I think about it… the more—'

'Yes,' he interrupted. 'If this is really over, then why can't we find our client? Until now, she's been easy to contact.'

Birdie sighed as Seb pulled out of the car park. 'We need to get to her apartment. If there's a trail to follow, it could be from there.'

Chapter 22

'She's not here,' Ernie said as he greeted Birdie at the reception of Florrie's apartment building. Seb had left her to speak to Ernie, saying something about walking around the building and CCTV cameras.

Unlike their previous encounters, when Ernie was in uniform, today he was wearing a pair of jeans and expensive trainers. Birdie had called him on the way over from the studio to ask for the name of the concierge who worked the day shift, because they might need urgent access to Florrie's apartment. They hadn't needed to call Rob or DS Johns in the end to get confirmation about Wilde's attack, because it was already in the media and on local radio, so the continued silence from Florrie was a concern. She hadn't intended to ask Ernie to meet them there, but when they'd spoken, he told her he was in the pub around the corner and offered to come over.

'Have you any idea the last time anyone saw her?'

'She left at six this morning when the car from the studio came to collect her, like it always does. She seemed fine then,' Ernie explained, before nodding at the tall woman in the same concierge uniform he usually wore. 'This is Ellen. She took over at seven.'

'Afternoon.' Ellen gave them a gruff nod, as if unsure why Ernie was being so forthcoming with two strangers. Since being discreet was part of their job too, Birdie really couldn't blame her.

'I appreciate your help. We've been hired by Florrie to look into a situation, which has now turned dangerous. We have real concerns for her safety, which is why this is so important and we need your help.'

'Why not go to the police then?' Ellen frowned. Next to her, Ernie flinched, as if worried they might actually do that.

'Because we need to confirm whether she's missing first.' Birdie hadn't intended to sound so impatient, but she was anxious to get moving. 'According to her assistant, she left the studio between eleven and twelve. Did she come back here?'

Ellen turned to Ernie, who gave a short nod. 'Okay, this isn't how we usually operate here, but since Ernie's vouching for you... I didn't see her come in, but she did leave the building about forty-five minutes ago, at one-thirty.'

'Did she say anything?' Birdie asked as Seb joined them. 'This is my colleague, by the way.'

'No. I was helping someone else so didn't speak to her at all.'

'But it was definitely her?'

Ellen gave a self-assured grin. 'No one else who lives here wears giant glasses and an oversized coat. It was definitely her.'

'Do you have any idea of the direction she took, or if she drove her own car?'

'Please.' The smile turned into an eye-roll. 'She never

drives her own car. I doubt it would even start. She usually gets picked up by a studio car, which is why she waits at the front of the building. And before you ask, no, I didn't see her get into any car.'

Birdie swore under her breath, but Seb pointed to the bank of computer screens behind the counter. 'There's a camera directly outside, which should have picked it up. Will you check it for us?'

'It's okay. I'll do it,' Ernie said. 'And if anything blows back, you can blame me.' Then he glared up at Seb. 'But I hope that won't happen.'

'It won't. Please, check the footage. That's all we care about,' Birdie told him.

'Fine. We'll go into the back office.'

They followed Ernie behind the reception to a small office with a desk, complete with computer screen. Ernie lowered himself into the chair, and Seb and Birdie stood to the side.

He brought up a camera feed and for several minutes didn't speak as he scrolled through the footage, going back and forth, as if he was playing a video game.

Birdie hopped from one foot to the other while, next to her, Seb's hands were clenched. Finally, Ernie looked at them. 'I've found her. But the car she's getting into isn't one belonging to the firm the studio uses. They're all Mercedes and this isn't.' He turned the screen until it was facing them. 'I'll replay from when she leaves the building.'

Florrie appeared on screen, dressed exactly as Ellen had described. The footage was in colour and after several seconds a silvery grey Fiat pulled up with a woman in the driver's seat. As soon as the car came to a halt, Florrie walked around the front and climbed into the passenger's side.

There appeared to be a short conversation and then the car pulled away.

'Can you zoom in on the driver?' Birdie leaned forward, as if it would somehow make the blurry image of the back of the person's head more visible.

'Sorry. This is the only camera we have for that part of the building. It could be an Uber or a friend collecting her?'

'Why would she get in the front seat if it was an Uber?' Birdie asked. 'I know some people do, but we know that Florrie values her privacy so I can't see her being one of them.'

'Yeah. Right. Want me to see if I can get the number plate?'

'Please.' She clenched her fists. If Florrie was in danger, then having to track down yet another car could take precious time that they didn't have.

Ernie dragged the mouse across the screen and then let the footage play before freezing the frame at the time the car pulled away from the pickup point. At least the registration plate was clear. She reached into her pocket for her notebook.

'I've got it,' Seb said.

Of course he had. She returned the notebook to her pocket and turned to Ernie. 'That's all we need. Thanks so much for your help.'

'I wish I could've done more. I hope you find Florrie. She's all right, she is.'

They left the office and hurried back across the marbled floor.

'I can't believe we have to start over again. It's best to call Twiggy for this one, rather than Rob. We've already asked him for too many favours.'

'No need,' Seb said, his mouth set in a tight line. 'I

know that plate. How could we have not seen what was right in front of our eyes?'

'I don't get it. What was?' Birdie stared at him. *Where* had he seen that car?

'The Fiat was outside Katie Wilson's mother's house the day we went to visit. When we left, it was parked in front of us but it wasn't there when we arrived.'

Birdie's chest tightened and her mouth went dry. There was no point asking him if he was sure, because of course he was.

'Do you think it belongs to Katie?'

'Yes. She didn't turn up until after us.'

'Bloody hell. Do you think she knew Jane was Florrie all the time? Except… when we spoke to her, there was no sign that she did.'

'Perhaps Florrie decided to reach out to Katie because she trusted her and felt safe?' Seb said as they reached the car.

'If that's the case, then it's crap timing,' Birdie muttered as she climbed in. 'Why wouldn't she tell us first?'

'I don't know, and that's what's worrying. We've had no luck contacting Florrie, so we'll call Katie instead to see if we can get to the bottom of it. Then we'll ask Rob to dig a little more into Katie's past.' Seb placed his phone in the dock and started up the engine.

'Agreed—' Birdie was cut off as a call came through the Bluetooth speakers and Rob's name flashed up on the screen. She broke into a laugh as she touched the screen to answer. 'Speak of the devil—we were just talking about you.'

'No wonder my ears were burning. You must have known I have news.'

'Is it about Duncan Wilde? We heard he was attacked and taken to the hospital. Has he been arrested?'

'No. But Harris' death is officially a murder investigation. They've already ruled Wilde out. They have multiple witnesses and CCTV footage to prove he was at an all-night club in Brixton and didn't leave until after six in the morning. There's no way he could have made it all the way back and killed Harris. They're now looking for a six-foot, thick-set, blond-haired man. He was seen entering the building several hours before you discovered Harris' body.'

Was it the same man who'd been following them the previous night? She exchanged a look with Seb, who seemed to confirm her thoughts.

Birdie's brow began to throb the way it sometimes did when bad news was on the way. 'Why do I get the feeling you have something else to tell us?'

'You're not going to like it,' Rob said, his voice grim.

'Go on,' Birdie said, tapping her fingers on her leg impatiently.

'Remember I tried to contact Colin Reeves, the officer who worked on the case involving Jane— Sorry, Florrie?'

'You said he was away on a cruise,' Seb said.

'Caribbean. Lucky sod. Anyway, he arrived back last night and called me a few minutes ago.'

Birdie's tapping increased. 'What did he say?'

'Your client, Jane Smith, didn't get off with community service because of her age and for being in the car instead of the house. She got off because she did a deal with the Crown Prosecution Service. She turned against Katie Wilson, Dean Knowles, Kyle Richards and Trevor Blackham, leaving them all with criminal records, while she got to walk away with community service and the chance to start a new life. It was very hush-hush and there's no record of this. Nowadays there would have been some digital trace, but it was different then.'

Birdie took a shuddering breath and stopped her tapping.

There was only one reason the CPS would consider a deal like that. If they didn't have enough evidence to successfully prosecute the case. In other words, if Jane hadn't cooperated with the police, there was a good chance her friends would have got away with it.

'I don't understand.' Seb was the first one to speak. 'Why were they so eager to do a deal with Jane? What was so important about the case?'

Rob sighed. 'According to Colin, Tom Winger, the victim, was close friends with the mayor back in the day. There was pressure to get a conviction. It seemed to be a case of money talks.'

'Neither Katie nor Dean mentioned this to us,' Seb said.

'Can't help you there, I'm afraid. Colin said it was done behind closed doors. But you know how these things work. Secrets don't stay buried forever. It's my belief that when Norman Harris accidentally stumbled upon Florrie's previous identity, he opened a whole can of worms, if you'll excuse the cliché.'

Birdie's heart pounded as Seb gave her a sharp nod. They needed to get to Peterborough pronto, because if they didn't, there could be a lot more than Florrie's reputation at stake.

Chapter 23

The early-evening sky was pale blue and the trees that flanked the road swayed with the breeze as they headed towards Peterborough. The remains of the sandwiches they'd grabbed when they'd stopped for petrol were stuffed into the brown paper bag they came in, and Birdie was once again staring at her phone.

They'd thought about phoning Wilson or Knowles but decided against it; if they did have Florrie and she was in danger, that could make matters worse. They needed to surprise them so they didn't have a chance to take off.

Birdie checked the map. They still had fifteen miles to go. But at least the traffic hadn't been heavy, thanks to ongoing roadworks, which the local radio station said had discouraged people taking this route. Thank goodness. Travelling up and down motorways was boring at the best of times.

In contrast, their last big case had taken them to art galleries, posh restaurants, and even across the channel to France, so it was hard not to feel like this was a let-down. Which was stupid, of course. It wasn't like her time on the force had been very exciting. Most of it had involved answering the phones thanks to the trouble she seemed to always land herself in.

She took a quick look at her inbox and did a double take.

Crap.

An email had come in from her birth mother. It was the reply she'd been waiting for all week, but now it had arrived, she was far too scared to open it.

And what lousy timing? Why couldn't Kim have replied when the case was over? Or at least when Birdie was in Seb's flat, with easy access to a tub of ice cream and Elsa's sweet nudges to keep her company.

'Should I be worried?' Seb broke the silence that had filled the car.

'About what?' She frowned and turned to him, only to see his lips twitch in amusement.

'You didn't finish the sandwich or muffin you bought, nor did you even smile when that truck went past with a twenty-foot fake cow on the trailer.'

'Wait? What? How did I miss a giant fake cow?'

'You tell me. It does seem like surveillance 101 to notice something like that. Especially when it was purple. Are you going to tell me what's wrong?'

Birdie closed her eyes. Her first instinct was to keep everything private. In a way, life was so much easier that way. But this was Seb. And he could stop her from driving herself crazy by overthinking things. He'd already been with her for so much of the journey that it didn't seem right to hide it from him.

'Okay, I'll tell you. Kim's emailed me back.'

'I see.' He nodded, eyes not leaving the road. 'What did she say?'

Birdie sucked in a breath and moved so she was facing his profile. 'I haven't read it yet. Is that stupid?'

He turned and fixed her with one of his *There's no such thing as a stupid question* looks. 'Don't be so hard on yourself, Birdie. This is new territory for you, and for Kim. Of course it's going to be scary. Terrifying even.'

'Yes, but you would've opened it straight away,' she pointed out.

Seb was organised and structured and he liked things neat and tidy, and while she'd never actually caught him with a to-do list, she was sure he had one in his mind, ticking off every task as he did it. Then again, so did she, most of the time.

'Not always. I once had an email from my sixth-form house master that I didn't read for days. I was convinced he'd found out about a stupid prank I'd been part of and told myself that if I didn't open the email, then it would just go away.'

Birdie blinked. 'Wait? You had an email back then?'

'Of course. Why do you think they were so worried about Y2K and all the computers crashing?' he protested, before letting out a low groan. 'Joke?'

'You've got it. I can't help it. And thanks for sharing. What happened? What was the email really about?'

'He wanted to know if I was interested in a summer-exchange programme with a school in the States. I would have been, but by the time I opened it, the deadline had passed and another boy went instead.'

'Yeah, but that's hardly a big deal. It's not like you couldn't afford to visit America, is it?'

'That's not the point. What I'm trying to say is that it's up to you when you open the email. It won't change the contents. If you'd prefer to wait until you're somewhere that feels safe, then do that: travelling along the A1 might not be the best of places to find out what your birth mother wants to do.'

Birdie leaned back in the seat and let her focus go wide so that it felt like she was part of the car as the sky and trees flashed by around her. Seb was right. It was up to her when she read it, and right now, with everything going on, wasn't the time.

She turned back to him. 'Thanks. You're pretty good at this stuff.'

'I've learnt from my mistakes.'

He turned right and drove past an endless row of terraced houses until they pulled up outside the house where Katie's mum lived. The silver Fiat from the surveillance footage was parked outside, and the mustard front door was half open while a woman wearing a dusky pink tracksuit was hunched over a phone, a thin roll-up cigarette in her hand.

Katie.

At the sound of the car doors slamming, she looked up and muttered something under her breath.

'She's going to make a run for it.' Birdie sprinted down the path, careful to jump over the discarded skateboard that lay across the paving stones. An all-too-familiar bark greeted her as Bluebell, the little terrier from next door, appeared at the hedge.

'Shut it, Bluebell,' Katie snapped as she lunged for the front door, but Birdie reached it first and stood in front of it, blocking the way. 'What the hell?'

'My thoughts exactly.' Birdie took in Katie's dishevelled appearance. The smudges under her eyes had morphed into proper bags and her dyed blonde hair was dragged back from her lined face, clearly showing the dark roots. She looked terrible. 'Where's Florrie Hart? Is she here?'

'Who?' Katie said, a little too quickly before looking

away. It wasn't very convincing, and Birdie folded her arms and glared at her.

'Florrie Hart. The woman you picked up from her apartment building in London. What's going on?'

'No comment,' Katie retorted as Bluebell continued to bark and dance around, her head occasionally appearing over the hedge, as if she was on a trampoline.

'This isn't a police interview,' Birdie snapped. 'So "no comment" isn't going to wash. I'll ask you one more time. Where. Is. Florrie?'

Katie's face crumpled and her body slumped, the flight clearly gone out of her. 'I can't believe this is happening.'

Birdie's shoulders relaxed and she softened her voice. 'Let's start at the beginning. What do you actually know about Florrie Hart?'

Before the woman could answer, Seb joined them. He gave Birdie a concerned glance, as if wanting to know if he should back off? She shook her head.

Bluebell's bark turned into a mournful howl and Katie glared at the next-door hedge before sighing. 'That dog's going to be the death of me. Come on, you'd better come inside so we can hear ourselves think.'

There was no sign of her mother, but a hamper of laundry was scattered across the leather sofa and the howls and screams of kids playing a video game came from upstairs. Katie immediately began pacing the room, and Birdie's annoyance faded a little. Whatever was going on, it seemed Katie wasn't happy about it.

'Are you living here now?'

'No. I don't have a washing machine at my place. I do it all here, at Mum's. The kids are upstairs, keeping out of my way.'

'Look. I'm sorry for coming on strong before, but we're

concerned for Florrie's safety. Can you tell us why you were in London today?'

Katie pulled her lighter out of the pocket of her jeans and began to fiddle with it. 'First, you lot can tell *me* what's going on. When you came to see me last week, did you know that Jane Smith was Florrie Hart? And don't lie, because it's pretty bleedin' obvious now I think about it. I was stupid to believe about the inheritance.'

'You're right, we did lie,' Birdie said truthfully; it was the one part of the job that she still struggled with. 'Yes, we knew about Florrie. She's the one who hired us. And we certainly don't think you're stupid.'

'So you're not the police?'

'No. We're private investigators,' Seb said. 'That part of what we told you was correct. Is Florrie here?'

Katie's gaze drifted from Birdie to Seb and back again, before she finally shook her head. 'No. She was here at first, but about an hour ago Ginny came and got her, and—'

'You mean Ginny Knowles?' Birdie said, unable to hide her surprise.

'Yes.' Katie nodded.

'Why did she go with her? I didn't know they were friends.'

'Definitely not friends.' Katie snorted. 'Ginny hates everyone. She's always worried someone's going to steal her precious Dean. Please, like anyone would. Anyway, it's Dean who wanted to see Florrie… Or Jane… I can't think of her as some celebrity.'

'Why Dean?' Seb asked.

'She did something years ago. And he's angry as fuck about it, and before you ask, I haven't the foggiest idea what it was.'

Birdie frowned as she tried to piece it all together. 'So,

Dean told Ginny he wanted to talk to Florrie Hart, aka Jane Smith, and they asked you to go to London to fetch her? Did you—'

A glass shattered from somewhere upstairs, quickly followed by a shriek. 'Mum, he spilt juice all over Nan's rug.'

'Well, get a cloth and clean it up.'

'I don't want to. Can't you do it?'

'What did your last maid die of?' Katie yelled. She glanced at Birdie and Seb. 'Bloody kids. I could kill them sometimes. Sorry. You were saying.'

'Did you already know that Florrie was really Jane when we spoke to you?'

'I'd no idea.' Katie gave a frantic shake of her head, her messy blonde hair breaking free of the band so that it fell down her back. 'I didn't know until we talked in the car.'

'Why did you agree to go to London?' Birdie asked, biting down on her bottom lip. It wasn't making any sense.

'Ginny came round to my place this morning after I dropped the kids off to school and said I had to go to London to pick someone up.'

Seb frowned. 'Why did you agree to go such a long way?'

Katie was silent as she gathered her hair and tied it back using a second band that had been on her wrist. Then she studied the floor.

'Look, being a single mum is hard, and sometimes Dean gives me jobs to do. Nothing major. The occasional pickup or delivery. I never ask questions and he pays in cash, so it doesn't affect my benefits. He often sends Ginny with the details. They pay extra for petrol.'

'When did you find out it was Florrie Hart you were picking up?'

'Ginny told me I had to call her once I got into London. So I did. A-and that's when she said it, the fucking cow—' Katie broke off in a painful sob, and wrapped her hands around her chest, trying to stop herself from shaking.

Birdie glanced at Seb in alarm. What else had happened?

'Would you like a glass of water?' Birdie asked. 'We can sit down to talk.'

Katie shook her head and pushed back her shoulders. 'No. Sorry, I'm all good.'

'What did Ginny say?' Seb asked.

'She gave me the address and told me that I had to wait outside for Florrie Hart and if we weren't back here in two hours, then Dean would make sure I never saw my kids again.'

Birdie's jaw dropped as Harris' blood-soaked body flashed into her mind. What had started as a blackmail case was quickly turning into something a lot more sinister. And now they knew Florrie had helped the police in return for avoiding a prison sentence, there was a strong motive for revenge.

'Is Dean capable of harming your children?' Seb asked.

'He has a nasty streak in him, and prison only made him meaner.' Her voice shook and she used the back of her hand to brush away the tears. 'But I never thought he'd resort to threatening my kids.'

'What happened next?' Seb said, nodding in encouragement.

Katie took a couple of deep breaths. 'I asked her why Dean wanted to see Florrie. I mean, it's really weird. She's some big television celebrity and he's a nobody pawnbroker in Peterborough. But Ginny wouldn't answer. She told me to do it, or pay the price.'

'So, you definitely didn't know who Florrie really was when you got there?' Birdie pressed.

'I've already told you that.' Katie gave another vigorous shake of her head. 'She was nothing like Jane. That's what happens with plastic surgery and lots of money. Even the colour of her eyes and her accent are different. But the minute she got in the car, she knew it was me. She freaked and nearly got straight back out.'

Birdie nodded. They'd seen the camera footage and there had definitely been a pause before the car had driven off. 'How did you stop her from leaving?'

'I told her the truth. That Dean sent me and he was going to hurt my kids—' She broke off and her eyes filled with tears again. She angrily wiped them away. 'Prick that he is. Anyway, her whole face softened and the fancy accent disappeared. She said, "You have kids?" And that's when I realised it was Jane. I just can't believe it. A big television star. Back in the day, she was so shy and always stayed in the background. Anyway, when I told her about Dean's message, she seemed to accept it. She said she'd messed up big time, but could never live with herself if anything happened to my kids. We talked the whole way back to Peterborough.'

'How come Florrie came out to your car in the first place? It sounded like she had no idea what was going on,' Birdie asked, trying to piece everything together.

'She told me she was sent an anonymous text saying they'd tell everyone the truth about her if she didn't get in the car that was coming to collect her. We talked the whole time on the journey. It was great. Like we hadn't been away from each other for all these years.'

'We tried to call Florrie loads of times, but she didn't answer. Why not?'

Yet another question that needed answers. There were so many.

'She put her phone on silent because she didn't want any interruptions while we were talking. Well, that's what she said. But maybe it was because she didn't want to put me in danger. I don't know.'

'What happened when you got back to Peterborough?' Seb asked.

'When we got back to my flat, Ginny was waiting and she took Jane— I mean Florrie.'

'Where did she take her?' Seb asked.

'I don't know. When I asked Ginny she told me to shut up and be grateful I wasn't going with them.'

'Are you sure you don't know? Is there anywhere you can think of that she might be?' Birdie pushed.

Katie shook her head. 'I've told you I don't. W-w-what are you going to do? If you call the police, Dean will think I ratted him out, and—' She broke off with another sob. Birdie's skin prickled. They needed to find Florrie as quickly as possible, but they couldn't ignore the fact that Katie and her kids could be in danger.

Seb took out his wallet and counted out two hundred pounds. 'Call your mother and ask her to come back home now. Then take her and the kids somewhere safe. Do you know anyone who lives out of town? Or go to a bed and breakfast somewhere well away from here. Once you get there, text us so we know where you are and that you're okay. As soon as it's safe to come back, we'll let you know.'

Katie stared at the notes in his hand for several moments before taking them. 'Okay. And tell Jane I'm sorry. I really didn't want to be part of it.'

'We know. Do you have Dean and Ginny's phone

numbers and their home address? We won't tell them that we got them from you,' Birdie said.

Katie stuffed the notes into the pocket of her tracksuit and unlocked her phone. She rattled off two mobile numbers and an address, which she told them was a few streets away, and showed them to Seb.

'Though I can't see them going there with Jane. Their neighbours are even worse than my mum's. You could try the shop, I suppose. Sorry, I didn't think of that until now.'

'Thanks. Did you get all that?' Birdie asked, turning to Seb.

'Yes,' he replied, nodding.

Katie looked at them, puzzled.

'Seb remembers everything. Saves having to write stuff down,' Birdie said, with a wave of her hand. If she had a pound for every time she had to explain his *gift* to people, she'd be rich. 'Now gather the kids together so you can get going. Where's your mum?'

'She popped to the shops for some milk. I'll get the kids ready and we'll leave as soon as she comes back.'

Birdie and Seb hurried back to the car. Dean and Ginny Knowles already had an hour's head start on them. That wasn't good.

Chapter 24

It was almost six-thirty when Seb turned his car into a side road a few metres before the parade of shops where Knowles' shop was located; if that's where they'd taken Florrie, they didn't want to announce their presence.

It had started to drizzle after they'd left Katie Wilson, and that had turned into a heavy shower, making it hard to see without the help of the windscreen wipers. Seb reached for the waterproof jacket he always kept on the back seat. Next to him, Birdie dragged a woollen beanie over her red curls.

A cold blast of wind wrapped around Seb as he climbed out of the car. At this time of year, it wasn't usually dark until after seven, but the weather was so bad, it was already almost black. He dropped his shoulders and walked headlong into the rain, Birdie a step behind him.

When they reached the slip road leading to the shops, they stopped and scanned the area. There were no parked cars and the shops were all shut, their glass windows obscured by metal roller doors that reached down to the ground; it had the eerie effect of looking like a mouth of metal teeth. The pawnbroker's was second from the end and the metal door was covered in dull white graffiti, although someone had attempted to paint over them several times before, but finally seemed to have accepted the inevitable.

There was no light coming under the roller door and, while it didn't prove the place was empty, it wasn't encouraging, either.

'Damn.' Birdie wiped away the rain from her face, mouth set in a frustrated line. They hadn't expected it to be open, but had hoped to at least be able to look through the glass. 'Shall I call Katie to see if she has any other ideas as to where they might have taken Florrie?'

'She didn't before, so she probably doesn't now.'

'But she's had time to process it, so she might have thought of something. Or am I clutching at straws?'

They'd already stopped earlier at the house address Katie had given them for Knowles, but there had been no sign of life there. The shop was still the most obvious place.

'We'll take a look around first.' Seb moved closer and nodded to the betting shop next door, which was also shut up. 'That's the shop Harris' sister owns.'

'I wonder how she took the news. Her brother wasn't the most likeable of people.'

'Family is family and I imagine it would still be hard,' Seb said, thinking of all the funerals he'd been to over the years, many of them for people who moved in the same social circles as his parents, and while he hadn't always liked the deceased, it still wasn't pleasant to think about their demise.

None of which was helping them find Florrie.

'Let's go around the back.' Birdie headed over to a narrow path that ran down the side of the building.

The street lights didn't extend that far, so Seb retrieved

the torch he always carried, and Birdie used her phone. The narrow beams of light revealed sodden piles of litter and leaves that had been left covering the path. Maintenance obviously wasn't a high priority. There was more graffiti on the side wall and there was a collection of empty bottles and cans nearby, suggesting that it had been done recently.

The path ended at a steep bank, and to the left was a metal gate. It effectively blocked off access to the rear of the building. Undeterred, Birdie hurried over to it and held up her phone, shining her beam to where an unsecured padlock was swinging off the gate's metal crossbar. Did that mean there was someone inside? Or had whoever left the building last forgotten to lock it? Considering the nature of the businesses and the neighbourhood, that seemed unlikely.

Birdie raised an eyebrow and held a finger to her lips before holding up her torch again, so that Seb could slide the crossbar until the gate opened, the squeaking muffled by the pouring rain.

His nerves jangled as he surveyed the scene. This was too easy. And from the look on Birdie's face, she felt the same. Without speaking, they both turned off their lights and stepped over the threshold.

The rain had eased a little and another gust of wind swept past them, moving the clouds above and offering faint shafts of moonlight to illuminate the path, giving them a brief glimpse of their surroundings. Bins and unwanted wooden pallets filled the space along with the occasional chair that staff probably used on their breaks.

The pawnbroker's was the second shop in the strip and the back entrance was made of reinforced steel. There were no exterior windows and the place was in darkness. Seb took his phone from his pocket and brought up Florrie's number. If she was in there and still had her phone, there was a chance it would ring and they would hear it, confirming her presence. He held the screen up to Birdie so she could see what he was doing.

He pressed call and they both stepped closer to the door.

Nothing.

Damn.

They carefully retraced their steps and closed the gate before making their way back to the front of the shops. Seb clenched his jaw, no longer able to hide his concern for Florrie. Without more knowledge of where else Knowles might have taken her, they were working in the dark.

They could call the police, but with so little evidence that a crime had been committed, or that Florrie was even missing, it was futile.

And yet, every minute they wasted, increased the likelihood that Florrie could be in more danger.

'We need to find out what other properties Knowles has access to.' Birdie's voice was tight, mirroring his own concern. 'Let's go back to the car and get out of this rain, so we can think properly.'

Seb took one last look at the front of the pawnbroker's shop before they walked back down the road. Headlights flashed as a car drove past. Out of instinct, the pair of them stepped back into the shadows just in time to catch the car slowing down and turning into the slip road and coming to a halt outside Knowles shop, the brake lights like two blood-red eyes against the filthy weather.

Adrenaline flooded Seb's body as he leaned forward. Seconds went by without any movement until the driver's door opened and a tall man with a shock of blond hair stepped out of the car. Despite the rain, the man took his time as he lit a cigarette and then walked down the side path to the back of the shops.

Birdie gasped. 'Is that Blondie, the guy who followed us?'

'I believe so.'

'Right. Now we have a good reason to call the police. We'll phone DS Johns and not the local force because she knows us.'

Seb took out his phone and made the call. 'I hope she's still on duty.'

'DS Johns,' she answered on the second ring.

'It's Sebastian Clifford.'

'I see. Are you ready to come in to make a statement?'

'That's not possible right now. Birdie and I are in Peterborough outside a pawnbroker's and a betting shop. The latter of which is owned by Norman Harris' sister, Ingrid.'

The detective sucked in a breath, as if considering her words. 'And why exactly are you still interfering with my murder investigation?'

Seb grimaced. 'We're not. We're actually looking for our client. We were hired by Florrie Hart to find out who has been blackmailing her, and our investigations led us to Norman Harris, who once worked as a cameraman on the set of her show. He believed she was responsible for getting him fired and that led him to the extortion attempt. He discovered details regarding Florrie's past, that she previously went by the name Jane Smith.'

'I see,' DS Johns said. 'That explains the newspaper cuttings we found in the drawer of his flat. And by telling me this, you do realise it makes Florrie Hart a potential suspect in his murder—' She broke off and let out an exasperated laugh. 'Of course you realise. And the fact we're still having this conversation means something else has happened. Tell me everything.'

Seb succinctly explained everything, including the blond man—who at the very least was a suspect in DS Johns' murder investigation. Once he'd finished, she swore softly under her breath.

'I'm calling Peterborough CID. We need officers there as soon as possible.'

'Thank you.'

'Don't thank me, Clifford. You need to assure me that you and your colleague won't do anything stupid. Stay out of sight and wait until the police arrive. The man you've seen is dangerous and wanted for murder. It's not safe for you to be involved. Is that clear?'

'Yes,' Seb agreed and finished the call.

Even if they had wanted to do anything, there was no way they could get through the reinforced steel doors of Dean Knowles' shop.

Which now meant that all they could do was wait. And hope Florrie was safe.

Chapter 25

Birdie checked the time on her phone again, tapping her foot impatiently on the ground. It had been ten minutes since Seb had spoken to DS Johns and there was still no sign of the police.

Blondie hadn't reappeared, which wasn't good. What if he was harming Florrie? Torturing her… Or even…

Stop it.

The man was already wanted for Harris' murder but that didn't mean he was doing the same to Florrie. Then again… What if…?

'This is ridiculous. We can't stand here not knowing what's happening to Florrie. We should try and get inside the pawnshop.'

'Do you really want me to answer that?' Seb asked in an irritatingly calm voice.

'Yes,' she grunted, wiping the rain from her face, yet again. There had to be something they could do to get inside.

'Step back.' Seb's hand nudged her arm, encouraging

her back into the shadows when a delivery scooter whizzed by and veered onto the slip road.

The rider had a bright green hi-vis vest on as well as a telltale backpack with the name of a well-known food delivery service stamped on it. The scooter skidded to a halt outside the pawnbroker's.

Birdie's heart pounded. Unlike some parades of shops, this one had no flats above them. Whoever had ordered food was inside the shop itself.

'I've had an idea,' she said, turning to Seb. 'I'll take the food and use it to get inside.'

'You don't seriously believe that they've kidnapped Florrie and then ordered food, do you?'

'There's nowhere else the food could be going. The place is deserted. And everyone's got to eat. Come on.'

She jogged towards the shops, Seb following not far behind. The fact he hadn't tried to stop her meant that despite any reservations he might have, he was going to let her try.

The rain had lessened and as they reached the shopfronts, the delivery guy was busy opening an insulated food bag that was fitted to the back of the scooter. He finally managed it and lifted out two large pizza boxes. He closed the insulated box and then suddenly muttered something.

Birdie and Seb both froze before she noticed his headset. He'd obviously answered a phone call and seemed oblivious to the fact anyone else was around.

'Look, it's not my fault the last place was up ten flights of stairs with no working lift. I'll be there in ten minutes, so tell them to keep their hair on,' the delivery guy moaned. 'I'm about to make a delivery. Get this, they want me to go down some back alley and stop at the third door where I knock twice, then pause and then knock again... Yeah, I know, right? Weirdos. They're probably off their heads and think it's some bloody movie. And they paid online, so it's not like I'll get a tip.'

Birdie's mouth slackened.

The third door down at the back of the shops?

Had the guy made a mistake?

The pawnbroker's was the second shop along from the end. The third one belonged to the betting shop that Harris' sister owned.

Next to her, Seb stiffened. Had he figured it out as well?

She stepped in front of the delivery guy and plastered on a smile.

'Thank goodness, you're here. They've just sent me out to look for these.' She reached out for the boxes, hoping her approach would work.

'I was told to take them around the back,' he said, holding the boxes close to his chest.

'Yeah, yeah. To the third door and knock twice, wait and then knock again. You were also told to deliver them ten minutes ago,' Birdie said, voice still encouraging.

It had the desired result, and the guy loosened his grip.

By this time, Seb had joined her and was holding out a ten-pound note in his hand. At some stage, she really needed to have a chat with him about bribing people.

'We came out here to wait. Everyone's getting pretty hungry. Thanks for your trouble.' Seb held the note in the air.

'Sure. One Hawaiian without the pineapple. Which, for the record, just makes it a ham pizza. And one supreme, no mushrooms.'

'Great.' Birdie put her hands around the boxes and eased them out of his grip before he could change his mind. At the same time, Seb handed over the money. The guy snatched it from him and shoved it into one of his many pockets. He then sped off into the darkness.

'This is weird,' Birdie said, while holding the pizza boxes as they walked towards the front of the betting shop for a closer inspection. 'Do you think that Harris' sister was in on the whole thing?'

He shrugged and then searched for something on his phone. He let out a sharp breath.

'Of course. We should have checked this earlier.'

'Checked what?'

'The opening times. A betting shop shouldn't be closed at this time of night. They're usually open until ten at night—this one included. Perhaps Harris' sister and her husband have shut up shop to travel to London because of Harris' death? Knowing the shop was empty, maybe Knowles thought it would be safer to take Florrie there instead of his own place, where people might look for her.'

'That makes total sense. And for all we know, they could have given Knowles the keys and asked him to keep an eye on the place.'

'All the more reason to be careful then,' Seb reminded her. 'You've met Knowles before and if he recognises you, it could make matters worse.'

'I doubt my own mother would recognise me like this.' Birdie rolled her eyes to indicate she was referring to the soaking-wet black beanie that was wedged tightly on her head and concealing her red hair.

She understood his concern, but was aware of the real reason he was worried: that there was a killer in the building.

'I don't like this one bit,' Seb said, shaking his head.

'I know, and I promise I won't go inside. This is surveillance, that's all. So we can report back to the police when they do arrive.'

Seb's mouth tightened, but he didn't argue with her. Thank goodness, because she couldn't stand around doing nothing. The boxes were warm and helped to defrost her fingers as she jogged to the side of the shops. Next to her, Seb retrieved his torch and held it out so they could navigate the piles of rubbish.

The gate was still open and they walked past the pawnbroker's to the betting shop. The rear was also metal, although the frame was scuffed and bent in places. Had there been a burglary in the past?

Without needing to be asked, Seb dropped back out of sight, close enough to help but not so close as to draw attention or arouse suspicions. Once he was in place, Birdie balanced the pizzas in one hand and knocked twice on the door, before pausing. Her heart banged heavily against her chest as she gave another single knock.

Energy fizzed through her entire body as the world seemed to stand still.

Suddenly, there was a click and the door cracked open, releasing a sliver of light into the deserted alley.

'What?' a male voice snapped from the other side.

'Don't be a moron. It's the bloody food,' a second voice said, this one distinctly female. Birdie forced herself to concentrate on her breathing—knowing all too well how easy it was to make simple mistakes when your adrenaline was high. The man muttered something unintelligible before the door slowly swung open and a figure appeared in the doorway.

Blondie.

Up close, his skin was overly tanned against his blond hair. Nicotine and stale sweat wafted from him, and Birdie did her best not to gag as she tried to peer past his broad shoulders. The door led into a long room that was illuminated by a single light bulb. A makeshift kitchen bench ran down one wall and was stacked high with boxes. There was a hum from a refrigerator and a round table sat to the left of the man's shoulder.

He grunted, reminding her to focus.

'I have an order for two pizzas,' she said, putting on a Birmingham accent and not letting go of the boxes while she tried to see past him. It looked like there were two women sitting at the table, one almost buried under a large black jacket. Florrie? The second woman shifted slightly, her long black hair and sharp eyes were familiar. Ginny Knowles. But where was her husband? 'One Hawaiian without the pineapple, and the other—'

'Yeah, yeah. I don't need a commentary.' Blondie snatched the two boxes out of her hands and gave her a gentle shove away, but not before she caught sight of Dean Knowles prostrate on the floor. 'Now piss off and make sure you close the gate on the way out.'

The door slammed shut and the alley was once again in darkness. *Crap.* Birdie stood there for several seconds before Seb appeared at her side. He touched her lightly on the elbow and nodded to the gate.

She swallowed hard. They needed to leave in case Blondie decided to open the door and make sure she was gone. They jogged away, and she let the gate clang shut for good measure before resuming their position up the road.

'Did you see inside?' Seb asked, his usual calmness gone. 'Is Florrie there?'

'I think so. She was sitting at the table but I couldn't quite see her face. But that's not all. Dean Knowles was on the floor and looked unconscious. At least I hope that's all he was.' She shuddered. 'Ginny was there, too. Sitting at the table next to Florrie.'

Seb's mouth dropped. 'You think Ginny's behind this?'

'It does make sense. Katie kept talking about how paranoid Ginny was. And we both saw her at the shop when we mentioned Jane's name.'

'But how did she find out who Florrie really was?'

'My guess is from Harris. How else could she have known?' Birdie said, with a shrug.

'It seems extreme to harbour a grudge over something that happened so long ago, to the extent that she'd mastermined a blackmail plot.'

'Maybe if Jane Smith had ended up cleaning toilets, Ginny wouldn't have minded. But she's gorgeous and rich,' Birdie pointed out. 'This way she can ensure Florrie stays away from Dean and make a lot of money in the process. Occam's razor. Right?'

Seb was quiet as he considered her theory. 'You're right. But why is her husband unconscious on the floor?'

'Maybe he tried to stop her? But whatever it is, we can't stand here and do nothing. Florrie isn't safe.' Birdie began to pace, the adrenaline still fizzing through her veins. 'Where the hell are the police? If they're not here in—'

Seb nodded towards a line of cars speeding towards them that turned into the slip road. 'It's okay, they've arrived. Come on, let's go over.'

Chapter 26

'Are you Clifford?'

'I am.' Seb joined the detective who'd taken up residence behind the police car. The man was about sixty with the look of someone who had been in the job too long.

There was an ambulance, a police van, and two other police cars all stationed close by. Twelve armed officers had silently fanned out around the slip road with two more guarding the metal gate at the back of the shops. DS Johns had obviously done a convincing job when she'd spoken to the local police.

The detective had a surly expression as he eyed Seb up and down. What else had DS Johns told him? That Seb needed to be watched?

'I'm DS Bell, senior investigating officer. So don't get any funny ideas about doing anything heroic.' His tone implied that his request was non-negotiable, and he backed it up by folding his tree-trunk arms in front of his chest. His gaze landed on Birdie, whose cheeks were bright red even against the dark night. 'What have you done?'

'Nothing,' Birdie retorted before seeming to think

better of it. 'Fine. We had an opportunity to deliver pizzas, so we took it. We weren't discovered and it did let me see inside. There's a tall, blond-haired man in there, who we believe is responsible for the murder of Norman Harris. Also in there is a woman called Ginny Knowles. Her husband, Dean, was lying on the floor—I couldn't see if he was conscious or not—and our client, Florrie Hart, is also there.'

The detective turned to Seb, as if wanting an explanation for Birdie's rapid-fire approach. He shrugged. She was fast but efficient. He couldn't have summed it up better himself.

'Stay here and don't move,' Bell barked, before leaving them to join one of the other officers.

Birdie waited until he was out of earshot. 'Who knew that Sarge had a doppelgänger? Do you think they have a factory where they make hundreds of cranky old sergeants?'

Seb resisted the urge to smile. It was no secret that while Birdie adored and respected her old boss, she'd certainly riled against his need for order and timekeeping. It was one of the reasons she suited private investigator work; she was able to utilise her skills without having to follow some of the more mundane rules that she'd always struggled with.

A flurry of movement captured their attention, and they both turned to where six officers in bulletproof vests were standing by the back door, two of them holding a battering ram. Once the door was pushed open, they all charged inside.

Seb moved from foot to foot, anxious to learn the outcome of the raid. It seemed like they were in the building for ages.

'Come on,' Birdie groaned. 'What's taking so long?

That's the trouble with not being in there with them. We have to wait… Oh, hang on… here they are. They've got him.' She pointed at two officers who'd appeared from around the side of the building, escorting a handcuffed blond-haired man.

Seb shone his torch in their direction. Blondie had a face like thunder, his mouth set in a thin line. Seb doubted he'd say much when he got to the station, but if DS Johns had enough physical evidence implicating him for Harris' murder, they wouldn't need a confession.

As the officer herded the man into the back of the police car, DS Bell appeared and walked over to them, followed by a paramedic who was walking with a small figure in an oversized black jacket. Florrie. Her face was pale, and her eyes were flat with exhaustion. At the sight of her, the tension in Seb's shoulders eased.

They hadn't been too late.

'Thank goodness. Florrie, are you okay?' Birdie asked.

'Miss Hart appears to be fine,' the paramedic said. 'We've checked her over, but would like her to go to the hospital as a precaution.'

'You're both here?' Florrie croaked, her gaze suddenly sweeping over them as she reached their side.

Her mouth crumpled and tears filled her eyes. Seb stiffened. He'd never been great with tears, but Birdie appeared unphased and quickly drew Florrie into a hug.

'Of course we are.' Birdie finally stepped away. 'That was the deal, remember. Are you really okay? Did they hurt you?'

'N-n-no, they didn't hurt me,' Florrie stammered. 'It's been a long day and I want to go home.'

'No can do. You heard the guy. You need to be checked out at the hospital and then we need you at the station to make a statement,' DS Bell informed her in a blunt voice.

Another paramedic appeared, pushing a trolley with Dean Knowles strapped in.

'Is he alive?' Seb asked, nodding in their direction.

'Yes, he'll live, though I'm not sure how his marriage will survive.' DS Bell raised an eyebrow as another group of officers appeared from the side of the shops, this time flanking a woman.

Ginny Knowles.

The woman's eyes were two narrow slits, and her mouth twisted into a furious snarl as she caught sight of Florrie. 'You'd better let me go this instant, you bloody animals. I'm not the villain here. It's her, she's a fucking tart. She's been trying to steal my husband for years. Little Miss Muck thinks she's too good for the likes of us. Dean and Katie might have been fooled by her but me and Blake knows the truth.'

'I was right. It was Ginny.' Birdie's expression was tight. 'Is Blake Blondie's real name?'

'Blake Richards,' Bell said. 'Unfortunately, we know him far too well. He's been causing trouble almost since before he could talk.'

'Richards?' Seb turned to him, immediately recalling the name from the original newspaper reports of one of the other men involved in the assault on Winger. 'Is he related to Kyle Richards?'

'Kyle's his big brother, but he's been locked up for years.'

Birdie let out a gasp as she turned to Seb. 'There's the connection. Blake wanted revenge as much as Ginny did.'

'He's just not as vocal about it,' Seb said, while Ginny continued to fight the officers who had almost reached the patrol car. As if she heard him, Ginny's head swung back around.

'Tell that stupid bitch she's not fooling me. Ask her

about the diamonds? Go on... ask her. Because—' The rest of her words were lost as the officers finally managed to push her into the back of the car.

'Diamonds?' DS Bell's eyes were narrowed. 'If you've left anything out, then I'm going to be dragging the pair of you down to the station.'

'It's news to us,' Birdie said, swinging her attention to Florrie and arching a questioning eyebrow.

'The only diamonds I have are these.' Her finger shook as she pointed to the diamond solitaire studs she always wore. 'I swear they're mine. I bought them from Tiffany's when I got my first big contract. You can check my insurance documents if you don't believe me.'

'So what was she talking about then?' DS Bell glared at Florrie, but she didn't falter.

'For some reason, she believes that Dean gave them to me and that they should be hers. She wouldn't believe me when I said I haven't seen Dean for over twenty years and he hasn't given me anything.' The pressure of the day seemed to finally catch up with her, and several tears rolled down her cheek.

It was clear that she needed to get a good night's rest before anyone could try to question her properly about what had happened.

Seb gestured to the sergeant for a private conversation, and then stepped to one side while Birdie stayed with Florrie. 'Look, I know you want Florrie to go to the hospital, but if she does, she'll be poked and prodded and kept awake for hours when it seems clear that all she needs is some time to rest. We can book into a hotel and bring her down to the station to be interviewed tomorrow. Is that okay with you?'

DS Bell rubbed his chin before giving Seb a sharp nod. 'Fine. But I expect to see you there at nine on the dot. And make sure you monitor her in case she needs any medical attention. Are we clear?'

'Perfectly,' Seb assured him before returning to where Florrie and Birdie were standing. 'Let's go. He's agreed for you to come with us and will postpone taking statements until tomorrow.'

'Thank you.' Florrie's eyes filled with gratitude. 'Both of you. I really don't know what I would have done without you.'

'We're just relieved we got here in time.' Birdie put a comforting arm around their client as they walked back to the car. 'Some food and a good night's sleep and you'll be feeling as good as new.'

Chapter 27

'I hope you enjoy your stay. Check-out is at ten a.m. and breakfast is served in the dining room between six and nine.' The receptionist at the hotel they'd found in the centre of Peterborough gave Seb a wide smile and handed over the key cards for both rooms.

The hotel's décor was reminiscent of something from the 1980s, which gave it a gloomy feel. But considering the time, Seb was pleased they were open and had vacancies.

He booked a single room for himself and a double with twin beds for Birdie and Florrie to share. Despite Florrie no longer being in danger, they decided it would still be a good idea for Birdie to be with her.

He made his way back to the velvet sofa where Florrie was scrolling through her phone with the vigour of a twelve-year-old child who'd been without it for twenty minutes, and Birdie clutched at the bag containing the Chinese takeaway they'd picked up on the way over.

'We're on the first floor and the stairs are over there.' He handed Birdie one of the key cards. 'You walk, and I'll take Florrie up in the lift.'

'I hate lifts,' Birdie said to Florrie by way of explanation, who nodded. 'I'll see you up there.'

'How are you feeling?' Seb asked Florrie, on their way to the lift.

'Like I've been hit by a bus.' She gingerly stepped forward and stood next to him. 'And it's not like anything bad happened to me. Not really.'

'I'm not surprised. You might not have been physically hurt, but mentally you've been through a difficult experience. Your body is trying to remind you of the fact,' he explained.

Several of Seb's friends had been in the army and had come back with various degrees of trauma. Seb had taken a great interest in how it was treated these days.

'Well, someone needs to tell my body that I don't have time for a breakdown. I have the press conference at ten tomorrow. I've been messaging Brian to ask what will happen if all this ends up out there.'

The lift arrived, and they both stepped in, but Seb waited until the steel doors closed in front of them before answering. 'You won't make the press conference. We're due at the station at nine. You must contact Brian to rearrange it.'

'You don't understand.' Florrie's eyes widened in alarm. 'I can't stay here. The whole point of hiring you was so that this thing didn't hijack my life. Can't I just call the police once I'm back in London? I can do the interview from there.'

'That's not an option,' Seb told her firmly as the lift doors opened on the first floor. 'DS Bell wouldn't take kindly to a witness leaving town before speaking to him. Especially when he'd only agreed for you to come with us because we promised to be responsible for you.'

'But I need to be there. To see if there's any way I can

stop this nightmare from hitting the papers. My absence would only add to the speculation,' Florrie implored as Birdie appeared in the hallway.

'It's a murder and kidnapping investigation, Florrie. With the best will in the world, we can't stop it from hitting the news.' Birdie held the bag with one hand and swiped the key card before turning to Seb. 'Shall we eat in our room?'

'Sounds good,' he agreed, trying to ignore the mutinous expression on Florrie's face. But Birdie was already in the room and didn't seem to catch it.

The rooms were in a better condition than the reception area, and while the light pine furniture was out of date, the room was well aired and smelt clean.

'Let's eat before the food gets even colder,' Birdie said, putting the takeaway on the small table by the window, opening the bag, and handing it out.

Seb joined her at the table, and Florrie perched on the edge of one of the beds, but she didn't eat much. Instead, she spent most of the time chasing her rice around the box with the chopsticks.

'Before we go to the station tomorrow, I'd like to know what else Ginny told you. Did she mention Norman Harris?' Seb asked once they'd stopped eating.

Florrie winced, as if remembering it was painful. 'According to her, Norman visited his sister a few months after he was fired from the set last year. He was still fuming about what had happened and blamed it entirely on me. It seems he got some temp work while he was here, filing old case notes for a solicitor and somehow saw an article about the case. The more he looked at the photo of me, the more familiar it became, especially as he remembered my comment about knowing Dean's shop.'

'Talk about bad luck,' Birdie said, wrinkling her nose.

'Sorry, I didn't mean to offend you. But the chances of it happening are so slim.'

Florrie gave a tired laugh. 'When Norman approached Dean with the news of my new identity, Dean didn't want to blackmail me, but Ginny contacted him privately and was all in. She kept ranting about how she was sick of living off the smell of an oily rag, and that she deserved so much better.'

'So Dean didn't have anything to do with it?' Birdie asked.

Florrie shook her head. 'I don't think so. Ginny must have used Dean's phone to text Katie, and that's how she threatened her kids. I can't forgive her for that.'

'Did Ginny say how Harris managed to get the last letter into your dressing room, because that's still baffling?' Birdie said.

'As usual, money talks. Norman was still in contact with one of the contractors and he paid him to deliver it. He did it during the recording when the coast was clear.'

'Do you know who it was?'

'No. And there's no point in finding out. Not now.'

'And what about Blake Richards? How did he get involved?'

'Right time, right place? Although if you ask me, there's something going on between him and Ginny. There were plenty of secret looks.'

'Really?' Birdie said, leaning forward, clearly interested in what Florrie was saying. 'I thought Ginny was super possessive of Dean.'

Florrie shrugged. 'Just because she didn't want Dean, didn't mean that anyone else could have him. That's not uncommon, is it?'

'True.' Birdie nodded. 'But why was Harris murdered?'

Florrie bit down on her trembling bottom lip. 'It was all my fault.'

'No. That's not true,' Birdie said, vehemently.

'The blackmail letters said not to contact anyone. But I ignored it and got in touch with you. They sussed it when you went to Peterborough and starting asking about me. When Norman told Ginny that he had a last-minute meeting with a TV producer, she suspected it was you and sent Blake to check. And… well, you know the rest. He wasn't going to risk losing the money, if Norman had blabbed to you.'

'There was someone else in the car when we were being followed. Do you know who that was?' Seb asked.

'No. He might have taken someone with him. I don't know. There wasn't anyone else in the betting shop with us.' She let out a long yawn as the tiredness crept back into her eyes. 'Now do you see why it's my fault Norman's dead?'

'What happened isn't down to you. Harris knew the risk when he set the ball rolling,' Birdie said.

'Birdie's right,' Seb agreed. 'Now, it's time we retired to bed. Tomorrow's going to be a long day.'

Chapter 28

A pang of nostalgia coursed through Birdie as the uncomfortable plastic chair dug into her lower back. The police station was so similar to Market Harborough that she almost expected to see Twiggy hurrying past, clutching a bag from the local bakery in one hand, hoping no one would notice. That had always been impossible because they were trained detectives, not to mention he usually had flakes of pastry on his chin from the extra sausage roll he'd consumed on his way back to the station.

Birdie glanced at the old clock on the wall. DS Bell had interviewed her and Seb separately, and now Florrie was with him. She'd also seen a couple of officers from the previous night and longed for an update from them. Had Blake Richards confessed? What else had Ginny Knowles said about the mystery diamonds? Was Dean Knowles okay?

Birdie suspected she could find out the answer to the last question from Katie Wilson, who'd been texting her all morning to thank them for putting in a good word with DS

Bell about her part in it all. The family had returned home late last night after Birdie had told Katie it was all over.

Maybe DS Bell would tell them more when he'd finished with Florrie… and perhaps he'd let something else slip. It was hopeful at the best, and delusional at the worst, especially as the case was linked to the murder investigation in London.

She let out a sigh, and Seb, who was awkwardly crammed into the plastic chair next to hers, turned to her.

'You're on edge. What's wrong?'

'Just wishing I could be a fly on the wall. This is the one part I miss about being in the force. I hate being sidelined. What do you think Ginny told the police?'

Seb shrugged. 'I've no idea. No police reports or newspaper articles from around the time of the attack have referred to anything being stolen.'

'In which case, why did Ginny mention diamonds?'

'It's possible something was taken without the police knowing. It would explain why Florrie was so eager to leave Peterborough and take on a new identity.'

'Are you saying that you don't believe Florrie's story?'

'It's certainly something worth considering.'

'If she did have a stash of diamonds, it would make it much easier to start a new life,' Birdie said, as she tried to tease it out in her mind. 'Do you think she's been playing us?'

'It did cross my mind.' Seb nodded.

'But her remorse over Harris was genuine. I'm sure of it.'

'I agree, but that's a different matter. How was she last night after I left the room and went to bed?'

'On edge. She took ages in the bathroom and then kept checking her phone all night. She tried to hide it by leaning over the side of the bed, but, of course, the screen was so bright I knew what she was doing. Not to mention it kept me awake. I think she was texting someone. It could have been Brian. I asked her this morning when we were getting dressed, but she was evasive.'

'Something's definitely going on,' he said as a door opened up and Florrie appeared alongside DS Bell.

'Ms Hart is all yours. DS Johns is on her way and she said to remind you to go to the station to make a statement when you're back in London. She also needs to interview Ms Hart in the next couple of days. But in the meantime, you're all free to go,' he said in a gruff voice before his mouth softened into something that almost resembled a smile. 'And good work. While I don't approve of your antics with the pizza, I do appreciate you calling us in before things got out of hand. With resources stretched, this investigation could have taken a lot longer.'

Birdie, who was more than used to back-handed compliments, especially from her old sergeant, was tempted to give DS Bell a hug. Then she looked at his folded arms and slightly raised eyebrow and thought better of it. Instead, she grinned and reached into her pocket for one of the lovely business cards that Seb had insisted she always carry with her.

'Any time… and don't forget we're currently based not too far away in Market Harborough, so if you ever want some outside help…'

'I bet you were a handful when you were on the force,' the DS grumbled, but all the same, he took the card and let out a rueful smile. 'And I guess stranger things have happened at sea.'

~

Florrie didn't speak as they walked back to the car, but by the time Seb had pulled in for coffee and petrol, she finally seemed to have recovered enough to face them.

'I know we didn't discuss this last night, but I take it you know about the deal I did with the police when it first happened and the real reason I was given community service?' She stirred her coffee, though didn't appear to be interested in drinking it. There were still dark shadows under her eyes and her cheeks were hollowed out, making her look more like the photographs of Jane Smith than Florrie Hart.

'Our friend in the Met told us yesterday, after speaking to the original detective in charge of the case,' Birdie said, flatly. 'You should have been straight with us.'

Florrie stopped stirring and finally looked up. 'I know. And I'm so sorry. It sounds stupid now, but they said I couldn't tell anyone. They kept drilling it into me how important it was to stay silent. Not that I wanted to tell anyone, anyway. All I could think of was getting out of there and never seeing Peterborough again—' She broke off with a dry laugh. 'Yet, here I am.'

'They always say you can't outrun your past,' Birdie said.

Florrie nodded. 'I guess they're right. Though I've spent the last twenty years pretending that the past never happened and, in some ways, it feels like it didn't. Have you ever tried to talk about an old movie and you can only remember a few of the big set pieces?'

Birdie had, on occasion, fallen asleep in the middle of a movie, especially if it was a boring one, so she did know what Florrie was talking about.

'Our minds can get very good at believing our own lies,' Seb answered. His voice was mild but Birdie could tell by the tilt of his head that he was studying Florrie closely. 'Did Ginny say how Dean knew about your deal?'

'What will happen to Ginny and Blake Richards?'

'Richards will be charged with murdering Harris and, depending on Ginny's involvement, she might very well be an accessory. There are also the blackmail and kidnapping charges. When we're back in London, DS Fiona Johns will go through everything with you and—'

Florrie's phone rang, interrupting him.

Their client studied the screen and then declined the call. Seconds later, the sound of a text message pinged and Florrie glared at it before putting her phone back into her handbag.

'Everything okay?' Birdie checked.

'Yes. It's Brian. But I don't want to talk to him right now. I'll call him once I'm back home.'

'Is it about the press conference for *Hands On?* Did it go ahead?' Birdie asked.

Florrie's shoulders slumped. 'No. They decided to cancel it until things have calmed down. But I'm sure that's an excuse. They really want to see if this all becomes public. It's like I'm being punished twice. So much for hoping that once this was all over, things would go back to normal.'

'You need to give it a bit of time,' Birdie said. 'A lot has happened, and when you speak to Brian, you might discover it's not as bad as you thought.'

'Maybe.' Florrie let out a dramatic sigh before getting to her feet. 'I'm going to use the loo before we head back. I won't be long.'

Once she'd disappeared into the bathroom at the far end of the cafeteria, Birdie leaned back in her chair. 'Something's definitely going on. I bet she's gone into the bathroom to return the call. Shall I go and listen?'

Seb shook his head. 'That's not necessary. There's a nervous energy about her and I suspect that the moment we drop her back at her apartment building, she'll make a move.'

'What are you suggesting? That we follow our own client?'

Seb nodded. 'If she's breaking the law or involved in anything illegal, then we need to know about it. Otherwise we're just enabling her. Are you in agreement?'

'I certainly am.' Birdie gave him an approving nod before standing up. 'Hopefully we'll find out what's really going on by the end of the day.'

'I'll second that. I also want to see Elsa—it seems ages since we've been with her.'

Not to mention she wanted to find out what was happening with her birth mother.

Chapter 29

'You were right about Florrie,' Birdie said, several hours later, putting down the binoculars she'd been using and leaning back in the passenger seat.

'It looks like she's heading for the Tube. Let's leave the car here and follow her. We've already spent a small fortune on parking so what's a few more pounds?'

'Nothing, as long as you charge it to our client.' Birdie grabbed her jacket and joined him. Florrie was a good two hundred yards ahead of them. Yet again, hidden beneath a large jacket. This time it was navy and her blonde hair was crammed under a matching beret. 'We can't get too close. She'll spot you a mile away because of your height.'

'I should have brought my short legs along.'

'Did you just make a joke?' Birdie stared up at him, but he just gave her a vague shrug.

'It's been known to happen occasionally. Now come on, we don't want to miss her.'

'Well, if you *did* bring your short legs, then it wouldn't be so hard keeping up with you.' Birdie jogged alongside him, which actually felt good. Not surprising, after all the time she'd been stuck in the car recently.

She'd go for a proper run once she got home. That, and some all-night dancing.

They turned the corner as a flash of a navy beret disappeared down the escalator leading to the Tube station. After her last visit to London, Birdie had come to understand that the capital was virtually always full of people. And while sometimes it could be annoying, right now it was proving useful since the constant sea of bodies between them and Florrie made it easier to trail her without being seen.

'She's going to the Jubilee line,' Seb announced, his height enabling him to keep track of her.

'Okay. We need to make sure she doesn't spot us on the platform,' Birdie said as they went through the barrier, swiping their credit cards.

'We'll stand around the corner until the train pulls up.' Seb came to a halt and dropped his head, obviously trying to blend into the crowd. Birdie did the same as they waited. 'She's getting into the fourth carriage at the far end.'

They joined the rush of people and slipped in behind a group of loud Australian tourists. From her position, Birdie could just make out Florrie's profile. Thankfully, she kept her head bowed and didn't seem interested in looking around. She got off at Green Park and then went onto the Piccadilly line.

'I hope you know where we are,' Birdie said as Florrie once again stood up and got off the carriage. 'I've completely lost my bearings.'

'We're in Knightsbridge. You might remember it from our last visit.' His eyes twinkled as they waited several moments before going up the escalator.

Birdie groaned. Knightsbridge was where his parents lived when they were in town, and to say that she'd been nervous about meeting a viscount and viscountess was an understatement. As it happened, his mother had been okay, although his father still made her feel like she was going to trip over her tongue.

They got off the escalator and passed through the barrier before stepping out into the early-afternoon sunshine. Birdie shielded her eyes as the fancy shops came into view. Another thought hit her. One that was almost as bad as meeting his parents.

'What if we've followed her all this way just to get dragged along on some horrible shopping expedition?' It wasn't that she was opposed to the shopping, but going to department stores where everything cost more than she earned in a month would have her living in fear of breaking something.

'Some people do find retail therapy can help with trauma or a shock,' he said, but the small wrinkles around his eyes suggested he was also confused. 'Though I do agree. I'd much rather be taking Elsa for a walk. Never mind. She's heading in the other direction.'

Birdie looked over. The throngs of people had lessened, and she caught a glimpse of Florrie's navy coat before she disappeared into a doorway. There was a sign above it and she held up her phone to take a photo. She grabbed Seb's arm when she realised he was trying to get closer.

'It's okay. Look.' She stepped back under the awning of a shop and showed him the screen. 'We can keep an eye on her from here and that way if she does suddenly come out or look through a window, she won't spot us. The place is called KSL. Do you know what it is?'

'It's a vault… Interesting.' He turned to her. 'Within

the vault itself are safety deposit boxes that are protected by highly advanced security. My father uses one on Threadneedle Street.'

Birdie looked at the photo again. It was a nondescript brick wall with a plain doorway, and the sign was just a blue circle with the lettering in the middle. 'Are you sure? It doesn't look like much.'

His lips turned up into a tiny smile. 'It might not look like much on the outside, but trust me, the inside is something else. Next time we're in town and have some free time, I'll take you to the family one. It's an entirely different world.'

'One full of bars of gold and diamond necklaces,' she quipped, and then froze as her words echoed back in her mind. She turned to Seb. 'Diamonds. Do you think Florrie has stashed them here?'

'A very good question.' Seb stepped out from the protective embrace of the shopfront as Florrie reappeared from the inauspicious doorway. 'Let's find out.'

Chapter 30

Seb had grown up having good manners drummed into him, but it had been a long couple of days and he hated being lied to. Which was why when Florrie Hart emerged from the vault with her handbag clutched tightly to her side, he simply stepped in front of her and folded his arms.

Florrie glanced up and down the street, as if trying to decide what her chances were of running. She obviously concluded they weren't high, and finally let out a long sigh.

'I take it you know.'

'We have a pretty good idea, but why don't you explain?' Seb said.

'And this time try not to leave anything out.' Birdie bristled, her tone icy. 'We deserve the truth.'

'You're right. There's a café two doors down. Can we at least go there to talk?' Florrie asked.

'Yes, but you're paying,' Birdie retorted. 'And you can pay our invoice at the same time.'

'Oh, yes, of course.' Florrie flinched. 'But I swear, this isn't what you think. I wasn't trying to run away or not pay you. It's just—' This time, when her voice cracked, it was genuine, though Birdie's frosty expression didn't change.

'Come on.' Seb touched his partner lightly on the arm.

It seemed to work, and Birdie huffed. 'Fine.'

The Victorian-themed café was one he'd been into before. The tables were well spaced out and the chairs comfortable. Perfect for what they needed.

Birdie ordered at the counter, and once the waitress had brought over the pots of tea and cake, Seb nodded to Florrie.

'Okay, we're listening.'

'First of all. Nothing I've told you has been a lie.'

'Ever heard of lying by omission?' Birdie scowled.

'I'm not a bad person. Well… I don't think I am.' Florrie's eyes were bright with unshed tears. 'But I've definitely made enough stupid mistakes to last a lifetime. The first one was getting into that bloody car with Dean, Trevor, Kyle, and Katie. Even though I never went into the house, I was still part of it. When the police offered me a deal if I told them what happened, it seemed like the best way to make sure my life wasn't ruined. The thing I really regret… well… that's the diamonds.'

'Finally,' Birdie muttered before jabbing her cake fork into a mound of cream.

'What I didn't tell you was that when Dean and I dated, I'd—'

'I thought you didn't date,' Birdie interrupted.

'Well, it was only occasionally. And more like friends.'

'Okay, carry on.'

'When I was with Dean, sometimes I'd tag along when he did jobs for his Uncle Les.'

Seb's mind started to put the pieces of the puzzle together. Les's Pawnbrokers. There'd been several newspaper articles about his uncle's involvement in fencing stolen goods, especially gemstones and jewellery. Dean Knowles had specifically said that he'd worked hard to change the reputation of the business. *'Everything goes through the books now.'*

'What kind of jobs?' Seb asked.

'There was some kind of syndicate where jewellery, gems, and precious metals would get stolen in one city and sent on somewhere else to be broken down or melted, and then sold off. His uncle was... He was a bad man—' Florrie swallowed and her eyes clouded over, as if stuck in a memory. She shuddered and then looked up. 'Sorry. It's been a long time. I wasn't expecting it to affect me like that after all these years.'

'What did he do to you?' Birdie's mouth was set in a grim line.

'It's not as bad as it could have been. It happened one night when I'd arranged to meet Dean outside the shop. Except he was late and his uncle told me to come inside and wait. It was just the two of us. Then suddenly he was all over me. Like a bloody octopus. I only got away because I jabbed him with my nail file and then scratched at his eye. A teacher had once taught us what to do.'

'Did you report it?' Birdie asked, her voice softer than before.

'No. That's not how things were when I grew up. And it would only have made things worse. I didn't tell anyone. Not even Katie.'

Anger grew in Seb. Florrie would have only been sixteen at the time and with an alcoholic father and a checked-out mother, she must have felt so alone. Her determination to protect her new life and forget about her past suddenly made a lot more sense.

'So where do the diamonds fit in?' Birdie asked, the heat gone from her eyes.

'The night before we all got arrested, Dean had a pickup. He didn't tell me what was in the parcels and I didn't ask, but for some reason, this time, he decided to show me. It was a small leather pouch full of diamonds.'

Birdie leaned forward. 'Why would he have shown them to you?'

'I've no idea. Maybe to show off? Anyway, they were the most beautiful things I'd ever seen. It was like gazing at a night sky full of stars. They could have been fakes for all I knew, but I wouldn't have cared. To me, they were perfect and for one second I forgot about how ugly my life had become. I remember thinking how unfair it was that a bastard like Leslie Knowles would make money from them. And then I thought of all those snooty people who used to look down on me, who probably only wore diamonds to show the world they were rich. And in that moment, I hated them all.'

'So you took them?' Seb asked quietly.

'Not exactly. That night, we delivered them to his uncle. After what happened, I wasn't prepared to go inside, so I waited in the car, which was parked outside the shop. But they took ages and I was desperate to go to the loo, so I got out and went around the back. It's not like it was when you saw it. Twenty years ago, there was no gate and at the far end was an outside toilet. Seems archaic now, but that's how it was. Anyway, I'd just finished and was about to open the toilet door when I heard footsteps in the alley. I looked over the top of door and could see Les. He was holding the leather pouch in his hand. He pulled out a brick from the old wall that ran behind the shops.'

'He hid stolen diamonds behind a brick?' Birdie spluttered. 'Was he crazy?'

'Quite possibly. Dean reckons he was paranoid that his shop would be broken into, so I guess it made sense to him.

227

The next night, we were arrested and I thought my life was over. That's why I took the deal they offered. After I'd finished my community service, I heard Les Knowles had been killed in a car accident. I remembered the diamonds. It was almost like they were calling to me. I went to see if they were still there. And sure enough, they were. So I took them. After all, Dean was in prison and Les Knowles was dead. If I hadn't taken them, they might have been lost there forever.'

Seb closed his eyes. His instincts had been correct.

And so had Ginny's accusations. But how?

'There's one thing I don't understand,' Seb asked. 'If Dean knew you were the one to take the diamonds, why did he refuse to take part in Norman Harris' plan to blackmail you?'

Florrie's brows drew together. 'I'm not entirely sure. Ginny was ranting the whole time I was there, but from what I could make out, she was the one who worked out it was me. After she and Dean got together, he told her about the missing diamonds, and when they found out who I was from Harris, she put two and two together. She thought I'd used them to turn myself into the new me. But she was wrong. It was hard work that got me here...' She paused. 'Okay... and the deal, but they don't know about that. I still feel responsible for what happened to Norman. I should have reached out to him at the time he was fired and made sure he was okay.'

'It wasn't up to you,' Seb assured her, hoping he could at least take some of the guilt off her shoulders.

Florrie had been weighed down with so many secrets and troubles for far too long, but despite Seb having a better understanding of Florrie and what she'd been through, it didn't change the fact she'd stolen something of great value.

'What did you do with the diamonds after you took them?'

His question acted like a blanket, and silence descended. Florrie dropped her head and studied the table. Then, without a word, she dug into her handbag and carefully lifted out a rough-hewn leather pouch.

'They're here. I've kept them ever since. Like my good-luck charm.' Her touch was almost reverent and a flicker of joy crossed her features as she tugged at the leather string.

Seb peered in, not wanting to draw too much attention to them. He wasn't an expert on precious stones, but there were several sets of necklaces and earrings that had come down the family line and his father had taken great care to make sure Seb understood their value. He knew enough to recognise the clarity and cut of first-rate stones.

'Bloody hell,' Birdie exclaimed in her typical fashion. 'There are hundreds of them.'

'Fifty-two,' Florrie corrected, her gaze still lovingly fixed on the glittering stones.

'Fifty-two?' He paused, as his memory shifted with its usual efficiency to a particular news article he'd read about a robbery at a City vault twenty three years ago, when thieves had stolen a diamond necklace, better known as The Winter Diamonds because the design of the necklace was based on a constellation seen only in the winter sky. It had contained fifty-two white diamonds. The police believed the necklace had been broken down and sold. 'You haven't taken any?'

'Of course not.' Florrie turned to him, her eyes filled with shock. 'I would never separate them. That's not why I took them. Well, maybe it was. But once I got to London, I was too scared to sell them, and after I got my job and changed my name, I managed to do it all on my own. But I loved having them there. W-why? Do you know their origin?'

'I'm guessing yes,' Birdie cut in. 'Seb has HSAM. It's a memory thing and means he never forgets anything. Most of the time, it's very useful.'

Most of the time? He must remember to follow up on that later. He gently took the leather bag from Florrie, and nodded.

'There was a robbery two years before Leslie Knowles came into possession of these diamonds. At the time, they were thought to be worth half a million pounds,' he said, before explaining what had happened. When he was finished, Florrie's eyes were bright with tears.

'The Winter Diamonds? So I was right. They really are like stars?'

'Yes, they are. Is that why you didn't want to separate them?'

She nodded. 'I did consider it many times, but could never bring myself to go through with it. But I knew I couldn't return them without getting into all sorts of trouble, so I kept hold of them. As my plan B.'

'Did you take them out today because you have a plan B in mind?' Seb asked.

This time, colour stained her cheeks, and she nodded. 'The writing's on the wall. Brian still hasn't returned any of my calls, and now Ginny's been arrested, there's no way the truth won't come out. Knowing her, she'll scream it from the rooftops. My career will be over and I'll be famous for all the wrong reasons. I can't stay.'

'I understand.' He nodded before fixing his gaze firmly on hers. 'Which leaves us with the real question. What are we going to do now?'

Chapter 31

Birdie's head was spinning. They'd worked out that Florrie had been keeping secrets from them, but she would never have guessed the truth.

There was no way they could allow her to keep the diamonds. But did Florrie realise that?

She studied their client, who hadn't spoken since Seb had asked his question. Instead, her gaze kept flickering back to the leather pouch in Seb's hand, her eyes full of longing.

'I had planned to go to New Zealand and start again. A radio station in Auckland is looking for a producer and when I spoke to them last week, they offered me the job. I'll get to do what I love, but my face won't be all over the television, and in time, people will forget I even existed. It will be a fresh chance.' Florrie looked directly at Seb and then at Birdie, her eyes brimming with hope. 'But I guess that decision is up to you.'

'What about the diamonds?' Birdie jumped in. 'You know we can't let you take them, right?'

'Yes.' She took a resolute breath, and nodded. 'I've

always known that they weren't mine. Not really. But I have money. More than enough to set myself up. And speaking of which... I transferred your fee this morning. I didn't think you'd be wanting it in cash.' Florrie tapped her phone screen and held it up to show the bank transfer.

Birdie swallowed as she stared at the screen. It was 20 per cent more than the agreed fee.

'I take it that you want to leave the country and have us return the diamonds once you've left?' Seb said.

Florrie pressed her lips together, as if making a silent prayer. 'Yes, please. You must think I'm a terrible person. I keep running and hiding from the truth. But I want a chance to be happy. Does that make sense?'

Birdie shut her eyes. Did it? Florrie had broken the law when she'd taken the diamonds. But she'd also tried to make a life for herself that was bigger than the life she'd been born into. And she'd been honest enough to tell them at the end... even if it was because they'd caught her out.

So the question remained. What to do?

She glanced at Seb and was about to see if he wanted to discuss it. But instead, he just gave a slight nod of his head. Birdie smiled at him. For all his fancy posh upbringing, he believed in an even playing field and giving people second chances. And sometimes third.

She nodded back at him and then coughed. 'You can't leave the country until you've given a full statement to DS Johns in respect of Norman Harris. We'll take you tomorrow. Once that's done and Johns has given her permission, you can leave. We'll wait two weeks after you've flown out of the country before handing the diamonds over to the police.'

Florrie was silent as she considered the offer, then said, 'I can do that.'

'Good.'

Birdie glanced over at Seb. There was still one more thing. They had to tell her about her father being in a care home with dementia. It didn't take them long, and once Birdie had finished, Florrie stared ahead, as if in a trance.

'I can give you the address of the home he's in if you'd like to make contact,' Seb said, which seemed to bring Florrie back to the present.

'Yes. Thank you. That will be good.'

'Does that mean you'll go to see him?' Birdie asked, considering Florrie hadn't gone home for her mother's funeral.

'I-I'm not sure. I'll need to think it over.' Florrie got to her feet. 'Thank you. If you could collect me on your way to the station tomorrow, that would be most appreciated. And now, if you don't mind, I'd better get going. I have a lot to organise and very little time in which to do it.'

Seb, ever the gentleman, stood up and shook hands with Florrie and slid the diamonds into the inside pocket of his suit jacket as he sat down. Birdie supposed it was one good reason to wear something so posh on a London stake-out.

'Will she keep her word?' he asked.

Birdie had wondered the same thing, but as she watched Florrie leave the café, the nervous energy that had always hovered around her was gone. It was like the weight of her secret was no longer with her.

'I think she will. Without the diamonds and the fear that her past will catch up with her, she'll finally be able to be herself. She looks happier all ready. And, even better, we got paid.'

'We did. I think that calls for a celebration. How about we go back to my flat and take Elsa for a walk and then you can pick a restaurant? Anywhere you like.'

'It's like you read my mind. But first there's one thing I

have to do.' Birdie pulled out her phone and brought up her inbox. The email from Kim was still sitting there, unopened.

She couldn't ignore it forever. She didn't want to. After all, she was the one who started the search. The longer she avoided it, the more she'd become like Florrie—full of secrets.

She clicked on it.

Dear Birdie,

I've been trying to write this message for the last few days. No, that's a lie. I've been trying to write it for almost twenty-seven years. I still don't have the words, and I'm not sure I'll ever be able to answer your questions in a way that makes sense to you. But... it's something I'd like to try.

I moved back from Canada with my two daughters and their father, a man who has given me the kind of life I always wanted for myself. The kind of life I wanted to give to you. And it sounds like you've had that. My heart is eased.

For so long, I've been too scared to look for you, worried about what you might think or feel. But it's not about me. It's about you, and if you still want to meet at the Royal Oak on Saturday, I'll be there. And now I need to hit send before I delete this entire message and start again.

Kim

PS You play cricket? So did I when I was at school.

Birdie closed her eyes and let it all sink in.

Kim had said yes. She wanted to meet up. After all this time, she'd finally get some answers.

Seb was quiet, as if he understood what she was doing. It's what made him such a good detective. And friend.

'We might need to change our plans because it looks like I'll be going to the pub on Saturday, after all. I had better start looking at the train timetable and working out how to get there.'

A wide smile broke out across his mouth and, for a moment, Birdie almost thought he was going to hug her. Then he seemed to collect himself and patted her arm instead.

'I'm pleased for you. You don't need to take the train. Elsa and I will drive you and go for a walk in the park. That way, you don't need to worry about being late.'

'Hey! Who said anything about being late?' she protested, before catching the glint in his eyes. She groaned. 'I think I've created a monster. Besides, for all we know, that's where I got it from. She might be even later than me.'

He didn't answer. But he didn't have to. Because soon Birdie would know exactly what her birth mother was like.

Chapter 32

Seb put the vacuum away and joined Elsa on the couch. Definitely one of the advantages of his place in London was that it only took ten minutes to vacuum, as opposed to Sarah's house. Maybe that's why she hadn't been in a hurry to return home.

Now that the case was over and Florrie's payment was safely in their bank account, the business definitely felt a lot more viable. DS Johns had called earlier and said they had enough evidence to charge Blake Richards with Harris' murder but they didn't have sufficient evidence to connect him to the blackmail and they weren't pursuing it further.

When he told Florrie, she'd accepted it, especially as murder came with a much stiffer penalty. She said she was more concerned with getting ready for her move to New Zealand and her new life.

Seb had also decided to continue working for Rob because his friend was desperate and he could hardly refuse, after all the help he'd given them.

He went over to the table and was about to open his laptop when Birdie appeared in the doorway.

'How do I look?' she asked nervously, doing a twirl. She'd forgone her usual jeans and was wearing a pair of wide-legged linen trousers and an emerald green T-shirt, along with her denim jacket.

'You look fine.'

'Only fine,' she said, pouting.

'Okay, you look great. Perfect for meeting your birth mother. Speaking of which, are you sure you don't want us to drive you?'

'No. I'd rather take the train. It gives me some thinking time on the way there… and on the way back. But you can walk me to the station to make sure I arrive on time.'

'Done. I'll get Elsa's lead.'

~

Despite the lack of oak trees, the Royal Oak was set off the road in a two-storey white building with hanging baskets and a high-pitched roof.

Birdie had been getting more nervous the closer she got to the pub. But now she was there, she was determined to walk inside… as soon as her heart stopped thumping loudly in her ears.

'Come on, love. Some of us actually want to go in,' a man growled as they swept past her, obviously not appreciating the fact she was having a life-changing moment.

'So sorry. I wouldn't want you to be three seconds late,' she retorted before she could stop herself. The man glared at her for a moment before marching into the pub, muttering under his breath. Though at least his rudeness had settled her nerves.

She hadn't been there for several years but when she entered, she immediately recognised the rough brick walls and striped wooden floors. The wall panels were painted a soft pistachio green and the window sashes were white, giving the whole place a modern but cosy feel. A huge bar ran the length of the wall, and it overlooked wide glass doors that opened out onto a courtyard.

The air was filled with the aroma of roasting meat and the sweet tang of fried onions, but for the first time in her life, Birdie wasn't hungry. There was a serving station by the glass door and she made her way over to where a middle-aged woman stood, dressed in black jeans and a T-shirt with an oak tree embroidered into the top corner.

'Hi, I have a booking for twelve-thirty. For two people.'

'Sure, love. What's your name?'

'It's—' She broke off as her mind went momentarily blank. What was wrong with her? She needed to get it together. Breath in. Breath out. Then she gave the woman an apologetic smile. 'Sorry, it's Birdie. I booked online and I'm not sure if my… guest is here yet?'

The woman consulted the tablet in her hand and then shook her head. 'It looks like you're the first to arrive. I'll take you over. The menus are on the table.'

'Thanks.' Birdie followed her through the busy courtyard to a table overlooking the grassy reserve that ran next to the pub. Her mouth was dry, and she was grateful when a waiter brought over a bottle of cold water and two glasses. After she poured herself a drink, she dared to look around.

Would she recognise Kim when she came in? She'd only seen a photo of her when she was young. Should she have asked for a more recent one? Then again, maybe that was rude? She patted her own hair. She'd taken extra care to try to make it sit flat, though she could already feel the curls battling their way back to the surface. At least her outfit was nice.

But suddenly she felt overdressed and her heart started to thump again. This was definitely a—

'H-hello, Birdie?'

A wave of nausea coursed through her and Birdie swallowed hard before daring to look up. A woman was standing behind the opposite seat. She was about five foot three and had the physique of someone who worked out a lot. Her face was framed by shoulder-length brown hair with a wide mouth and a nose that was... *like hers.*

Kim.

She realised she hadn't answered.

'Yes. That's me. I'm Birdie.' She pushed back her chair and stood up, her heart still racing as if she'd had a triple-shot espresso. 'Thanks for meeting me. I wasn't sure if you were going to come.'

'That makes two of us,' Kim admitted before smoothing down her already-smooth hair. Her hands were shaking. Was she as nervous as Birdie? 'So, um, how do you want to do this?'

'I guess we should sit down first. Otherwise we might look a little stupid,' Birdie said, and then winced. 'Crap. Sorry, that probably sounded rude. I don't always think before I speak.'

She half expected Kim to look horrified, but her birth mother grinned. 'I guess I know where you got that from. You have no idea how worried I've been that I might blurt out something dumb.' She looked around. 'You're right. We should definitely sit.'

Birdie awkwardly dropped back down into the seat, beads of perspiration gathering on her brow. Why had she picked an outside table? 'Would you like a drink? I could get us something from the bar?'

Kim shook her head. 'Water's fine. Did you come down from Market Harborough today?'

'No. I've been working in London, so it was easier to stay a couple of days longer, rather than go home first.'

'Yes, that makes sense.' Kim studied her hands, as if she was too scared to look up. 'You said you'd just started working as a private investigator. Did you have a case in London?'

'Yes. I was in the middle of it when I got your email… which was one of the reasons I didn't reply straight away. Though to be honest, the main reason was that I was scared. Which is so dumb. I've been wanting to meet you for ages. But the closer it got—'

'The harder it became?' This time, Kim looked up and met her gaze. 'I don't think there's an easy way to do this, so I'm going to leave it up to you. You ask me whatever questions you want and I'll try my best to answer them.'

Birdie traced a line around her water glass, her thoughts all rushing together, hustling for a place at the front of the queue. But some of the questions were big and hard, and she wasn't sure she was ready for the answers. It was like when she was conducting an interview; sometimes it was easier to start with the smaller things and go from there.

'Okay. So, I guess we could start with now. You said you were married?'

A flash of relief crossed Kim's face. She'd obviously been having the same concerns. This seemed like a question she was happy to answer.

'Yes. Ken and I met when I was twenty-four. I studied physical education at university in Canada and he was a music teacher at the first school I worked in. We got married a couple of years later. That's why I was so thrilled when you said you played cricket. Do you like other sports?'

'Does night-club dancing count?' Birdie grinned, and Kim matched her smile.

'Absolutely. I still sneak out now and then on a girl's night. No better way to let off steam.'

'Exactly. I love it. And I do play a bit of netball with friends when one of their social teams need a stand-in. I loved basketball as well but my legs decided to stop growing.'

'Tell me about it.' Kim rolled her eyes as if it was a problem she'd been dealing with her whole life. 'I think I mentioned in my email that I have two other daughters. Lottie is ten and Micha is twelve. I have photos, if you'd like to see them.'

'I'd like that very much.' Birdie's mouth went dry, but she nodded her head so much, her curls tumbled down onto her cheeks. The two girls had brown hair and pale skin with a scattering of freckles. Like Birdie's own. They were holding hula hoops and had the excited smiles that came from an afternoon of running around. Her breathing quickened.

Her half-sisters.

'This was taken a few weeks ago while we were on holiday in Wales. The first two days, they hardly left the cottage—more interested in their phones—but by the third day, they got bored and ventured outside. From there, they hardly stopped for food.'

'That sounds like the kind of holidays we used to have,' Birdie said, some of the tension easing in her chest. 'I have two younger brothers. Arthur is about to turn twenty-one and Thomas is nineteen and thinks he's a world expert on everything. I love them both… but I've always wondered what it would be like to have sisters.'

'I grew up with two sisters and a brother. They have

their moments. Especially when it comes to sharing a bath-room.' Kim grimaced.

'It's the worst,' Birdie agreed as the waitress returned to get their order, and suddenly she was starving. Kim picked up her own menu and scanned it, then looked up at the girl.

'Fish and chips for me, and hold the salad. No offence, but I can't stand vegetables. What about you, Birdie?'

Birdie found herself grinning. She'd been right to start with the small stuff. To create a relationship before delving into the bigger questions she had. She looked up at the waitress and then back at her birth mother. 'Sounds good. I'll have the same.'

Claim your free book

GET ANOTHER BOOK FOR FREE!
To instantly receive **Nowhere to Hide,** a free novella
from the Detective Sebastian Clifford series, featuring DC
Lucinda Bird when she first joined CID, sign up for Sally
Rigby's free author newsletter at www.sallyrigby.com

Read the Sebastian Clifford Series

WEB OF LIES: A Midlands Crime Thriller (Detective Sebastian Clifford - Book 1)

A trail of secrets. A dangerous discovery. A deadly turn.

Police officer Sebastian Clifford never planned on becoming a private investigator. But when a scandal leads to the disbandment of his London based special squad, he finds himself out of a job. That is, until his cousin calls on him to investigate her husband's high-profile death, and prove that it wasn't a suicide.

Clifford's reluctant to get involved, but the more he digs, the more evidence he finds. With his ability to remember everything he's ever seen, he's the perfect person to untangle the layers of deceit.

He meets Detective Constable Bird, an underutilised detective at Market Harborough's police force, who refuses to give him access to the records he's requested unless he allows her to help with the investigation. Clifford isn't thrilled. The last time he worked as part of a team it ended his career.

But with time running out, Clifford is out of options. Together they must wade through the web of lies in the hope that they'll find the truth before it kills them.

Web of Lies is the first in the new Detective Sebastian Clifford series. Perfect for readers of Joy Ellis, Robert Galbraith and Mark Dawson.

~

SPEAK NO EVIL: A Midlands Crime Thriller (Detective Sebastian Clifford - Book 2)

What happens when someone's too scared to speak?

Ex-police officer Sebastian Clifford had decided to limit his work as a private investigator, until Detective Constable Bird, aka Birdie, asks for his help.

Twelve months ago a young girl was abandoned on the streets of Market Harborough in shocking circumstances. Since then the child has barely spoken and with the police unable to trace her identity, they've given up.

The social services team in charge of the case worry that the child has an intellectual disability but Birdie and her aunt, who's fostering the little girl, disagree and believe she's gifted and intelligent, but something bad happened and she's living in constant fear.

Clifford trusts Birdie's instinct and together they work to find out who the girl is, so she can be freed from the past. But as secrets are uncovered, the pair realise it's not just the child who's in danger.

Speak No Evil is the second in the Detective Sebastian Clifford series. Perfect for readers of Faith Martin, Matt Brolly and Joy Ellis.

~

NEVER TOO LATE: A Midlands Crime Thriller (Detective Sebastian Clifford - Book 3)

A vicious attack. A dirty secret. And a chance for justice

Ex-police officer Sebastian Clifford is quickly finding that life as a private investigator is never quiet. His doors have only been open a few weeks when DCI Whitney Walker approaches him to investigate the brutal attack that left her older brother, Rob, with irreversible brain damage.

For nearly twenty-five years Rob had no memory of that night, but lately things are coming back to him, and Whitney's worried that her brother might, once again, be in danger.

Clifford knows only too well what it's like be haunted by the past, and so he agrees to help. But the deeper he digs, the more secrets he uncovers, and soon he discovers that Rob's not the only one in danger.

Never Too Late is the third in the Detective Sebastian Clifford series, perfect for readers who love gripping crime fiction.

HIDDEN FROM SIGHT: A Midlands Crime Thriller (Detective Sebastian Clifford - Book 4)

A million pound heist. A man on the run. And a gang hellbent on seeking revenge.

When private investigator Detective Sebastian Clifford is asked by his former society girlfriend to locate her fiancé, who's disappeared along with some valuable pieces of art, he's reluctant to help. He'd left the aristocratic world behind, for good reason. But when his ex starts receiving threatening letters Clifford is left with no choice.

With the help of his partner Lucinda Bird, aka Birdie, they start digging and find themselves drawn into London's underworld. But it's hard to see the truth between the shadows and lies. Until a clue leads them in the direction of Clifford's nemesis and he realises they're all in more danger than he thought. The race is on to find the missing man and the art before lives are lost.

A perfect mix of mystery, intrigue and danger that will delight fans of detective stories. '**Hidden from Sight**' is the fourth in the bestselling, fast-paced, Midland Crime Thriller series, featuring Clifford and Birdie, and the most gripping yet. Grab your copy, and see if you can solve the crime.

~

FEAR THE TRUTH: A Midlands Crime Thriller (Detective Sebastian Clifford - Book 5)

The truth will set you free...except when it doesn't...

Private investigator Sebastian Clifford and his partner Birdie, step into the world of celebrity when a star of children's TV turns to them for help. She's being blackmailed by someone who knows about her murky past and she's desperate to keep it hidden. But silence comes at a price, and it's one she can't afford to pay.

Clifford, who knows better than anyone what it's like to be punished for one mistake, agrees to help. But, as they dig deeper, they discover that everyone has secrets, and some are dark enough to kill for. Can they find the blackmailer before it's too late and save the reputation...and the life...of a beloved star?

'**Fear the Truth**' is the fifth in the best-selling Sebastian Clifford thriller series, and is a perfect blend of mystery, mayhem and danger. Grab your copy now and see if *you* can face the truth.

Also by Sally Rigby: The Cavendish & Walker Series

DEADLY GAMES - Cavendish & Walker Book 1

A killer is playing cat and mouse....... and winning.

DCI Whitney Walker wants to save her career. Forensic psychologist, Dr Georgina Cavendish, wants to avenge the death of her student.

Sparks fly when real world policing meets academic theory, and it's not a pretty sight.

When two more bodies are discovered, Walker and Cavendish form an uneasy alliance. But are they in time to save the next victim?

Deadly Games is the first book in the Cavendish and Walker crime fiction series. If you like serial killer thrillers and psychological intrigue, then you'll love Sally Rigby's page-turning book.

Pick up *Deadly Games* today to read Cavendish & Walker's first case.

∽

FATAL JUSTICE - Cavendish & Walker Book 2

A vigilante's on the loose, dishing out their kind of justice...

A string of mutilated bodies sees Detective Chief Inspector Whitney Walker back in action. But when she discovers the victims have all been grooming young girls, she fears a vigilante is on the loose. And while she understands the motive, no one is above the law.

Once again, she turns to forensic psychologist, Dr Georgina Cavendish, to unravel the cryptic clues. But will they be able to save the next victim from a gruesome death?

Fatal Justice is the second book in the Cavendish & Walker crime fiction series. If you like your mysteries dark, and with a twist, pick up a copy of Sally Rigby's book today.

∾

DEATH TRACK - Cavendish & Walker Book 3

Catch the train if you dare...

After a teenage boy is found dead on a Lenchester train, Detective Chief Inspector Whitney Walker believes they're being targeted by the notorious Carriage Killer, who chooses a local rail network, commits four murders, and moves on.

Against her wishes, Walker's boss brings in officers from another force to help the investigation and prevent more deaths, but she's forced to defend her team against this outside interference.

Forensic psychologist, Dr Georgina Cavendish, is by her side in an attempt to bring to an end this killing spree. But how can they get into the mind of a killer who has already killed twelve times in two years without leaving a single clue behind?

For fans of Rachel Abbott, L J Ross and Angela Marsons, *Death Track* is the third in the Cavendish & Walker series. A gripping serial killer thriller that will have you hooked.

~

LETHAL SECRET - Cavendish & Walker Book 4

Someone has a secret. A secret worth killing for....

When a series of suicides, linked to the Wellness Spirit Centre, turn out to be murder, it brings together DCI Whitney Walker and forensic psychologist Dr Georgina Cavendish for another investigation. But as they delve deeper, they come across a tangle of secrets and the very real risk that the killer will strike again.

As the clock ticks down, the only way forward is to infiltrate the centre. But the outcome is disastrous, in more ways than one.

For fans of Angela Marsons, Rachel Abbott and M A Comley, *Lethal Secret* is the fourth book in the Cavendish & Walker crime fiction series.

~

LAST BREATH - Cavendish & Walker Book 5

Has the Lenchester Strangler returned?

When a murderer leaves a familiar pink scarf as his calling card, Detective Chief Inspector Whitney Walker is forced to dig into a cold case, not sure if she's looking for a killer or a copycat.

With a growing pile of bodies, and no clues, she turns to forensic psychologist, Dr Georgina Cavendish, despite their relationship being at an all-time low.

Can they overcome the bad blood between them to solve the

unsolvable?

For fans of Rachel Abbott, Angela Marsons and M A
Comley, *Last Breath* is the fifth book in the Cavendish & Walker
crime fiction series.

~

FINAL VERDICT - Cavendish & Walker Book 6

The judge has spoken......everyone must die.

When a killer starts murdering lawyers in a prestigious law firm,
and every lead takes them to a dead end, DCI Whitney Walker
finds herself grappling for a motive.

What links these deaths, and why use a lethal injection?

Alongside forensic psychologist, Dr Georgina Cavendish, they
close in on the killer, while all the time trying to not let their
personal lives get in the way of the investigation.

For fans of Rachel Abbott, Mark Dawson and M A Comley,
Final Verdict is the sixth in the Cavendish & Walker series. A fast
paced murder mystery which will keep you guessing.

~

RITUAL DEMISE - Cavendish & Walker Book 7

Someone is watching.... No one is safe

The once tranquil woods in a picturesque part of Lenchester
have become the bloody stage to a series of ritualistic murders.
With no suspects, Detective Chief Inspector Whitney Walker is

once again forced to call on the services of forensic psychologist Dr Georgina Cavendish.

But this murderer isn't like any they've faced before. The murders are highly elaborate, but different in their own way and, with the clock ticking, they need to get inside the killer's head before it's too late.

For fans of Angela Marsons, Rachel Abbott and L J Ross. Ritual Demise is the seventh book in the Cavendish & Walker crime fiction series.

$\sim$

MORTAL REMAINS - Cavendish & Walker Book 8

Someone's playing with fire…. There's no escape.

A serial arsonist is on the loose and as the death toll continues to mount DCI Whitney Walker calls on forensic psychologist Dr Georgina Cavendish for help.

But Lenchester isn't the only thing burning. There are monumental changes taking place within the police force and there's a chance Whitney might lose the job she loves. She has to find the killer before that happens. Before any more lives are lost.

Mortal Remains is the eighth book in the acclaimed Cavendish & Walker series. Perfect for fans of Angela Marsons, Rachel Abbott and L J Ross.

$\sim$

SILENT GRAVES - Cavendish & Walker Book 9

Nothing remains buried forever…

When the bodies of two teenage girls are discovered on a building site, DCI Whitney Walker knows she's on the hunt for a killer. The problem is the murders happened in 1980 and this is her first case with the new team. What makes it even tougher is that with budgetary restrictions in place, she only has two weeks to solve it.

Once again, she enlists the help of forensic psychologist Dr Georgina Cavendish, but as she digs deeper into the past, she uncovers hidden truths that reverberate through the decades and into the present.

Silent Graves is the ninth book in the acclaimed Cavendish & Walker series. Perfect for fans of L J Ross, J M Dalgliesh and Rachel Abbott.

KILL SHOT - Cavendish & Walker Book 10

The game is over…..there's nowhere to hide.

When Lenchester's most famous sportsman is shot dead, DCI Whitney Walker and her team are thrown into the world of snooker.

She calls on forensic psychologist Dr Georgina Cavendish to assist, but the investigation takes them in a direction which has far-reaching, international ramifications.

Much to Whitney's annoyance, an officer from one of the Met's special squads is sent to assist.

But as everyone knows…three's a crowd.

Kill Shot is the tenth book in the acclaimed Cavendish & Walker series. Perfect for fans of Simon McCleave, J M Dalgliesh, J R Ellis and Faith Martin.

∼

DARK SECRETS - Cavendish & Walker Book 11

An uninvited guest...a deadly secret....and a terrible crime.

When a well-loved family of five are found dead sitting around their dining table with an untouched meal in front of them, it sends shockwaves throughout the community.

Was it a murder suicide, or was someone else involved?

It's one of DCI Whitney Walker's most baffling cases, and even with the help of forensic psychologist Dr Georgina Cavendish, they struggle to find any clues or motives to help them catch the killer.

But with a community in mourning and growing pressure to get answers, Cavendish and Walker are forced to go deeper into a murderer's mind than they've ever gone before.

Dark Secrets is the eleventh book in the Cavendish & Walker series. Perfect for fans of Angela Marsons, Joy Ellis and Rachel McLean.

∼

BROKEN SCREAMS - Cavendish & Walker Book 12

Scream all you want, no one can hear you....

When an attempted murder is linked to a string of unsolved sexual attacks, Detective Chief Inspector Whitney Walker is incensed. All those women who still have sleepless nights because the man who terrorises their dreams is still on the loose.

Calling on forensic psychologist Dr Georgina Cavendish to help, they follow the clues and are alarmed to discover the victims all had one thing in common. Their birthdays were on the 29th February. The same date as a female officer on Whitney's team.

As the clock ticks down and they're no nearer to finding the truth, can they stop the villain before he makes sure his next victim will never scream again.

Broken Screams is the twelfth book in the acclaimed Cavendish & Walker series and is perfect for fans of Angela Marsons, Helen H Durrant and Rachel McClean.

Psychological Series

Sally also writes psychological thrillers in collaboration with Amanda Ashby.

∾

REMEMBER ME?: A brand new addictive psychological thriller that you won't be able to put down in 2021

A perfect life...

Paul Henderson leads a normal life. A deputy headteacher at a good school, a loving relationship with girlfriend Jenna, and a baby on the way. Everything *seems* perfect.

A shocking message...

Until Paul receives a message from his ex-fiance Nicole. Beautiful, ambitious and fierce, Nicole is everything Jenna is not. And now it seems Nicole is back, and she has a score to settle with Paul...

A deadly secret.

But Paul can't understand how Nicole is back. Because he's pretty sure he killed her with his own bare hands....

Which means, someone else knows the truth about what happened that night. And they'll stop at nothing to make Paul pay...

A brand new psychological thriller that will keep you guessing till the end! Perfect for fans of Sue Watson, Nina Manning, Shalini Boland

~

I WILL FIND YOU: An addictive psychological crime thriller to keep you gripped in 2022

Three sisters...One terrible secret

Ashleigh: A creative, free spirit and loyal. But Ash is tormented by her demons and a past that refuses to be laid to rest.

Jessica: Perfect wife and loving mother. But although Jessica might seem to have it all, she lives a secret life built on lies.

Grace: An outsider, always looking in, Grace has never known the love of her sisters and her resentment can make her do bad things.

When Ashleigh goes missing, Jessica and Grace do all they can to find their eldest sister. But the longer Ashleigh is missing, the more secrets and lies these women are hiding threaten to tear this family apart.

Can they find Ashleigh before it's too late or is it sometimes safer to stay hidden?

~

THE EX-WIFE

"Dark, gripping and with a smart twist, The Ex-Wife kept me turning the pages. I thought I'd managed to guess the ending, but for once was thrilled to be wrong." Bestselling author M A Hunter

My life was perfect until she came along. Norah.

Younger, prettier and about to marry my own ex-husband, they are a walking cliché.

I hate her. I hate them both.

She's taken everything from me – my husband, my life, my home - but I refuse to allow her to take Cassie, my beautiful daughter. That's a step too far.

Now I've discovered that Norah plans to have a baby of her own and that causes me no end of problems. She could destroy everything and reveal my deepest, darkest secrets.

That can never be allowed to happen.

No matter what it costs…

A brand new psychological thriller that will keep you guessing till the end! Perfect for fans of Sue Watson, Nina Manning, Shalini Boland

Acknowledgments

No book is produced in a vacuum and I'd like to acknowledge all of those who have helped with the production of this one.

First, enormous thanks go to Amanda Ashby for her invaluable input. I'd have been lost without it.

I'd also like to thank Rebecca Millar for being such an insightful and incredible editor. Thanks, also, to Victoria Goldman for your edit.

The cover is one of my favourites, and I'd like to thank, as usual, the amazing Stuart Bache.

To my Advanced Reader Teams, thanks so much for your input. I truly appreciate it.

Finally, thanks to my family for your continued support.

About the Author

Sally Rigby was born in Northampton, UK. After leaving university she worked in magazines and radio, before finally embarking on a career lecturing in both further and higher education.

Sally has always had the travel bug and after living in Manchester and London moved overseas. From 2001 she has lived with her family in New Zealand (apart from five years in Australia), which she considers to be the most beautiful place in the world.

Sally is the author of the acclaimed Cavendish and Walker series, and the more recent Detective Sebastian Clifford series. In collaboration with another author, she also writes psychological thrillers in collaboration with Amanda Ashby for Boldwood Books.

Sally has always loved crime fiction books, films and TV programmes. She has a particular fascination with the psychology of serial killers.

Sally loves to hear from her readers, so do feel free to get in touch via her website www.sallyrigby.com

Made in the USA
Middletown, DE
21 September 2023

38962683R00161